THE WILD PALMS

THE
Wild Palms

———

WILLIAM
FAULKNER

VINTAGE BOOKS
A DIVISION OF RANDOM HOUSE
New York

THE WILD PALMS

Wild Palms

THE KNOCKING SOUNDED AGAIN, AT ONCE DISCREET AND peremptory, while the doctor was descending the stairs, the flashlight's beam lancing on before him down the brown-stained stairwell and into the brown-stained tongue-and-groove box of the lower hall. It was a beach cottage, even though of two stories, and lighted by oil lamps—or an oil lamp, which his wife had carried up stairs with them after supper. And the doctor wore a night shirt too, not pajamas, for the same reason that he smoked the pipe which he had never learned and knew that he would never learn to like, between the occasional cigar which clients gave him in the intervals of Sundays on which he smoked the three cigars which he felt he could buy for himself even though he owned the beach cottage as well as the one next door to it and the one, the residence with electricity and plastered walls, in the village four miles away. Because he was now forty-eight years old and he had been sixteen and eighteen and twenty at the time when his father could tell him (and he believe it) that cigarettes and pajamas were for dudes and women.

It was after midnight, though not much. He could tell that, even apart from the wind, the taste and smell and feel of wind even here behind the closed and locked doors and shutters. Because he had been born here, on

3

this coast though not in this house but in the other, the
residence in town, and had lived here all his life, including the four years at the State University's medical
school and the two years as an intern in New Orleans
where (a thick man even when young, with thick soft
woman's hands, who should never have been a doctor
at all, who even after the six more or less metropolitan
years looked out from a provincial and insulated amazement at his classmates and fellows: the lean young men
swaggering in their drill jackets on which—to him—they
wore the myriad anonymous faces of the probationer
nurses with a ruthless and assured braggadocio like
decorations, like flower trophies) he had sickened for
it. So he graduated, nearer the foot of the class than the
head though not at either, and came home and within
the year married the wife his father had picked out for
him and within four years owned the house which his
father had built and assumed the practice which his
father had created, losing nothing from it and adding
nothing to it, and within ten years owned not only the
beach house where he and his wife spent their childless
summers but the adjoining property as well, which he
rented to summer visitors or even parties—picnickers
or fishermen. On the evening of the wedding he and his
wife went to New Orleans and spent two days in a hotel
room, though they never had a honeymoon. And though
they had slept in the same bed for twenty-three years
now they still had no children.

But even apart from the wind he could still tell the
approximate time by the staling smell of gumbo now

cold in the big earthen pot on the cold stove beyond the
flimsy kitchen wall—the big pot of it which his wife
had made that morning in order to send some over to
their neighbors and renters in the next house: the man
and the woman who four days ago had rented the cottage
and who probably did not even know that the donors of
the gumbo were not only neighbors but landlords too—
the dark-haired woman with queer hard yellow eyes in a
face whose skin was drawn thin over prominent cheek-
bones and a heavy jaw (the doctor called it sullen at
first, then he called it afraid), young, who sat all day
long in a new cheap beach chair facing the water, in a
worn sweater and a pair of faded jean pants and canvas
shoes, not reading, not doing anything, just sitting there
in that complete immobility which the doctor (or the
doctor in the Doctor) did not need the corroboration of
the drawn quality of the skin and the blank inverted
fixity of the apparently unseeing eyes to recognise at
once—that complete immobile abstraction from which
even pain and terror are absent, in which a living creature seems to listen to and even watch some one of its
own flagging organs, the heart say, the secret irreparable
seeping of blood; and the man young too, in a pair of
disreputable khaki slacks and a sleeveless jersey undershirt and no hat in a region where even young people
believed the summer sun to be fatal, seen usually walking barefoot along the beach at tide-edge, returning
with a faggot of driftwood strapped into a belt, passing
the immobile woman in the beach chair with no sign

from her, no movement of the head or perhaps even of the eyes.

But it was not the heart, the doctor told himself. He decided that on the first day from where, without intending to eavesdrop, he watched the woman through the screen of oleander bushes which separated the two lots. Yet this very postulation of what it was not seemed to him to contain the secret, the answer. It seemed to him that he saw the truth already, the shadowy indefinite shape of truth, as though he were separated from the truth only by a veil just as he was separated from the living woman by the screen of oleander leaves. He was not eavesdropping, not spying; perhaps he thought, *I will have plenty of time in which to learn just which organ it is she is listening to; they have paid their rent for two weeks* (perhaps at that time also the doctor in the Doctor knowing that it would not require weeks but just days), thinking how if she should need assistance it would be fortunate that he, the landlord, was also a doctor until it occurred to him that since they probably did not even know he was the landlord, they would probably not know either that he was a doctor.

The real estate agent told him over the telephone of the renting of the house. "She's got on pants," the agent said. "I mean, not these ladies' slacks but pants, man's pants. I mean, they are too little for her in just exactly the right places any man would want to see them too little but no woman would unless she had them on herself. I reckon Miss Martha aint going to like that much."

"That will be all right with her if they pay their rent on time," the doctor said.

"No damn fear," the agent said. "I saw to that. I aint been in this business this long for nothing. I said, 'It will have to be in advance,' and he said, 'All right. All right. How much?' like he was Vanderbilt or somebody, in them dirty fishing pants and nothing but an undershirt under his coat, hauling the wad of money out and one of the bills wasn't but a ten and I just gave him ten change back out of the other one and there wasn't but two of them to begin with and I says 'Of course if you want to take the house like it is, with just what furniture is in it now, you can get out pretty cheap,' and he says 'All right. All right. How much?' I believe I could have got more than I did because if you ask me he dont want any furniture, all he wants is four walls to get inside of and a door to close afterward. She never even got out of the taxi. She just sat there, waiting, in them pants that was just exactly too little for her in just exactly the right places." The voice ceased; the doctor's head filled now with suspended wirehum, the rising inflection of a risible silence, so that he said almost sharply:

"Well? Do they want more furniture or not? There's nothing in the house but one bed, and the mattress on it aint—"

"No, no, they dont want any more. I told him the house had a bed and a stove in it, and they had a chair with them—one of these canvas ones that fold up in the taxi along with the grip. So they are all fixed." Now that

suspension of silent laughing filled the doctor's head
again.

"Well?" the doctor said. "What is it? What's the
matter with you?" though he seemed to know already,
before the other spoke, what the voice would say:

"I reckon Miss Martha is going to have something
that will set heavier on her stomach than them pants
even. I dont think they are married. Oh, he says they are
and I dont think he is lying about her and maybe he
aint even lying about himself. The trouble is, they aint
married to each other, she aint married to him. Because
I can smell a husband. Show me a woman I never saw
before on the streets of Mobile or New Orleans either
and I can smell whether—"

They took possession that afternoon of the cottage,
the shack, which contained the one bed whose springs
and mattress were not very good, and the stove with its
one frying pan incrusted by generations of cooking fish,
and the coffee pot and the meager collection of mis-
matched iron spoons and forks and knives and cracked
cups and saucers and drinking vessels which had once
been containers of bought jams and jellies, and the new
beach chair in which the woman lay all day long apparently watching the palm fronds clashing with their
wild dry bitter sound against the bright glitter of the
water while the man carried driftwood into the kitchen.
Two mornings ago the milk wagon which made the
beach route stopped there and the doctor's wife saw the
man once returning up the beach from a small grocery
store owned by a Portuguese ex-fisherman, carrying a

loaf of bread and a bulky paper sack. And she told the
doctor about watching him cleaning (or trying to clean)
a mess of fish at the kitchen steps, told the doctor about
it with bitter and outraged conviction—a shapeless
woman yet not fat, not anywhere near as plump as the
doctor himself, who had begun to turn gray all over
about ten years ago, as if hair and complexion both
were being subtly altered, along with the shade of her
eyes, by the color of the house dresses which she apparently chose to match them. "And a mess of it he was
making!" she cried. "A mess outside the kitchen and a
mess on the stove too probably!"

"Maybe she can cook," the doctor said mildly.

"Where, how? Sitting out there in the yard? When he
carries stove and all out to her?" But even that was not
the real outrage, though she did not say so. She did not
say "They are not married" though it was in both their
minds. They both knew that, once it was said aloud between them, he would turn the renters out. Yet they both
refused to say it and for more reason than because when
he turned them out he would feel conscience-bound to
return the rent money; more than this on his part anyway, who was thinking *They had only twenty dollars.
And that was three days ago. And there is something
wrong with her,* the doctor now speaking louder than the
provincial protestant, the Baptist born. And something
(perhaps the doctor here too) talking louder than the
provincial Baptist in her too because this morning she
waked the doctor, calling him from the window where
she stood shapeless in the cotton nightgown shaped like

a shroud and with her gray hair screwed into papers, to show him the man coming up the beach at sunrise with his belted faggot of driftwood. And when he (the doctor) came home at noon she had the gumbo made, an enormous quantity of it, enough for a dozen people, made with that grim Samaritan husbandry of good women, as if she took a grim and vindictive and masochistic pleasure in the fact that the Samaritan deed would be performed at the price of its remainder which would sit invincible and inexhaustible on the stove while days accumulated and passed, to be warmed and rewarmed and then rewarmed until consumed by two people who did not even like it, who born and bred in sight of the sea had for taste in fish a predilection for the tuna, the salmon, the sardines bought in cans, immolated and embalmed three thousand miles away in the oil of machinery and commerce.

He delivered the bowl himself—a shortish fattish untidy man with linen not quite fresh, sidling a little clumsily through the oleander hedge with the bowl covered by a yet-creased (and not yet even laundered, it was that new) linen napkin, lending an air of awkward kindliness even to the symbol which he carried of the uncompromising Christian deed performed not with sincerity or pity but through duty—and lowered it (she had not risen from the chair nor moved save the hard cat's eyes) as if the bowl contained nitro-glycerin, the fattish unshaven mask beaming foolishly but behind the mask the eyes of the doctor within the Doctor shrewd, missing nothing, examining without smiling and without diffidence the face of the woman who was not thin but actually gaunt, thinking *Yes. A degree or two. Perhaps three. But not the heart* then waking, rousing, to find the blank feral eyes staring at him, whom to his certain knowledge they could scarcely have seen before, with profound and illimitable hatred. It was quite impersonal, as when the person in whom joy already exists looks out at any post or tree with pleasure and happiness. He (the doctor) was without vanity; it was not at him the hatred was directed. *It's at the whole human race,* he thought. *Or no, no. Wait. Wait*—the veil about to break, the cogs of deduction about to mesh—*Not at the race of mankind but at the race of man, the masculine. But why? Why?* His wife would have noticed the faint mark of the absent wedding ring, but he, the doctor, saw more than that: *She has borne children,* he thought. *One, anyway; I would stake my degree on that. And if Cofer* (he was the agent) *is right about his not being her husband—and he should be, should be able to tell, smell, as he says, since he is apparently in the business of renting beach cottages for the same reason or under the same compulsion, vicarious need, which drives certain people in the cities to equip and supply rooms to clandestine and fictitious names. . . . Say she had come to hate the race of men enough to desert husband and children; good. Yet, to have gone not only to another man, but to live apparently in penury, and herself sick, really sick. Or to have deserted husband and children for another man and poverty, and then to have—to have—to . . .* He could feel, hear them: the cogs, clicking, going fast; he felt a need for terrific haste in order to keep up, a premonition that the final cog would click and the bell of comprehension ring and he would not be quite near enough to see and hear: *Yes. Yes. What is it that man as a race can have done to her that she would look upon such a manifestation of it as I, whom she has never seen before and would not look at twice if she had, with that same hatred through which he must walk each time he comes up from the beach with an armful of firewood to cook the very food which she eats?*

She did not even offer to take the dish from him. "It's not soup, it's gumbo," he said. "My wife made it. She —we . . ." She did not move, looking at him as he stooped fatly in his crumpled seersucker, with the careful tray; he did not even hear the man until she spoke to him.

"Thanks," she said. "Take it into the house, Harry." Now she was not even looking at the doctor any more. "Thank your wife," she said.

He was thinking about his two tenants as he descended the stairs behind the jerking pencil of light, into the staling odor of gumbo in the lower hall, toward the door, the knocking. It was from no presentiment, premonition that the knocker was the man named Harry. It was because he had thought of nothing else for four days—this snuffy middleaging man in the archaic sleeping garment now become one of the national props of comedy, roused from slumber in the stale bed of his childless wife and already thinking of (perhaps having

been dreaming of) the profound and distracted blaze
of objectless hatred in the strange woman's eyes; and
he again with that sense of imminence, of being just
beyond a veil from something, of groping just without
the veil and even touching but not quite, almost seeing
but not quite, the shape of truth, so that without being
aware of it he stopped dead on the stairs in his old-
fashioned list slippers, thinking swiftly: *Yes. Yes. Something which the entire race of men, males, has done to
her or she believes has done to her.*

The knocking came again now, as if the knocker had
become aware that he had stopped through some alteration of the torch's beam seen beneath the door itself and
now began to knock again with that diffident insistence
of a stranger seeking aid late at night, and the doctor
moved again, not in response to the renewed knocking,
who had had no presentiment, but as though the re-
newal of the knocking had merely coincided with the
recurrent old stale impasse of the four days' bafflement
and groping, capitulant and recapitulant; as though
instinct perhaps moved him again, the body capable of
motion, not the intellect, believing that physical advance-
ment might bring him nearer the veil at the instant when
it would part and reveal in inviolable isolation that truth
which he almost touched. So it was without premonition
that he opened the door and peered out, bringing the
torch's beam on the knocker. It was the man called
Harry. He stood there in the darkness, in the strong
steady seawind filled with the dry clashing of invisible
palm fronds, as the doctor had always seen him, in the

soiled ducks and the sleeveless undershirt, murmuring the conventional amenities about the hour and the need, asking to use the telephone while the doctor, his night-shirt streaming about his flabby calves, peered at the caller and thought in a fierce surge of triumph: *Now I am going to find out what it is.* "Yes," he said, "you wont need the telephone. I am a doctor myself."

"Oh," the other said. "Can you come at once?"

"Yes. Just let me slip on my pants. What's the trouble? So I shall know what to bring."

For an instant the other hesitated; this familiar to the doctor too who had seen it before and believed he knew its source: that innate and ineradicable instinct of mankind to attempt to conceal some of the truth even from the doctor or lawyer for whose skill and knowledge they are paying. "She's bleeding," he said. "What will your fee—"

But the doctor did not notice this. He was talking to himself: *Ah. Yes. Why didn't I . . . Lungs, of course. Why didn't I think of that?* "Yes," he said. "Will you wait here? Or perhaps inside? I wont be but a minute."

"I'll wait here," the other said. But the doctor did not hear that either. He was already running back up the stairs; he trotted into the bedroom where his wife rose on one elbow in the bed and watched him struggle into his trousers, his shadow, cast by the lamp on the low table by the bed, antic on the wall, her shadow also monstrous, gorgonlike from the rigid paper-wrapped twists of gray hair above the gray face above the high-necked night-dress which also looked gray, as if every garment she owned had partaken of that grim iron-color of her implacable and invincible morality which, the doctor was to realise later, was almost omniscient. "Yes," he said, "bleeding. Probably hemorrhage. Lungs. And why in the world I didn't—"

"More likely he has cut or shot her," she said in a cold quiet bitter voice. "Though from the look in her eyes the one time I saw her close I would have said she would be the one to do the cutting and shooting."

"Nonsense," he said, hunching into his suspenders. "Nonsense." Because he was not talking to her now either. "Yes. The fool. To bring her here, of all places. To sealevel. To the Mississippi coast—Do you want me to put out the lamp?"

"Yes. You'll probably be there a long time if you are going to wait until you are paid." He blew out the lamp and descended the stairs again behind the torch. His black bag sat on the hall table beside his hat. The man Harry still stood just outside the front door.

"Maybe you better take this now," he said.

"What?" the doctor said. He paused, looking down, bringing the torch to bear on the single banknote in the other's extended hand. *Even if he has spent nothing, now he will have only fifteen dollars,* he thought. "No, later," he said. "Maybe we had better hurry." He bustled on ahead, following the torch's dancing beam, trotting while the other walked, across his own somewhat sheltered yard and through the dividing oleander hedge and so into the full sweep of the unimpeded seawind which thrashed among the unseen palms and

hissed in the harsh salt grass of the unkempt other lot;
now he could see a dim light in the other house. "Bleeding, hey?" he said. It was overcast; the invisible wind
blew strong and steady among the invisible palms, from
the invisible sea—a harsh steady sound full of the murmur of surf on the outside barrier islands, the spits and
scars of sand bastioned with tossing and shabby pines.
"Hemorrhage?"

"What?" the other said. "Hemorrhage?"

"No?" the doctor said. "She's just coughing a little
blood then? Just spitting a little blood when she coughs,
eh?"

"Spitting?" the other said. It was the tone, not the
words. It was not addressed to the doctor and it was
beyond laughter, as if that which it addressed were
impervious to laughter; it was not the doctor who
stopped; the doctor still trotted onward on his short
sedentary legs, behind the jolting torch-beam, toward
the dim waiting light, it was the Baptist, the provincial,
who seemed to pause while the man, not the doctor
now, thought not in shock but in a sort of despairing
amazement: *Am I to live forever behind a barricade of
perennial innocence like a chicken in a pen?* He spoke
aloud quite carefully; the veil was going now, dissolving now, it was about to part now and now he did not
want to see what was behind it; he knew that for the
sake of his peace of mind forever afterward he did not
dare and he knew that it was too late now and that he
could not help himself; he heard his voice ask the ques-

tion he did not want to ask and get the answer he did not want to hear:

"You say she is bleeding. Where is she bleeding?"

"Where do women bleed?" the other said, cried, in a harsh exasperated voice, not stopping. "I'm no doctor. If I were, do you think I would waste five dollars on you?"

Nor did the doctor hear this either. "Ah," he said. "Yes. I see. Yes." Now he stopped. He was aware of no cessation of motion since the steady dark wind still blew past him. *Because I am at the wrong age for this,* he thought. *If I were twenty-five I could say, Thank God I am not him because I would know it was only my luck today and that maybe tomorrow or next year it will be me and so I will not need to envy him. And if I were sixty-five I could say, Thank God, I am not him because then I would know I was too old for it to be possible and so it would not do me any good to envy him because he has proof on the body of love and of passion and of life that he is not dead. But now I am forty-eight and I did not think that I deserved this.* "Wait," he said; "wait." The other paused; they stood facing one another, leaning a little into the dark wind filled with the wild dry sound of the palms.

"I offered to pay you," the other said. "Isn't five enough? And if it isn't, will you give me the name of someone who will come for that and let me use your telephone?"

"Wait," the doctor said. *So Cofer was right,* he thought. *You are not married. Only why did you have to tell me so?* He didn't say that, of course, he said, "You haven't . . . You are not . . . What are you?"

The other, taller, leaned in the hard wind, looking down at the doctor with that impatience, that seething restraint. In the black wind the house, the shack, stood, itself invisible, the dim light shaped not by any door or window but rather like a strip of dim and forlorn bunting dingy and rigidly immobile in the wind. "What am I what?" he said. "I'm trying to be a painter. Is that what you mean?"

"A painter? But there is no building, no boom, no development here any more. That died nine years ago. You mean, you came here without any offer of work, any sort of contract at all?"

"I paint pictures," the other said. "At least, I think I do—Well? Am I to use your phone or not?"

"You paint pictures," the doctor said; he spoke in that tone of quiet amazement which thirty minutes later and then tomorrow and tomorrow would vacillate among outrage and anger and despair: "Well. She's probably still bleeding. Come along." They went on. He entered the house first; even at the moment he realised that he had preceded the other not as a guest, not even as owner, but because he believed now that he alone of the two of them had any right to enter it at all so long as the woman was in it. They were out of the wind now. It merely leaned, black, imponderable and firm, against the door which the man called Harry had closed behind them: and now and at once the doctor smelled again the odor of stale and cooling gumbo. He even knew where it

would be; he could almost see it sitting uneaten (*They
have not even tasted it,* he thought. *But why should they?
Why in God's name should they?*) on the cold stove
since he knew the kitchen well—the broken stove, the
spare cooking vessels, the meager collection of broken
knives and forks and spoons, the drinking receptacles
which had once contained gaudily labelled and machine-
made pickle and jam. He knew the entire house well, he
owned it, he had built it—the flimsy walls (they were
not even tongue-and-groove like the one in which he
lived but were of ship-lap, the synthetic joints of which,
weathered and warped by the damp salt air, leaked all
privacy just as broken socks and trousers do) murmur-
ous with the ghosts of a thousand rented days and nights
to which he (though not his wife) had closed his eyes,
insisting only that there be always an odd number in
any mixed party which stayed there overnight unless the
couple were strangers formally professing to be man
and wife, as now, even though he knew better and knew
that his wife knew better. Because this was it, this the
anger and outrage which would alternate with the despair
tomorrow and tomorrow: *Why did you have to tell me?*
he thought. *The others didn't tell me, upset me, didn't
bring here what you brought, though I dont know what
they might have taken away.*

At once he could see the dim lamplight beyond the
open door. But he would have known which door without the light to guide him, the one beyond which the bed
would be, the bed in which his wife said she would not
ask a nigger servant to sleep; he could hear the other

behind him and he realised for the first time that the
man called Harry was still barefoot and that he was
about to pass and enter the room first, thinking (the
doctor) how he who actually had the only small portion
of right to enter of either of them must hold back, feeling a dreadful desire to laugh, thinking, *You see, I dont
know the etiquette in these cases because when I was
young and lived in the cities where apparently such as
this occurs, I suppose I was afraid, too afraid,* pausing
because the other paused: so that it seemed to the doctor, in a steady silent glare of what he was never to
know was actual clairvoyance, that they had both paused
as if to allow the shade, the shadow, of the absent outraged rightful husband to precede them. It was a sound
from within the room itself which moved them—the
sound of a bottle against a glass.

"Just a minute," the man named Harry said. He entered the room quickly; the doctor saw, flung across the
beach chair, the faded jeans that were too small for her
in exactly the right places. But he did not move. He just
heard the swift passage of the man's bare feet on the
floor and then his voice, tense, not loud, quiet, quite
gentle: so that suddenly the doctor believed he knew why
there had been neither pain nor terror in the woman's
face: that the man was carrying that too just as he carried the firewood and (doubtless) cooked with it the
food she ate. "No, Charlotte," he said. "You mustn't.
You cant. Come back to bed now."

"Why cant I?" the woman's voice said. "Why bloody
cant I?" and now the doctor could hear them struggling.

"Let me go, you bloody bungling bastard" (it was "rat," the noun, which the doctor believed he heard). "You promised, rat. That was all I asked and you promised. Because listen, rat—" the doctor could hear it, the voice cunning, secret now: "It wasn't him, you see. Not that bastard Wilbourne. I ratted off on him like I did you. It was the other one. You cant, anyway. I'll plead my ass like they used to plead their bellies and nobody ever knows just where the truth is about a whore to convict anybody—" The doctor could hear them, the two pairs of bare feet; it sounded as if they were dancing, furiously and infinitesimally and without shoes. Then this stopped and the voice was not cunning, not secret. *But where's the despair?* the doctor thought. *Where's the terror?* "Jesus, there I went again. Harry! Harry! You promised."

"I've got you. It's all right. Come back to bed."

"Give me a drink."

"No. I told you no more. I told you why not. Do you hurt bad now?"

"Jesus, I dont know. I cant tell. Give me the drink, Harry. Maybe that will start it again."

"No. It cant now. It's too late for that to. Besides, the doctor's here now. He'll start it again. I'm going to put your gown on you so he can come in."

"And risk bloodying up the only nightgown I ever owned?"

"That's why. That's why we got the gown. Maybe that's all it will take to start it again. Come on now."

"Then why the doctor? Why the five dollars? Oh,

you damned bloody bungling—No no no no. Quick.
There I go again. Stop me quick. I am hurting. I cant
help it. Oh, damn bloody bloody—" she began to laugh;
it was hard laughing and not loud, like retching or
coughing. "There. That's it. It's like dice. Come seven
come eleven. Maybe if I can just keep on saying it—"
He (the doctor) could hear them, the two pair of bare
feet on the floor, then the rusty plaint of the bed springs,
the woman still laughing, not loud, just with that ab-
stract and furious despair which he had seen in her eyes
over the bowl of gumbo at noon. He stood there, holding
his little scuffed worn serviceable black bag, looking at
the faded jeans among the wadded mass of other garments on the beach chair; he saw the man called Harry
reappear and select from among them a night gown and
vanish again; the doctor looked at the chair. *Yes* he
thought. *Just like the firewood.* Then the man called
Harry was standing in the door.

"You can come in now," he said.

Old Man

ONCE (IT WAS IN MISSISSIPPI, IN MAY, IN THE FLOOD
year 1927) there were two convicts. One of them was
about twenty-five, tall, lean, flat-stomached, with a sunburned face and Indian-black hair and pale, china-col-
ored outraged eyes—an outrage directed not at the men
who had foiled his crime, not even at the lawyers and
judges who had sent him here, but at the writers, the
uncorporeal names attached to the stories, the paper
novels—the Diamond Dicks and Jesse Jameses and such
—whom he believed had led him into his present predicament through their own ignorance and gullibility
regarding the medium in which they dealt and took
money for, in accepting information on which they
placed the stamp of verisimilitude and authenticity (this
so much the more criminal since there was no sworn
notarised statement attached and hence so much the
quicker would the information be accepted by one who
expected the same unspoken good faith, demanding, asking, expecting no certification, which he extended along
with the dime or fifteen cents to pay for it) and retailed
for money and which on actual application proved to
be impractical and (to the convict) criminally false;
there would be times when he would halt his mule and
plow in midfurrow (there is no walled penitentiary in
Mississippi; it is a cotton plantation which the convicts

23

work under the rifles and shotguns of guards and trus-
ties) and muse with a kind of enraged impotence, fumbling among the rubbish left him by his one and only
experience with courts and law, fumbling until the
meaningless and verbose shibboleth took form at last
(himself seeking justice at the same blind fount where
he had met justice and been hurled back and down):
Using the mails to defraud: who felt that he had been
defrauded by the third-class mail system not of crass and
stupid money which he did not particularly want anyway, but of liberty and honor and pride.

He was in for fifteen years (he had arrived shortly
after his nineteenth birthday) for attempted train robbery. He had laid his plans in advance, he had followed
his printed (and false) authority to the letter; he had
saved the paper-backs for two years, reading and re-
reading them, memorising them, comparing and weighing story and method against story and method, taking
the good from each and discarding the dross as his work-
able plan emerged, keeping his mind open to make the
subtle last-minute changes, without haste and without
impatience, as the newer pamphlets appeared on their
appointed days as a conscientious dressmaker makes the
subtle alterations in a court presentation costume as
the newer bulletins appear. And then when the day came,
he did not even have a chance to go through the coaches
and collect the watches and the rings, the brooches and
the hidden money-belts, because he had been captured
as soon as he entered the express car where the safe and
the gold would be. He had shot no one because the pistol

which they took away from him was not that kind of a pistol although it was loaded; later he admitted to the District Attorney that he had got it, as well as the dark lantern in which a candle burned and the black handkerchief to wear over the face, by peddling among his pine-hill neighbors subscriptions to the *Detectives' Gazette*. So now from time to time (he had ample leisure for it) he mused with that raging impotence, because there was something else he could not tell them at the trial, did not know how to tell them. It was not the money he had wanted. It was not riches, not the crass loot; that would have been merely a bangle to wear upon the breast of his pride like the Olympic runner's amateur medal—a symbol, a badge to show that he too was the best at his chosen gambit in the living and fluid world of his time. So that at times as he trod the richly shearing black earth behind his plow or with a hoe thinned the sprouting cotton and corn or lay on his sullen back in his bunk after supper, he cursed in a harsh steady unrepetitive stream, not at the living men who had put him where he was but at what he did not even know were pen-names, did not even know were not actual men but merely the designations of shades who had written about shades.

The second convict was short and plump. Almost hairless, he was quite white. He looked like something exposed to light by turning over rotting logs or planks and he too carried (though not in his eyes like the first convict) a sense of burning and impotent outrage. So it did not show on him and hence none knew it was there.

But then nobody knew very much about him, including
the people who had sent him here. His outrage was
directed at no printed word but at the paradoxical fact
that he had been forced to come here of his own free
choice and will. He had been forced to choose between
the Mississippi State penal farm and the Federal Penitentiary at Atlanta, and the fact that he, who resembled
a hairless and pallid slug, had chosen the out-of-doors
and the sunlight was merely another manifestation of
the close-guarded and solitary enigma of his character,
as something recognisable roils momentarily into view
from beneath stagnant and opaque water, then sinks
again. None of his fellow prisoners knew what his crime
had been, save that he was in for a hundred and ninety-
nine years—this incredible and impossible period of
punishment or restraint itself carrying a vicious and
fabulous quality which indicated that his reason for
being here was such that the very men, the paladins and
pillars of justice and equity who had sent him here had
during that moment become blind apostles not of mere
justice but of all human decency, blind instruments not
of equity but of all human outrage and vengeance, acting in a savage personal concert, judge, lawyer and
jury, which certainly abrogated justice and possibly
even law. Possibly only the Federal and State's Attorneys knew what the crime actually was. There had been
a woman in it and a stolen automobile transported
across a State line, a filling station robbed and the at-
tendant shot to death. There had been a second man in
the car at the time and anyone could have looked once

at the convict (as the two attorneys did) and known he
would not even have had the synthetic courage of alcohol to pull trigger on anyone. But he and the woman
and the stolen car had been captured while the second
man, doubtless the actual murderer, had escaped, so
that, brought to bay at last in the State's Attorney's
office, harried, dishevelled and snarling, the two grimly
implacable and viciously gleeful attorneys in his front
and the now raging woman held by two policemen in
the anteroom in his rear, he was given his choice. He
could be tried in Federal Court under the Mann Act and
for the automobile, that is, by electing to pass through
the anteroom where the woman raged he could take his
chances on the lesser crime in Federal Court, or by accepting a sentence for manslaughter in the State Court
he would be permitted to quit the room by a back entrance, without having to pass the woman. He had
chosen; he stood at the bar and heard a judge (who
looked down at him as if the District Attorney actually
had turned over a rotten plank with his toe and exposed
him) sentence him to a hundred and ninety-nine years
at the State Farm. Thus (he had ample leisure too; they
had tried to teach him to plow and had failed, they had
put him in the blacksmith shop and the foreman trusty
himself had asked to have him removed: so that now, in
a long apron like a woman, he cooked and swept and
dusted in the deputy wardens' barracks) he too mused at
times with that sense of impotence and outrage though it
did not show on him as on the first convict since he

leaned on no halted broom to do it and so none knew it
was there.

It was this second convict who, toward the end of
April, began to read aloud to the others from the daily
newspapers when, chained ankle to ankle and herded by
armed guards, they had come up from the fields and had
eaten supper and were gathered in the bunkhouse. It
was the Memphis newspaper which the deputy wardens
had read at breakfast; the convict read aloud from it to
his companions who could have had but little active interest in the outside world, some of whom could not
have read it for themselves at all and did not even
know where the Ohio and Missouri river basins were,
some of whom had never even seen the Mississippi River
although for past periods ranging from a few days to
ten and twenty and thirty years (and for future periods
ranging from a few months to life) they had plowed
and planted and eaten and slept beneath the shadow of
the levee itself, knowing only that there was water beyond it from hearsay and because now and then they
heard the whistles of steamboats from beyond it and,
during the last week or so had seen the stacks and pilot
houses moving along the sky sixty feet above their
heads.

But they listened, and soon even those who like the
taller convict had probably never before seen more
water than a horse pond would hold knew what thirty
feet on a river gauge at Cairo or Memphis meant and
could (and did) talk glibly of sandboils. Perhaps what
actually moved them were the accounts of the con-
scripted levee gangs, mixed blacks and whites working

in double shifts against the steadily rising water; stories of men, even though they were negroes, being
forced like themselves to do work for which they received no other pay than coarse food and a place in a
mudfloored tent to sleep on—stories, pictures, which
emerged from the shorter convict's reading voice: the
mudsplashed white men with the inevitable shot-guns,
the antlike lines of negroes carrying sandbags, slipping
and crawling up the steep face of the revetment to hurl
their futile ammuntion into the face of a flood and return
for more. Or perhaps it was more than this. Perhaps
they watched the approach of the disaster with that same
amazed and incredulous hope of the slaves—the lions
and bears and elephants, the grooms and bathmen and
pastrycooks—who watched the mounting flames of Rome
from Ahenobarbus' gardens. But listen they did and
presently it was May and the wardens' newspaper began
to talk in headlines two inches tall—those black stac-
cato slashes of ink which, it would almost seem, even
the illiterate should be able to read: *Crest Passes Memphis at Midnight 4000 Homeless in White River Basin
Governor Calls out National Guard Martial Law De-
clared in Following Counties Red Cross Train with Sec-
retary Hoover Leaves Washington Tonight*; then, three
evenings later (It had been raining all day—not the
vivid brief thunderous downpours of April and May,
but the slow steady gray rain of November and Decem-
ber before a cold north wind. The men had not gone
to the fields at all during the day, and the very second-
hand optimism of the almost twenty-four-hour-old news
seemed to contain its own refutation.): *Crest Now Below*

Memphis 22,000 Refugees Safe at Vicksburg Army Engineers Say Levees Will Hold.

"I reckon that means it will bust tonight," one convict said.

"Well, maybe this rain will hold on until the water gets here," a second said. They all agreed to this because what they meant, the living unspoken thought among them, was that if the weather cleared, even though the levees broke and the flood moved in upon the Farm itself, they would have to return to the fields and work, which they would have had to do. There was nothing paradoxical in this, although they could not have expressed the reason for it which they instinctively perceived: that the land they farmed and the substance they produced from it belonged neither to them who worked it nor to those who forced them at guns' point to do so, that as far as either—convicts or guards—were concerned, it could have been pebbles they put into the ground and papier-mâché cotton- and corn-sprouts which they thinned. So it was that, what between the sudden wild hoping and the idle day and the evening's headlines, they were sleeping restlessly beneath the sound of the rain on the tin roof when at midnight the sudden glare of the electric bulbs and the guards' voices waked them and they heard the throbbing of the waiting trucks.

"Turn out of there!" the deputy shouted. He was fully dressed—rubber boots, slicker and shotgun. "The levee went out at Mound's Landing an hour ago. Get up out of it!"

Wild Palms

When the man called Harry met Charlotte Rittenmeyer, he was an intern in a New Orleans hospital. He was the youngest of three children, born to his father's second wife in his father's old age; there was a difference of sixteen years between him and the younger of his two half sisters. He was left an orphan at the age of two and his older half sister had raised him. His father had been a doctor before him. He (the father) had begun and completed his medical training at a time when the designation Doctor of Medicine covered everything from pharmacology through diagnostics to surgery and when an education could be paid for in kind or in labor; the elder Wilbourne had been janitor of his dormitory and had also waited on table in commons and had completed his four-year course at a cash outlay of two hundred dollars. Thus when his will was opened, the last paragraph read:

> *To my son, Henry Wilbourne, and realizing that conditions as well as the intrinsic value of money have changed and therefore he cannot be expected to obtain his degree in Surgery and Medicine for the same outlay of money which obtained in my day, I hereby bequeath and set aside the sum of two thousand dollars, to be used for the furthering*

and completing of his college course and the ac-
quiring of his degree and license to practise in Sur-
gery and Medicine, believing that the aforesaid
sum will be amply sufficient for that purpose.

The will was dated two days after Harry's birth in
1910, and his father died two years later of toxemia got-
ten from sucking a snake bite on the hand of a child in
a country cabin and his half sister took him. She had
children of her own and was married to a man who
died still a clerk in a grocery store in a small Oklahoma
town, so by the time Harry was ready to enter medical
school that two thousand dollars to be stretched over
four years, even in the modest though well-rated school
which he chose, was not much more than his father's
two hundred had been. It was less, because there was
steam heat in the dormitories now and the college was
served by a cafeteria requiring no waiters and the only
way a young man could earn money in school now was
by carrying a football or stopping the man who did
carry it. His sister helped him—an occasional money
order for one or two dollars or even a few stamps folded
carefully into a letter. This bought his cigarettes and by
stopping tobacco for a year he saved enough to pay his
fee into his medical fraternity. There was nothing left
over for squiring girls (the school was coeducational)
but then he had no time for that; beneath the apparent
serenity of his monastic life he waged a constant battle
as ruthless as any in a Wall Street skyscraper as he
balanced his dwindling bank account against the turned
pages of his text books.

But he did it, he came in under the wire with enough of the two thousand dollars left either to return to the Oklahoma town and present his sheepskin to his sister, or to go straight to New Orleans and assume his internship, but not enough to do both. He chose New Orleans. Or rather, there was no choice; he wrote his sister and her husband a letter of gratitude and thanks, inclosing a signed note for the full amount of the postage stamps and the money orders, with interest (he also sent the diploma with its Latin and its spidery embossed salutation and its cramped faculty signatures, of which his sister and brother-in-law could decipher only his name) and mailed it to them and bought his ticket and rode fourteen hours in a day coach. He reached New Orleans with one bag and a dollar and thirty-six cents.

He had been in the hospital almost two years now. He lived in the intern's quarters with the others who, like him, had no private means; he smoked once a week now: a package of cigarettes over the week-end and he was paying the note which he had executed to his half sister, the one- and two-dollar money orders in reverse now, returning to source; the one bag would still hold all he owned, including his hospital whites—the twenty-six years, the two thousand dollars, the railroad ticket to New Orleans, the one dollar and thirty-six cents, the one bag in a corner of a barracks-like room furnished with steel army cots; on the morning of his twenty-seventh birthday he waked and looked down his body toward his foreshortened feet and it seemed to him that he saw the twenty-seven irrevocable years diminished and foreshortened beyond them in turn, as if his life were to lie passively on his back as though he floated effortless and without volition upon an unreturning stream. He seemed to see them: the empty years in which his youth had vanished—the years for wild oats and for daring, for the passionate tragic ephemeral loves of adolescence, the girl- and boy-white, the wild importunate fumbling flesh, which had not been for him; lying, so he thought, not exactly with pride and certainly not with the resignation which he believed, but rather with that peace with which a middleaged eunuch might look back upon the dead time before his alteration, at the fading and (at last) edgeless shapes which now inhabited only the memory and not the flesh: *I have repudiated money and hence love. Not abjured it, repudiated. I do not need it; by next year or two years or five years I will know to be true what I now believe to be true: I will not even need to want it.*

That evening he was a little late in going off duty; when he passed the dining room he heard already the clash of cutlery and the voices, and the interns' quarters were empty save for a man named Flint who in evening trousers and shirt was tying a black tie before the mirror and who turned as Wilbourne entered and pointed to a telegram on Wilbourne's pillow. It had been opened. "It was lying on my cot," Flint said. "I was in a hurry to dress so I didn't take time to look at the name good. I just picked it up and opened it. I'm sorry."

"That's all right," Wilbourne said. "Too many people have already seen a telegram for it to be very pri-

vate." He removed the folded yellow sheet from the
envelope. It was decorated with symbols—garlands and
scrolls; it was from his sister: one of those stereotyped
birthday greetings which the telegraph company sends
to any distance within the boundaries of the United
States for twenty-five cents. He found that Flint was still
watching him.

"So this is your birthday," Flint said. "Celebrating?"

"No," Wilbourne said. "I guess not."

"What? Listen. I'm going to a party down in French
Town. Why not come along?"

"No," Wilbourne said. "Thanks, though." He did
not yet begin to think, *Why not?* "I'm not invited."

"That dont matter. It's not that kind of a party. It's
at a studio. Painting guy. Just a mob sitting around on
the floor in each other's laps, drinking. Come on. You
dont want to stick here on your birthday." Now he did
begin to think, *Why not? Why really not?* and now he
could almost see the guardian of the old trained peace
and resignation rise to arms, the grim Moses, not
alarmed, impervious to alarm, just gauntly and fanat-
ically interdicting: *No. You will not go. Let well enough
alone. You have peace now; you want no more.*

"Besides, I haven't any dress clothes."

"You wont need them. Your host will probably be
wearing a bathrobe. You've got a dark suit, haven't
you?"

"But I dont—"

"All right," Flint said. "De Montigny has a tux. He's

about your size. I'll get it." He went to the closet which
they used in common.

"But I dont—" Wilbourne said.

"All right," Flint said. He laid the second dinner
suit on the cot and slipped his braces and began to re-
move his own trousers. "I'll wear de Montigny's and
you can wear mine. We're all three about standard."

An hour later, in a borrowed costume such as he had
never worn before, he and Flint halted in one of the
narrow, dim, balcony-hung one-way streets between
Jackson Square and Royal Street in the Vieux Carre—
a wall of soft muted brick above which the crest of a
cabbage palm exploded raggedly and from beyond
which came a heavy smell of jasmine which seemed to
lie visible upon the rich stagnant air already impreg-
nated with the smell of sugar and bananas and hemp
from the docks, like inert wisps of fog or even paint.
A wooden gate hung slightly awry, beside it a wire bell
pull which under Flint's hand produced a remote mel-
low jangling. They could hear a piano, it was something of Gershwin's. "There," Flint said. "You dont need
to worry about this party. You can already hear the
home-made gin. Gershwin might have painted his pictures for him too. Only I bet Gershwin could paint what
Crowe calls his pictures better than Crowe plays what
Gershwin calls his music."

Flint jerked the bell again, again nothing came of it.
"It's not locked, anyway," Wilbourne said. It was not,
they entered: a court paved with the same soft, quietly
rotting brick. There was a stagnant pool with a terra-

cotta figure, a mass of lantana, the single palm, the thick rich leaves and the heavy white stars of the jasmine bush where light fell upon it through open French doors, the court balcony—overhung too on three sides, the walls of that same annealing brick lifting a rampart broken and nowhere level against the glare of the city on the low eternally overcast sky, and over all, brittle, dissonant and ephemeral, the spurious sophistication of the piano like symbols scrawled by adolescent boys upon an ancient decayed rodent-scavengered tomb.

They crossed the court and entered the French windows and the noise—the piano, the voices—a longish room, uneven of floor, the walls completely covered with unframed paintings which at the moment impacted upon Wilbourne with that inextricable and detailless effect of an enormous circus poster seen suddenly at close range, from which vision the very eyeballs seem to start violently back in consternation. It contained no furniture except a piano at which a man sat in a Basque cap and a bathrobe. Perhaps a dozen other people sat or stood about on the floor with glasses; a woman in a sleeveless linen frock shrieked, "My God, where was the funeral?" and came and kissed Flint, still carrying her glass.

"This is Doctor Wilbourne, boys and girls," Flint said. "Watch him. He's got a pad of blank checks in his pocket and a scalpel in his sleeve." His host did not even turn his head, though a woman brought him a drink presently. It was his hostess, though no one had told him that; she stood and talked to him for a mo-

ment, or at him because he was not listening, he was
looking at the pictures on the wall; presently he stood
alone, still holding his glass, before the wall itself. He
had seen photographs and reproductions of such in
magazines before, at which he had looked completely
without curiosity because it was completely without
belief, as a yokel might look at a drawing of a dinosaur.
But now the yokel was looking at the monster itself and
Wilbourne stood before the paintings in complete ab-
sorption. It was not at what they portrayed, the method
or the coloring; they meant nothing to him. It was in a
bemusement without heat or envy at a condition which
could supply a man with the obvious leisure and means
to spend his days painting such as this and his evenings
playing the piano and feeding liquor to people whom
he ignored and (in one case, at least) whose names he
did not even bother to catch. He was still standing there
when someone behind said, "Here's Rat and Charley";
he was still standing there when Charlotte spoke at his
shoulder:

"What do you think about it, mister?" He turned and
saw a young woman a good deal shorter than he and for
a moment he thought she was fat until he saw it was not
fat at all but merely that broad, simple, profoundly
delicate and feminine articulation of Arabian mares—
a woman of under twenty-five, in a print cotton dress,
a face which laid no claim even to prettiness and wore
no makeup save the painted broad mouth, with a faint
inch-long scar on one cheek which he recognised as an

old burn, doubtless from childhood. "You haven't decided yet, have you?"

"No," he said. "I dont know."

"Dont know what you think, or whether you are trying to decide or not?"

"Yes. Probably that. What do you think about it?"

"Marshmallows with horseradish," she said, too
promptly. "I paint too," she added. "I can afford to
say. I can afford to say I can beat that, too. What's your
name, and what have you got all this on for, just to come
slumming? So we can all know you are slumming?"

He told her and now she looked at him and he saw
that her eyes were not hazel but yellow, like a cat's, staring at him with a speculative sobriety like a man might,
intent beyond mere boldness, speculative beyond any
staring. "I borrowed this suit. It's the first time in my
life I ever had one on." Then he said, he did not intend
to, he didn't even know he was going to say it, he
seemed to be drowning, volition and will, in the yellow
stare: "This is my birthday. I'm twenty-seven years
old."

"Oh," she said. She turned, she took him by the
wrist, a grasp simple, ruthless and firm, drawing him
after her. "Come on." He followed, awkwardly, not to
tread on her heels, then she released him and went on
before him, across the room to where three men and two
women stood about the table on which the bottles and
glasses sat. She stopped, she grasped his wrist again and
drew him toward a man of his own age about, in a dark
double-breasted suit, with blond wavy hair going a little

thin, a face not quite handsome and reasonably insensi-
tive and shrewder than intelligent yet on the whole gen-
tler than not, assured, courteous and successful. "This
is Rat," she said. "He is the senior living ex-freshman
of the University of Alabama. That's why we still call
him Rat. You can call him Rat too. Sometimes he is."

Later—it was after midnight and Flint and the woman
who had kissed him were gone—they stood in the court
beside the jasmine bush. "I've got two children, both
girls," she said. "That's funny, because all my family
were brothers except me. I liked my oldest brother the
best but you cant sleep with your brother and he and
Rat roomed together in school so I married Rat and
now I've got two girls, and when I was seven years old
I fell in the fireplace, my brother and I were fighting,
and that's the scar. It's on my shoulder and side and
hip too and I got in the habit of telling people about it
before they would have time not to ask and I still do it
even when it doesn't matter anymore."

"Do you tell everybody like this? At first?"

"About the brothers or about the scar?"

"Both. Maybe the scar."

"No. That's funny too. I had forgotten. I haven't told
anybody in years. Five years."

"But you told me."

"Yes. And that's funny twice. No, three times now.
Listen. I lied to you. I dont paint. I work with clay, and
some in brass, and once with a piece of stone, with a
chisel and maul. Feel." She took his hand and drew his
finger-tips along the base of her other palm—the broad,

blunt, strong, supple-fingered hand with nails as closely trimmed as if she had bitten them down, the skin at the base and lower joints of the fingers not calloused exactly but smoothly hardened and toughened like the heel of a foot. "That's what I make: something you can touch, pick up, something with weight in your hand that you can look at the behind side of, that displaces air and displaces water and when you drop it, it's your foot that breaks and not the shape. Not poking at a piece of cloth with a knife or a brush like you were trying to put together a jig-saw puzzle with a rotten switch through the bars of a cage. That's why I said I could beat that," she said. She didn't move, she didn't even indicate by a motion of her head the room behind them. "Not just something to tickle your taste buds for a second and then swallowed and maybe not even sticking to your entrails but just evacuated whole and flushed away into the damned old sewer, the Might-just-as-well-not-have-been. Will you come to supper tomorrow night?"

"I cant. I'm on duty tomorrow night."

"The next night then? Or when?"

"Dont you have engagements yourself?"

"There are some people coming the night after to-morrow. But they wont bother you." She looked at him. "All right, if you dont want a lot of people, I'll put them off. The night after tomorrow? At seven? Do you want me to come to the hospital for you in the car?"

"No. Dont do that."

"I can, you know."

"I know it," he said. "I know it. Listen—"

"Let's go in," she said. "I'm going home. And dont wear that. Wear your own clothes. I want to see."

Two evenings later he went to dinner. He found a modest though comfortable apartment in an irreproachable neighborhood near Audubon Park, a negro maid, two not particularly remarkable children of two and four, with her hair but otherwise looking like the father (who in another dark obviously expensive double-breasted suit made a cocktail not particularly remarkable either and insisted that Wilbourne call him Rat) and she in something he knew had been purchased as a semi-formal garment and which she wore with the same ruthless indifference as she had the garment in which he had first seen her, as if both of them were overalls. After the meal, which was considerably better than the cocktails, she went out with the older child, who had dined with them, but she returned presently to lie on the sofa smoking while Rittenmeyer continued to ask Wilbourne questions about his profession such as the president of a college fraternity might ask of a pledge from the medical school. At ten oclock Wilbourne said he must go. "No," she said, "not yet." So he remained; at half past ten Rittenmeyer said he must work tomorrow and was going to bed and left them. Then she crushed out the cigarette and rose and came to where he stood before the cold hearth and stopped, facing him. "What to—Do they call you Harry? What to do about it, Harry?"

"I dont know. I never was in love before."

"I have been. But I dont know either.—Do you want me to call a cab for you?"

"No." He turned; she moved beside him across the room. "I'll walk."

"Are you that poor? Let me pay for the cab. You cant walk to the hospital. It's three miles."

"That's not far."

"It wont be his money, if that's what you mean. I have some of my own. I have been saving it for something, I dont know what." She handed him his hat and stood with her hand on the door knob.

"Three miles is not far. I would walk—"

"Yes," she said. She opened the door, they looked at one another. Then the door closed between them. It was painted white. They did not shake hands.

During the next six weeks they met five times more. This would be downtown for lunch, because he would not again enter her husband's house and his destiny or luck (or ill-luck, since otherwise he might have discovered that love no more exists just at one spot and in one moment and in one body out of all the earth and all time and all the teeming breathed, than sunlight does) brought him no more second-hand invitations to parties. It would be in Vieux Carre places where they could lunch on the weekly two dollars which he had been sending to his sister to apply on the note. At the third of these she said abruptly, out of nothing: "I have told Rat."

"Told him?"

"About lunches. That I have been meeting you."

After that she never mentioned her husband again. The fifth time they did not lunch. They went to a hotel, they planned it the day before. He discovered that he knew next to nothing about the proper procedure other than, supposition and imagination; because of his ignorance he believed that there was a secret to the successful performance of the business, not a secret formula to be followed but rather a kind of white magic: a word or some infinitesimal and trivial movement of the hand such as that which opens a hidden drawer or panel. He thought once of asking her how to go about it because he was certain that she would know, just as he was certain that she would never be at a loss about anything she wished to do, not only because of her absolute coordination but because even in this short time he had come to realise that intuitive and infallible skill of all women in the practical affairs of love. But he did not ask her because he told himself that, when she told him how to do, which she would, and it would be correct, he might at some later time believe that she had done this before and that even if she had, he did not want to know it. So he asked Flint.

"Jesus," Flint said. "You have come out, haven't you? I didn't even know you knew a girl." Wilbourne could almost watch Flint thinking swiftly, casting backward. "Was it that brawl at Crowe's that night? But hell, that's your business, aint it? It's easy. Just take a bag with a couple of bricks wrapped up in a towel so they wont rattle, and walk in. I wouldn't pick the Saint Charles or the Roosevelt, of course. Take one of the smaller ones, not too small of course. Maybe that one down toward the station. Wrap the bricks separately, see, then roll them up together. And be sure to carry a coat with you. Raincoat."

"Yes. Do you reckon I'd better tell her to bring a coat too?"

Flint laughed, one short syllable, not loud. "I guess not. I dont guess she'll need any coaching from you or me either.—Here," he said quickly, "hold your horses. I dont know her. I aint talking about her. I'm talking about women. She could turn up with a bag of her own and a coat and a veil and the stub of a Pullman ticket sticking out of her handbag and that wouldn't mean she had done this before. That's just women. There aint any advice that Don Juan or Solomon either could give the youngest fourteen-year-old gal ever foaled about this kind of phenagling."

"It doesn't matter," he said. "She probably wont come anyway." He found that he really believed that. He still believed it even when the cab drew up to the curb where he waited with the bag. She had a coat, but no bag nor veil. She came swiftly out of the cab when he opened the door, her face was hard, sober, her eyes extraordinarily yellow, her voice harsh:

"Well? Where?"

He told her. "It's not far. We can—" She turned, already getting back into the cab. "We can walk—"

"You damned pauper," she said. "Get in. Hurry." He got in. The cab moved on. The hotel was not far. A negro porter took the bag. Then it seemed to Wilbourne

that he had never been in his life, and would never be
again, so aware of her as he was while she stood in the
center of the dingy lobby raddled with the Saturday
nights of drummers and of minor race-track hangers-on
while he signed the two fictitious names on the pad and
gave to the clerk the sixth two dollars which were to
have gone to his sister but did not, waiting for him,
making no effort for effacement, quiet, contained, and
with a quality profoundly tragic which he knew (he was
learning fast) was not peculiar to her but was an at-
tribute of all women at this instant in their lives, which
would invest them with a dignity, almost a modesty, to
be carried over and clothe even the last prone and
slightly comic attitude of ultimate surrender. He followed her down the corridor and into the door which
the porter opened; he dismissed the porter and closed
the rented door behind him and watched her cross the
room to the single dingy window and, still in the hat
and coat, turn without pausing and exactly like a child
playing prisoner's base return to him, the yellow
eyes, the whole face which he had already come to call
beautiful, hard and fixed. "Oh, God, Harry," she said.
She beat her clenched fists on his chest. "Not like this.
Jesus, not like this."

"All right," he said. "Steady, now." He caught her
wrists and held them, still doubled into fists against his
chest while she still wrenched at them to free them to
strike his chest again. *Yes,* he thought. *Not like this and
never.* "Steady now."

"Not like this, Harry. Not back alleys. I've always

said that: that no matter what happened to me, whatever I did, anything, anything but not back alleys. If it had just been hot pants, somebody with a physique I just leched for all of a sudden so that I never looked nor thought higher than his collar. But not us, Harry. Not you. Not you."

"Steady now," he said. "It's all right." He led her to the edge of the bed and stood over her, still holding her wrists.

"I told you how I wanted to make things, take the fine hard clean brass or stone and cut it, no matter how hard, how long it took, cut it into something fine, that you could be proud to show, that you could touch, hold, see the behind side of it and feel the fine solid weight so when you dropped it it wouldn't be the thing that broke it would be the foot it dropped on except it's the heart that breaks and not the foot, if I have a heart. But Jesus, Harry, how I have bitched it for you." She extended her hand, then he realised what she was about and twisted his hips away before she touched him.

"I'm all right," he said. "You mustn't worry about me. Do you want a cigarette?"

"Please." He gave her a cigarette and a light, looking down at the foreshortened slant of her nose and jaw as she drew at it. He threw the match away. "Well," she said. "So that's that. And no divorce."

"No divorce?"

"Rat's a Catholic. He wont give me one."

"You mean that he—"

"I told him. Not that I was to meet you at a hotel. I just said, suppose I did. And he still said no soap."

"Cant you get the divorce?"

"On what grounds? He would fight it. And it would have to be here—a Catholic judge. So there's just one other thing. And it seems I cant do that."

"Yes," he said. "Your children."

For a moment she looked at him, smoking. "I wasn't thinking of them. I mean, I have already thought of them. So now I dont need to think of them any more because I know the answer to that and I know I cant change that answer and I dont think I can change me because the second time I ever saw you I learned what I had read in books but I never had actually believed: that love and suffering are the same thing and that the value of love is the sum of what you have to pay for it and any time you get it cheap you have cheated your-self. So I dont need to think about the children. I settled that a long time ago. I was thinking about money. My brother sends me twenty-five dollars every Christmas and for the last five years I have saved it. I told you the other night I dont know why I have saved it. Maybe it was for this and maybe this is the best joke of all: that I have saved for five years and it's only a hundred and twenty-five dollars, hardly enough to get two people to Chicago. And you have nothing." She leaned toward the table at the head of the bed and crushed the cigarette out with slow and infinite care, and rose. "So that's that. That's all of it."

"No," he said. "No! I'll be damned if it is."

"Do you want to go on like this, hanging around and staying green for me like an apple on a limb?" She took his raincoat from the chair and slung it across her arm and stood waiting.

"Dont you want to go first?" he said. "I'll wait about thirty minutes, then I—"

"And let you walk alone through that lobby carrying the bag for that clerk and that nigger to snigger at because they saw me leave before I would have even had time to take my clothes off, let alone put them back on?" She went to the door and put her hand on the key. He picked up the bag and followed. But she did not unlock the door at once. "Listen. Tell me again you haven't got any money. Say it. So I can have something my ears can listen to as making sense even if I cant understand it. Some reason why I—that I can accept as the strong reason we cant beat even if I cant believe or understand that it could be just that, just money, not anything but just money. Come on. Say it."

"I have no money."

"All right. It makes sense. It must make sense. It will have to make sense." She began to shake, not tremble, shake, like one with a violent ague, the bones themselves seeming to chatter rigid and silent inside the flesh. "It will have—"

"Charlotte," he said. He set the bag down and moved toward her. "Charlotte—"

"Dont you touch me!" she whispered in a kind of tense fury. "Dont you touch me!" Yet for an instant he believed she was coming to him; she seemed to sway

forward, she turned her head and looked toward the bed
with an expression of distraction and despair. Then the
key clicked, the door opened, and she was out of the
room.

They parted as soon as he found a cab for her. He was
about to follow her into it, to ride down town to the
parking lot where she had left her car. Then for the
first of the two times in their lives he saw her cry. She
sat there, her face harsh and wrung and savage beneath
the springing tears like sweat. "Oh, you pauper, you
damned pauper, you transparent fool. It's money again.
After you paid the hotel two dollars you should have
sent your sister and got nothing for it, now you want to
pay this cab with what you intended to take your other
shirt out of the laundry with and get nothing for that
either but the privilege of transporting my damned ass
that at the last refused, will always refuse—" She leaned
toward the driver. "Go on!" she said savagely. "Drive
on! Downtown!"

The cab went on fast; it disappeared almost at once,
though he was not looking after it. After a while he said
quietly, aloud, to nobody: "At least, there's no use in
carrying the bricks too." So he walked on to where a
trash bin sat at the curb-edge and, while the people
passing glanced at him with curiosity or briefly or not
at all, he opened the bag and removed the bricks from
the towel and dropped them into the bin. It contained a
mass of discarded newspapers and fruit skins, the casual
anonymous droppings of the anonymous who passed it
during the twelve hours like the refuse of birds in flight.

The bricks struck the mass without a sound; there was no premonitory buzz or whirr at all, the edges of the papers merely tilted and produced from among them, with the magical abruptness with which the little metal torpedo containing change from a sale emerges from its tube in a store, a leather wallet. It contained the stubs of five pari-mutuel tickets from Washington Park, a customer's identification from a national gasoline trust and another from a B.P.O.E. lodge at Longview, Texas, and twelve hundred and seventy-eight dollars in bills.

He discovered the exact amount only after he reached the hospital however, his first thought was merely, *I ought to keep out a dollar for the reward* as he walked on toward the branch post office, then (the post office was not only six blocks away, it was in the opposite direction from the hospital) *I could even keep out taxi-fare and he should not mind. Not that I want to ride but that I've got to make it last, make everything last so there wont be any gaps between now and six oclock when I can hide behind my white jacket again, draw the old routine up over my head and face like niggers do the quilt when they go to bed.* Then he stood before the locked Saturday afternoon doors of the branch station and he had forgotten that too, thinking, as he buttoned the wallet into his hip pocket, how when he waked the name of today had been in fire letters and no word out of a nursery jingle or off a calendar, walking on, carrying the light bag, walking the now twelve useless blocks out of his way, thinking, *Only I have beat that too; I have*

*saved myself at least forty-five minutes of time that
otherwise would have been filled with leisure.*

The dormitory was empty. He put the bag away and
hunted for and found a flat cardboard box stippled with
holly-sprigs in which his sister had sent him one hand-
embroidered handkerchief last Christmas; he found
scissors and a bottle of paste and made a neat surgeon's
packet of the wallet, copying the address neatly and
clearly from one of the identification cards and putting
it carefully away beneath the garments in his drawer;
and now that was done too. *Maybe I can read,* he
thought. Then he cursed, thinking, *That's it. It's all exactly backward. It should be the books, the people in
the books inventing and reading about us—the Does and
Roes and Wilbournes and Smiths—males and females
but without the pricks or cunts.*

He went on duty at six. At seven he was relieved
long enough to go to supper. While he was eating one
of the probationer nurses looked in and told him he
was wanted on the telephone. It would be long distance,
he thought. It would be his sister, he had not written
her since he had sent the last two-dollar money order
five weeks ago, and now she had called him, would
spend two dollars herself, not to reproach him (*She's
right,* he thought, not meaning his sister. *It's comic. It's
more than comic. It rolls you in the aisles. I fail to make
the one I love and I make myself a failure toward the one
who loves me.*) but to see that he was well. So when the
voice on the wire said "Wilbourne?" he thought it was

his brother-in-law until Rittenmeyer spoke again: "Charlotte wants to speak to you."

"Harry?" she said. Her voice was rapid but calm: "I told Rat about today, and that it was a bust. So he's right. It's his turn now. He gave me a free shot, and I didn't make it. So now it's no more than fair to give him a free shot. And it's no more than decent to tell you what the score is, only decent is such a bastard word to have to use between you and me—"

"Charlotte," he said. "Listen, Charlotte—"

"So it's good-bye, Harry. And good luck. And good God damn—"

"Listen, Charlotte. Can you hear me?"

"Yes? What? What is it?"

"Listen. This is funny. I have been waiting all afternoon for you to call me, only I didn't know it until just now. I even know now that I knew then it was Saturday all the time I was walking toward that post office— Can you hear me? Charlotte?"

"Yes? Yes?"

"I've got twelve hundred and seventy-eight dollars, Charlotte."

At four oclock the next morning, in the empty laboratory, he cut up the wallet and the identification cards with a razor blade and burned the shreds of paper and leather and flushed the ashes away in a bathroom. The next day at noon, the two tickets to Chicago and the remainder of the twelve hundred and seventy-eight dollars buttoned into his pocket and the single bag on the seat facing him, he peered out the window as the

train slowed into the Carrollton Avenue station. They
were both there, the husband and the wife, he in the
conservative, spuriously unassertive dark suit, the face
of a college senior revealing nothing, lending an air of
impeccable and formal rightness to the paradoxical act
of handing the wife to the lover almost identical with
the conventional mumbo-jumbo of father and bride at a
wedding in church, she beside him in a dark dress beneath the open coat, watching the slowing car windows
intently yet without doubt or nervousness, so that Wilbourne mused again upon that instinctive proficiency in
and rapport for the mechanics of cohabitation even of
innocent and unpractised women—that serene confidence in their amorous destinies like that of birds in
their wings—that tranquil ruthless belief in an imminent deserved personal happiness which fledges them
instantaneous and full-winged from the haven of respectability, into untried and unsupportive space where
no shore is visible (*not sin*, he thought. *I dont believe in
sin. It's getting out of timing. You are born submerged
in anonymous lockstep with the teeming anonymous
myriads of your time and generation; you get out of
step once, falter once, and you are trampled to death.*)
and this without terror or alarm and hence inferring
neither of courage nor hardihood: just an utter and
complete faith in airy and fragile and untried wings—
wings, the airy and fragile symbols of love which have
failed them once, since by universal consent and ac-
ceptance they brooded over the very ceremony which,
in taking flight, they repudiate. They slid past and van-

ished, Wilbourne saw the husband stoop and raise the bag as they vanished; the air hissed into the brakes and he sat thinking, *He will come in with her, he will have to do that, he will not want to any more than I* (*she?*) *will want him to but he will have to do it just as he has to wear those dark suits which I dont believe he wants to wear either, just as he had to stay at that party that first night and drink as much as any other man there yet not once sit on the floor with a wife* (*his own or someone else's*) *sprawled across his knees.*

So he looked up presently and they were both standing beside his seat; he rose too and now the three of them stood, blocking the aisle while other passengers crowded past them or waited for them to move, Rittenmeyer carrying the bag—this man who ordinarily would no more have carried a bag into a train in the presence of a red cap or Pullman porter than he would have got up and fetched himself a glass of water in a restaurant; looking at the frozen impeccable face above the impeccable shirt and tie Wilbourne thought with a kind of amazement, *Why, he's suffering, he's actually suffering,* thinking how perhaps it is not the heart at all, not even the sensibilities, with which we suffer, but our capacity for grief or vanity or self-delusion or perhaps even merely masochism. "Go on," Rittenmeyer said. "Get out of the aisle." His voice was harsh, his hand almost rough as he pushed her into the seat and set the bag beside the other one. "Remember now. If I dont hear by the tenth of each month, I'm going to give the detective the word. And no lies, see? No lies." He turned, he

did not even look at Wilbourne, he merely jerked his
head toward the end of the,car. "I want to talk to you,"
he said in that seething repressed voice. "Come on."
When they were half way down the car the train began
to move, Wilbourne expected the other to run for the
exit, he thought again, *He is suffering; even circumstance, a trivial railroad time table, is making comedy of
that tragedy which he must play to the bitter end or cease
to breathe.* But the other did not even hurry. He went
steadily on and swung aside the curtain to the smoking
room and waited for Wilbourne to enter. He seemed to
read the temporary surprise in Wilbourne's face. "I've
got a ticket as far as Hammond," he said harshly. "Dont
you worry about me." The unspoken question seemed
to set him off; Wilbourne could almost see him struggling physically to keep his voice down. "Worry about
yourself, see? Yourself. Or by God——" Now he did
check the voice again, holding it on some sort of curb
like a horse, yet forcing it on; he took a wallet from his
pocket. "If you ever——" he said. "If you dare——"

He cant say it, Wilbourne thought. *He cant even bear
to say it.* "If I'm not good to her, gentle with her. Is that
what you mean?"

"I'll know it," Rittenmeyer said. "If I dont hear from
her by the tenth of every month, I am going to give the
detective the word to go ahead. And I'll know lies too,
see? See?" He was trembling, the impeccable face
suffused beneath the impeccable hair which resembled a
wig. "She's got a hundred and twenty-five dollars of her
own, she wouldn't take more. But damn that, she

wouldn't use that, anyway. She wont have it by the time she came to need it enough to use it. So here." He removed from the wallet a check and gave it to Wilbourne. It was a cashier's check for three hundred dollars, payable to the Pullman Company of America and indorsed in the corner in red ink: *For one railroad ticket to New Orleans, Louisiana.*

"I was going to do that with some of my money," Wilbourne said.

"Damn that too," the other said. "And it's for the ticket. If it is ever cashed and returned to the bank and no ticket bought with it, I'll have you arrested for fraud. See? I'll know."

"You mean, you want her to come back? You will take her back?" But he did not need to look at the other's face; he said quickly, "I'm sorry. I retract that. That's more than any man can bear to answer."

"God," the other said; "God. I ought to sock you." He added, in a tone of incredulous amazement, "Why dont I? Can you tell me? Aint a doctor, any doctor, supposed to be an authority on human glands?"

Then suddenly Wilbourne heard his own voice speaking out of an amazed and quiet incredulity; it seemed to him that they both stood now, aligned, embattled and doomed and lost, before the entire female principle: "I dont know. Maybe it would make you feel better." But the moment passed. Rittenmeyer turned and produced a cigarette from his coat and fumbled a match from the box attached to the wall. Wilbourne watched him—the trim back; he caught himself on the point of asking if the other wished him to stay and keep him company until the train reached Hammond. But again Rittenmeyer seemed to read his mind.

"Go on," he said. "Get to hell out of here and let me alone." Wilbourne left him standing facing the window and returned to his seat. Charlotte did not look up, she sat motionless, looking out the window, an unlighted cigarette in her fingers. Now they were running beside the larger lake, soon they would begin to cross the trestle between Maurepas and Pontchartrain. Now the whistle of the engine drifted back, the train slowed as beneath the sound of it came the hollow reverberation of the trestle. Water spread on either hand now, swampbound and horizonless, lined with rotting wooden jetties to which small dingy boats were tied. "I love water," she said. "That's where to die. Not in the hot air, above the hot ground, to wait hours for your blood to get cool enough to let you sleep and even weeks for your hair to stop growing. The water, the cool, to cool you quick so you can sleep, to wash out of your brain and out of your eyes and out of your blood all you ever saw and thought and felt and wanted and denied. He's in the smoking room, isn't he? Can I go back and speak to him a minute?"

"Can you go?—"

"Hammond is the next station."

Why, he is your husband, he was about to say but caught himself. "It's the men's room," he said. "Maybe I had better—" But she had already risen and passed him; he thought, *If she stops and looks back at me it*

*will mean she is thinking, 'Later I can always know that
at least I told him good-bye'* and she did stop and they
looked at each other, then she went on. Now the water
slid away, the sound of the trestle ceased, the engine
whistled again and the train regained speed, and almost
at once they were running through an outskirt of shabby
houses which would be Hammond, and he ceased to look
out the window while the train stopped and stood and
then moved again; he did not even have time to rise as
she slipped past him and into the seat. "So you came
back," he said.

"You didn't think I was. Neither did I."

"But you did."

"Only it's not finished. If he were to get back on the
train, with a ticket to Slidell——" She turned, staring at
him though she did not touch him. "It's not finished. It
will have to be cut."

"Cut?"

" 'If thine eye offend thee, pluck it out, lad, and be
whole.' That's it. Whole. Wholly lost—something. I've
got to cut it. That drawing room back there was empty.
Find the conductor and engage it to Jackson."

"Drawing room? But that will cost——"

"You fool!" she said. *She doesn't love me now,* he
thought. *She doesn't love anything now.* She spoke in a
tense whisper, beating on his knee with her fist. "You
fool!" She rose.

"Wait," he said, catching her wrist. "I'll do it." He
found the conductor in the vestibule at the end of the
car; he was not gone long. "All right," he said. She rose

at once, taking up her bag and coat. "The porter will be here—" he said. She didn't pause. "Let me have it," he said, taking the bag from her and then his own and followed her down the aisle. Later he was to recall that interminable walk between the filled seats where people sat with nothing else to do but watch them pass, and it seemed to him that everyone in the car must have known their history, that they must have disseminated an aura of unsanctity and disaster like a smell. They entered the drawing room.

"Lock the door," she said. He set the bags down and locked the door. He had never been in a drawing room before and he fumbled at the lock for an appreciable time. When he turned she had removed her dress: it lay in a wadded circle about her feet and she stood in the scant feminine underwear of 1937, her hands over her face. Then she removed her hands and he knew it was neither shame nor modesty, he had not expected that, and he saw it was not tears. Then she stepped out of the dress and came and began to unknot his tie, pushing aside his own suddenly clumsy fingers.

Old Man

WHEN THE BELATED AND STREAMING DAWN BROKE THE
two convicts, along with twenty others, were in a truck.
A trusty drove, two armed guards sat in the cab with
him. Inside the high, stall-like topless body the convicts
stood, packed like matches in an upright box or like the
pencil-shaped ranks of cordite in a shell, shackled by
the ankles to a single chain which wove among the
motionless feet and swaying legs and a clutter of picks
and shovels among which they stood, and was riveted
by both ends to the steel body of the truck.

Then and without warning they saw the flood about
which the plump convict had been reading and they
listening for two weeks or more. The road ran south.
It was built on a raised levee, known locally as a dump,
about eight feet above the flat surrounding land, bordered on both sides by the barrow pits from which the
earth of the levee had been excavated. These barrow
pits had held water all winter from the fall rains, not to
speak of the rain of yesterday, but now they saw that the
pit on either side of the road had vanished and instead
there lay a flat still sheet of brown water which extended
into the fields beyond the pits, ravelled out into long
motionless shreds in the bottom of the plow furrows and
gleaming faintly in the gray light like the bars of a
prone and enormous grating. And then (the truck was

moving at good speed) as they watched quietly (they
had not been talking much anyway but now they were
all silent and quite grave, shifting and craning as one to
look soberly off to the west side of the road) the crests
of the furrows vanished too and they now looked at a
single perfectly flat and motionless steel-colored sheet
in which the telephone poles and the straight hedgerows
which marked section lines seemed to be fixed and rigid
as though set in concrete.

It was perfectly motionless, perfectly flat. It looked,
not innocent, but bland. It looked almost demure. It
looked as if you could walk on it. It looked so still that
they did not realise it possessed motion until they came
to the first bridge. There was a ditch under the bridge, a
small stream, but ditch and stream were both invisible
now, indicated only by the rows of cypress and bramble
which marked its course. Here they both saw and heard
movement—the slow profound eastward and upstream
("It's running backward," one convict said quietly.) set
of the still rigid surface, from beneath which came a
deep faint subaquean rumble which (though none in
the truck could have made the comparison) sounded like
a subway train passing far beneath the street and which
inferred a terrific and secret speed. It was as if the water
itself were in three strata, separate and distinct, the
bland and unhurried surface bearing a frothy scum and
a miniature flotsam of twigs and screening as though by
vicious calculation the rush and fury of the flood itself,
and beneath this in turn the original stream, trickle,
murmuring along in the opposite direction, following

undisturbed and unaware its appointed course and serving its Lilliputian end, like a thread of ants between the rails on which an express train passes, they (the ants) as unaware of the power and fury as if it were a cyclone crossing Saturn.

Now there was water on both sides of the road and now, as if once they had become aware of movement in the water the water seemed to have given over deception and concealment, they seemed to be able to watch it rising up the flanks of the dump; trees which a few miles back had stood on tall trunks above the water now seemed to burst from the surface at the level of the lower branches like decorative shrubs on barbered lawns. The truck passed a negro cabin. The water was up to the window ledges. A woman clutching two children squatted on the ridgepole, a man and a halfgrown youth, standing waist-deep, were hoisting a squealing pig onto the slanting roof of a barn, on the ridgepole of which sat a row of chickens and a turkey. Near the barn was a haystack on which a cow stood tied by a rope to the center pole and bawling steadily; a yelling negro boy on a saddleless mule which he flogged steadily, his legs clutching the mule's barrel and his body leaned to the drag of a rope attached to a second mule, approached the haystack, splashing and floundering. The woman on the housetop began to shriek at the passing truck, her voice carrying faint and melodious across the brown water, becoming fainter and fainter as the truck passed and went on, ceasing at last, whether because of distance or because she had stopped screaming those in the truck did not know.

Then the road vanished. There was no perceptible slant to it yet it had slipped abruptly beneath the brown surface with no ripple, no ridgy demarcation, like a flat thin blade slipped obliquely into flesh by a delicate hand, annealed into the water without disturbance, as if it had existed so for years, had been built that way. The truck stopped. The trusty descended from the cab and came back and dragged two shovels from among their feet, the blades clashing against the serpentining of the chain about their ankles. "What is it?" one said. "What are you fixing to do?" The trusty didn't answer. He returned to the cab, from which one of the guards had descended, without his shotgun. He and the trusty, both in hip boots and each carrying a shovel, advanced into the water, gingerly, probing and feeling ahead with the shovel handles. The same convict spoke again. He was a middle-aged man with a wild thatch of iron-gray hair and a slightly mad face. "What the hell are they doing?" he said. Again nobody answered him. The truck moved, on into the water, behind the guard and the trusty, beginning to push ahead of itself a thick slow viscid ridge of chocolate water. Then the gray-haired convict began to scream. "God damn it, unlock the chain!" He began to struggle, thrashing violently about him, striking at the men nearest him until he reached the cab, the roof of which he now hammered on with his fists, screaming. "God damn it, unlock us! Unlock us! Son of a bitch!" he screamed, addressing no one.

"They're going to drown us! Unlock the chain!" But for all the answer he got the men within radius of his voice might have been dead. The truck crawled on, the guard and the trusty feeling out the road ahead with the reversed shovels, the second guard at the wheel, the twenty-two convicts packed like sardines into the truck bed and padlocked by the ankles to the body of the truck itself. They crossed another bridge—two delicate and paradoxical iron railings slanting out of the water, travelling parallel to it for a distance, then slanting down into it again with an outrageous quality almost significant yet apparently meaningless like something in a dream not quite nightmare. The truck crawled on.

Along toward noon they came to a town, their destination. The streets were paved; now the wheels of the truck made a sound like tearing silk. Moving faster now, the guard and the trusty in the cab again, the truck even had a slight bone in its teeth, its bow-wave spreading beyond the submerged sidewalks and across the adjacent lawns, lapping against the stoops and porches of houses where people stood among piles of furniture. They passed through the business district; a man in hip boots emerged knee-deep in water from a store, dragging a flat-bottomed skiff containing a steel safe.

At last they reached the railroad. It crossed the street at right angles, cutting the town in two. It was on a dump, a levee, also, eight or ten feet above the town itself; the street ran blankly into it and turned at right angles beside a cotton compress and a loading platform on stilts at the level of a freight car door. On this platform was a khaki army tent and a uniformed National Guard sentry with a rifle and bandolier.

The truck turned and crawled out of the water and up the ramp which cotton wagons used and where trucks and private cars filled with household goods came and unloaded onto the platform. They were unlocked from the chain in the truck and shackled ankle to ankle in pairs they mounted the platform and into an apparently inextricable jumble of beds and trunks, gas and electric stoves, radios and tables and chairs and framed pictures which a chain of negroes under the eye of an unshaven white man in muddy corduroy and hip boots carried piece by piece into the compress, at the door of which another guardsman stood with his rifle, they (the convicts) not stopping here but herded on by the two guards with their shotguns, into the dim and cavernous building where among the piled heterogeneous furniture the ends of cotton bales and the mirrors on dressers and sideboards gleamed with an identical mute and unreflecting concentration of pallid light.

They passed on through, onto the loading platform where the army tent and the first sentry were. They waited here. Nobody told them for what nor why. While the two guards talked with the sentry before the tent the convicts sat in a line along the edge of the platform like buzzards on a fence, their shackled feet dangling above the brown motionless flood out of which the railroad embankment rose, pristine and intact, in a kind of paradoxical denial and repudiation of change and portent, not talking, just looking quietly across the track to where the other half of the amputated town seemed to float, house shrub and tree, ordered and pageant-like and without motion, upon the limitless liquid plain beneath the thick gray sky.

After a while the other four trucks from the Farm arrived. They came up, bunched closely, radiator to tail light, with their four separate sounds of tearing silk and vanished beyond the compress. Presently the ones on the platform heard the feet, the mute clashing of the shackles, the first truckload emerged from the compress, the second, the third; there were more than a hundred of them now in their bed-ticking overalls and jumpers and fifteen or twenty guards with rifles and shotguns. The first lot rose and they mingled, paired, twinned by their clanking and clashing umbilicals; then it began to rain, a slow steady gray drizzle like November instead of May. Yet not one of them made any move toward the open door of the compress. They did not even look toward it, with longing or hope or without it. If they thought at all, they doubtless knew that the available space in it would be needed for furniture, even if it were not already filled. Or perhaps they knew that, even if there were room in it, it would not be for them, not that the guards would wish them to get wet but that the guards would not think about getting them out of the rain. So they just stopped talking and with their jumper collars turned up and shackled in braces like dogs at a field trial they stood, immobile, patient, almost rumi-nant, their backs turned to the rain as sheep and cattle do.

After another while they became aware that the number of soldiers had increased to a dozen or more, warm and dry beneath rubberised ponchos, there was an officer with a pistol at his belt, then and without making any move toward it, they began to smell food and, turning to look, saw an army field kitchen set up just inside the compress door. But they made no move, they waited until they were herded into line, they inched forward, their heads lowered and patient in the rain, and received each a bowl of stew, a mug of coffee, two slices of bread. They ate this in the rain. They did not sit down because the platform was wet, they squatted on their heels as country men do, hunching forward, trying to shield the bowls and mugs into which nevertheless the rain splashed steadily as into miniature ponds and soaked, invisible and soundless, into the bread.

After they had stood on the platform for three hours, a train came for them. Those nearest the edge saw it, watched it—a passenger coach apparently running under its own power and trailing a cloud of smoke from no visible stack, a cloud which did not rise but instead shifted slowly and heavily aside and lay upon the surface of the aqueous earth with a quality at once weightless and completely spent. It came up and stopped, a single old fashioned open-ended wooden car coupled to the nose of a pushing switch engine considerably smaller. They were herded into it, crowding forward to the other end where there was a small cast iron stove. There was no fire in it, nevertheless they crowded about it—the cold and voiceless lump of iron stained with fading tobacco and hovered about by the ghosts of a thousand Sunday excursions to Memphis or Moorhead and return—the peanuts, the bananas, the soiled garments of infants—huddling, shoving for places near it. "Come on, come on," one of the guards shouted. "Sit down, now." At last three of the guards, laying aside their guns, came among them and broke up the huddle, driving them back and into seats.

There were not enough seats for all. The others stood in the aisle, they stood braced, they heard the air hiss out of the released brakes, the engine whistled four blasts, the car came into motion with a snapping jerk; the platform, the compress fled violently as the train seemed to transpose from immobility to full speed with that same quality of unreality with which it had appeared, running backward now though with the engine in front where before it had moved forward but with the engine behind.

When the railroad in its turn ran beneath the surface of the water, the convicts did not even know it. They felt the train stop, they heard the engine blow a long blast which wailed away unechoed across the waste, wild and forlorn, and they were not even curious; they sat or stood behind the rain-streaming windows as the train crawled on again, feeling its way as the truck had while the brown water swirled between the trucks and among the spokes of the driving wheels and lapped in cloudy steam against the dragging fire-filled belly of the engine; again it blew four short harsh blasts filled with the wild triumph and defiance yet also with repudiation and even

farewell, as if the articulated steel itself knew it did not
dare stop and would not be able to return. Two hours
later in the twilight they saw through the streaming
windows a burning plantation house. Juxtaposed to
nowhere and neighbored by nothing it stood, a clear
steady pyre-like flame rigidly fleeing its own reflection,
burning in the dusk above the watery desolation with a
quality paradoxical, outrageous and bizarre.

Sometime after dark the train stopped. The convicts
did not know where they were. They did not ask. They
would no more have thought of asking where they were
than they would have asked why and what for. They
couldn't even see, since the car was unlighted and the
windows fogged on the outside by rain and on the inside
by the engendered heat of the packed bodies. All they
could see was a milky and sourceless flick and glare of
flashlights. They could hear shouts and commands, then
the guards inside the car began to shout; they were
herded to their feet and toward the exit, the ankle chains
clashing and clanking. They descended into a fierce hissing of steam, through ragged wisps of it blowing past
the car. Laid-to alongside the train and resembling a
train itself was a thick blunt motor launch to which was
attached a string of skiffs and flat boats. There were
more soldiers; the flashlights played on the rifle barrels
and bandolier buckles and flicked and glinted on the
ankle chains of the convicts as they stepped gingerly
down into knee-deep water and entered the boats; now
car and engine both vanished completely in steam as
the crew began dumping the fire from the firebox.

After another hour they began to see lights ahead—a faint wavering row of red pin-pricks extending along the horizon and apparently hanging low in the sky. But it took almost another hour to reach them while the convicts squatted in the skiffs, huddled into the soaked garments (they no longer felt the rain any more at all as separate drops) and watched the lights draw nearer and nearer until at last the crest of the levee defined itself; now they could discern a row of army tents stretching along it and people squatting about the fires, the wavering reflections from which, stretching across the water, revealed an involved mass of other skiffs tied against the flank of the levee which now stood high and dark overhead. Flashlights glared and winked along the base, among the tethered skiffs; the launch, silent now, drifted in.

When they reached the top of the levee they could see the long line of khaki tents, interspersed with fires about which people—men, women and children, negro and white—crouched or stood among shapeless bales of clothing, their heads turning, their eyeballs glinting in the firelight as they looked quietly at the striped garments and the chains; further down the levee, huddled together too though untethered, was a drove of mules and two or three cows. Then the taller convict became conscious of another sound. He did not begin to hear it all at once, he suddenly became aware that he had been hearing it all the time, a sound so much beyond all his experience and his powers of assimilation that up to this point he had been as oblivious of it as an ant or a flea might be of the sound of the avalanche on which it rides; he had been travelling upon water since early afternoon and for seven years now he had run his plow and harrow and planter within the very shadow of the levee on which he now stood, but this profound deep whisper which came from the further side of it he did not at once recognise. He stopped. The line of convicts behind jolted into him like a line of freight cars stopping, with an iron clashing like cars. "Get on!" a guard shouted.

"What's that?" the convict said. A negro man squatting before the nearest fire answered him:

"Dat's him. Dat's de Ole Man."

"The old man?" the convict said.

"Get on! Get on up there!" the guard shouted. They went on; they passed another huddle of mules, the eyeballs rolling too, the long morose faces turning into and out of the firelight; they passed them and reached a section of empty tents, the light pup tents of a military campaign, made to hold two men. The guards herded the convicts into them, three brace of shackled men to each tent.

They crawled in on all fours, like dogs into cramped kennels, and settled down. Presently the tent became warm from their bodies. Then they became quiet and then all of them could hear it, they lay listening to the bass whisper deep, strong and powerful. "The old man?" the train-robber convict said.

"Yah," another said. "He dont have to brag."

At dawn the guards waked them by kicking the soles

of the projecting feet. Opposite the muddy landing and
the huddle of skiffs an army field kitchen was set up,
already they could smell the coffee. But the taller convict at least, even though he had had but one meal yesterday and that at noon in the rain, did not move at
once toward the food. Instead and for the first time he
looked at the River within whose shadow he had spent
the last seven years of his life but had never seen before; he stood in quiet and amazed surmise and looked
at the rigid steel-colored surface not broken into waves
but merely slightly undulant. It stretched from the levee
on which he stood, further than he could see—a slowly
and heavily roiling chocolate-frothy expanse broken
only by a thin line a mile away as fragile in appearance
as a single hair, which after a moment he recognised.
It's another levee, he thought quietly. *That's what we
look like from there. That's what I am standing on looks
like from there.* He was prodded from the rear; a guard's
voice carried forward: "Go on! Go on! You'll have
plenty of time to look at that!"

They received the same stew and coffee and bread as
the day before; they squatted again with their bowls and
mugs as yesterday, though it was not raining yet. During
the night an intact wooden barn had floated up. It now
lay jammed by the current against the levee while a
crowd of negroes swarmed over it, ripping off the
shingles and planks and carrying them up the bank;
eating steadily and without haste, the taller convict
watched the barn dissolve rapidly down to the very

water-line exactly as a dead fly vanished beneath the moiling industry of a swarm of ants.

They finished eating. Then it began to rain again, as upon a signal, while they stood or squatted in their harsh garments which had not dried out during the night but had merely become slightly warmer than the air. Presently they were haled to their feet and told off into two groups, one of which was armed from a stack of mud-clogged picks and shovels nearby, and marched away up the levee. A little later the motor launch with its train of skiffs came up across what was, fifteen feet beneath its keel, probably a cotton field, the skiffs loaded to the gunwales with negroes and a scattering of white people nursing bundles on their laps. When the engine shut off the faint plinking of a guitar came across the water. The skiffs warped in and unloaded; the convicts watched the men and women and children struggle up the muddy slope, carrying heavy towsacks and bundles wrapped in quilts. The sound of the guitar had not ceased and now the convicts saw him—a young, black, lean-hipped man, the guitar slung by a piece of cotton plow line about his neck. He mounted the levee, still picking it. He carried nothing else, no food, no change of clothes, not even a coat.

The taller convict was so busy watching this that he did not hear the guard until the guard stood directly beside him shouting his name. "Wake up!" the guard shouted. "Can you fellows paddle a boat?"

"Paddle a boat where?" the taller convict said.

"In the water," the guard said. "Where in hell do you think?"

"I aint going to paddle no boat nowhere out yonder," the tall convict said, jerking his head toward the invisible river beyond the levee behind him.

"No, it's on this side," the guard said. He stooped swiftly and unlocked the chain which joined the tall convict and the plump hairless one. "It's just down the road a piece." He rose. The two convicts followed him down to the boats. "Follow them telephone poles until you come to a filling station. You can tell it, the roof is still above water. It's on a bayou and you can tell the bayou because the tops of the trees are sticking up. Follow the bayou until you come to a cypress snag with a woman in it. Pick her up and then cut straight back west until you come to a cotton house with a fellow sitting on the ridgepole—" He turned, looking at the two convicts, who stood perfectly still, looking first at the skiff and then at the water with intense sobriety. "Well? What are you waiting for?"

"I cant row a boat," the plump convict said.

"Then it's high time you learned," the guard said. "Get in."

The tall convict shoved the other forward. "Get in," he said. "That water aint going to hurt you. Aint nobody going to make you take a bath."

As, the plump one in the bow and the other in the stern, they shoved away from the levee, they saw other pairs being unshackled and manning the other skiffs. "I wonder how many more of them fellows are seeing this much water for the first time in their lives too," the tall convict said. The other did not answer. He knelt in the bottom of the skiff, pecking gingerly at the water now and then with his paddle. The very shape of his thick soft back seemed to wear that expression of wary and tense concern.

Some time after midnight a rescue boat filled to the guard rail with homeless men and women and children docked at Vicksburg. It was a steamer, shallow of draft; all day long it had poked up and down cypress- and gum-choked bayous and across cotton fields (where at times instead of swimming it waded) gathering its sorry cargo from the tops of houses and barns and even out of trees, and now it warped into that mushroom city of the forlorn and despairing where kerosene flares smoked in the drizzle and hurriedly strung electrics glared upon the bayonets of martial policemen and the red cross brassards of doctors and nurses and canteen-workers. The bluff overhead was almost solid with tents, yet still there were more people than shelter for them; they sat or lay, single and by whole families, under what shelter they could find or sometimes under the rain itself, in the little death of profound exhaustion while the doctors and the nurses and the soldiers stepped over and around and among them.

Among the first to disembark was one of the penitentiary deputy wardens, followed closely by the plump convict and another white man—a small man with a gaunt unshaven wan face still wearing an expression of incredulous outrage. The deputy warden seemed to know exactly where he wished to go. Followed closely by his two companions he threaded his way swiftly among the piled furniture and the sleeping bodies and stood presently in a fiercely lighted and hastily established temporary office, almost a military post of command in fact, where the Warden of the Penitentiary sat with two army officers wearing majors' leaves. The deputy warden spoke without preamble. "We lost a man," he said. He called the tall convict's name.

"Lost him?" the Warden said.

"Yah. Drowned." Without turning his head he spoke to the plump convict. "Tell him," he said.

"He was the one that said he could row a boat," the plump convict said. "I never. I told him myself—" he indicated the deputy warden with a jerk of his head "—I couldn't. So when we got to the bayou—"

"What's this?" the Warden said.

"The launch brought word in," the deputy warden said. "Woman in a cypress snag on the bayou, then this fellow—" he indicated the third man; the Warden and the two officers looked at the third man "—on a cotton house. Never had room in the launch to pick them up. Go on."

"So we come to where the bayou was," the plump convict continued in a voice perfectly flat, without any inflection whatever. "Then the boat got away from him. I dont know what happened. I was just sitting there because he was so positive he could row a boat. I never saw any current. Just all of a sudden the boat whirled clean around and begun to run fast backward like it was

hitched to a train and it whirled around again and I
happened to look up and there was a limb right over
my head and I grabbed it just in time and that boat was
snatched out from under me like you'd snatch off a sock
and I saw it one time more upside down and that fellow
that said he knew all about rowing holding to it with one
hand and still holding the paddle in the other—" He
ceased. There was no dying fall to his voice, it just
ceased and the convict stood looking quietly at a half-
full quart of whiskey sitting on the table.

"How do you know he's drowned?" the Warden said
to the deputy. "How do you know he didn't just see his
chance to escape, and took it?"

"Escape where?" the other said. "The whole Delta's
flooded. There's fifteen foot of water for fifty miles, clean
back to the hills. And that boat was upside down."

"That fellow's drowned," the plump convict said.
"You dont need to worry about him. He's got his pardon;
it wont cramp nobody's hand signing it, neither."

"And nobody else saw him?" the Warden said. "What
about the woman in the tree?"

"I dont know," the deputy said. "I aint found her yet.
I reckon some other boat picked her up. But this is the
fellow on the cotton house."

Again the Warden and the two officers looked at the
third man, at the gaunt, unshaven wild face in which an
old terror, an old blending of fear and impotence and
rage still lingered. "He never came for you?" the Warden said. "You never saw him?"

"Never nobody came for me," the refugee said. He

began to tremble though at first he spoke quietly enough. "I set there on that sonabitching cotton house, expecting hit to go any minute. I saw that launch and them boats come up and they never had no room for me. Full of bastard niggers and one of them setting there playing a guitar but there wasn't no room for me. A guitar!" he cried; now he began to scream, trembling, slavering, his face twitching and jerking. "Room for a bastard nigger guitar but not for me—"

"Steady now," the Warden said. "Steady now."

"Give him a drink," one of the officers said. The Warden poured the drink. The deputy handed it to the refugee, who took the glass in both jerking hands and tried to raise it to his mouth. They watched him for perhaps twenty seconds, then the deputy took the glass from him and held it to his lips while he gulped, though even then a thin trickle ran from each corner of his mouth, into the stubble on his chin.

"So we picked him and—" the deputy called the plump convict's name now "—both up just before dark and come on in. But that other fellow is gone."

"Yes," the Warden said. "Well. Here I haven't lost a prisoner in ten years, and now, like this—I'm sending you back to the Farm tomorrow. Have his family notified, and his discharge papers filled out at once."

"All right," the deputy said. "And listen, chief. He wasn't a bad fellow and maybe he never had no business in that boat. Only he did say he could paddle one. Listen. Suppose I write on his discharge, Drowned while trying to save lives in the great flood of nineteen twenty-seven, and send it down for the Governor to sign it. It will be something nice for his folks to have, to hang on the wall when neighbors come in or something. Maybe they will even give his folks a cash bonus because after all they sent him to the Farm to raise cotton, not to fool around in a boat in a flood."

"All right," the Warden said. "I'll see about it. The main thing is to get his name off the books as dead before some politician tries to collect his food allowance."

"All right," the deputy said. He turned and herded his companions out. In the drizzling darkness again he said to the plump convict: "Well, your partner beat you. He's free. He's done served his time out but you've got a right far piece to go yet."

"Yah," the plump convict said. "Free. He can have it."

Wild Palms

On the second morning in the Chicago hotel Wilbourne waked and found that Charlotte was dressed and gone, hat coat and handbag, leaving a note for him in a big sprawling untrained hand such as you associate at first glance with a man until you realise an instant later it is profoundly feminine: *Back at noon. C.*, then, beneath the initial: *Or maybe later.* She returned before noon, he was asleep again; she sat on the side of the bed, her hand in his hair, rolling his head on the pillow to shake him awake, still in the open coat and the hat shoved back from her forehead, looking down at him with that sober yellow profundity, and now he mused indeed on that efficiency of women in the mechanics, the domiciling, of cohabitation. Not thrift, not husbandry, something far beyond that, who (the entire race of them) employed with infallible instinct, a completely uncerebrated rapport for the type and nature of male partner and situation, either the cold penuriousness of the fabled Vermont farmwife or the fantastic extravagance of the Broadway revue mistress as required, absolutely without regard for the intrinsic value of the medium which they saved or squandered and with little more regard or grief for the bauble which they bought or lacked, using both the presence and absence of jewel or checking account as pawns in a chess game whose prize was not security at all but respectability within the milieu in which they lived, even the love-nest under the rose to follow a rule and a pattern; he thought, *It's not the romance of illicit love which draws them, not the passionate idea of two damned and doomed and isolated forever against the world and God and the irrevocable which draws men; it's because the idea of illicit love is a challenge to them, because they have an irresistible desire to (and an unshakable belief that they can, as they all believe they can successfully conduct a boarding house) take the illicit love and make it respectable, take Lothario himself and trim the very incorrigible bachelor's ringlets which snared them into the seemly decorum of Monday's hash and suburban trains.* "I've found it," she said.

"Found what?"

"An apartment. A studio. Where I can work too."

"Too?" She shook his head again with that savage obliviousness, she actually hurt him a little; he thought again, *There's a part of her that doesn't love anybody, anything;* and then, a profound and silent lightning-clap—a white glare—ratiocination, instinct, he did not know which: *Why, she's alone. Not lonely, alone. She had a father and then four brothers exactly like him and then she married a man exactly like the four brothers and so she probably never even had a room of her own in all her life and so she has lived all her life in complete solitude and she doesn't even know it as a child who has never tasted cake doesn't know what cake is.*

"Yes, too. Do you think that twelve hundred dollars will last forever? You live *in* sin; you cant live on it."

"I know it. I thought of that before I told you over the phone that night I had twelve hundred dollars. But this is honeymoon; later will be—"

"I know that too." She grasped his hair again, hurting him again though now he knew she knew she was hurting him. "Listen: it's got to be all honeymoon, always. Forever and ever, until one of us dies. It cant be anything else. Either heaven, or hell: no comfortable safe peaceful purgatory between for you and me to wait in until good behavior or forbearance or shame or repentance overtakes us."

"So it's not me you believe in, put trust in; it's love." She looked at him. "Not just me; any man."

"Yes. It's love. They say love dies between two people. That's wrong. It doesn't die. It just leaves you, goes away, if you are not good enough, worthy enough. It doesn't die; you're the one that dies. It's like the ocean: if you're no good, if you begin to make a bad smell in it, it just spews you up somewhere to die. You die anyway, but I had rather drown in the ocean than be urped up onto a strip of dead beach and be dried away by the sun into a little foul smear with no name to it, just *This Was* for an epitaph. Get up. I told the man we would move in today."

They left the hotel with their bags within the hour, by cab; they mounted three flights of stairs. She even had the key; she opened the door for him to enter; he knew she was looking not at the room but at him. "Well?" she said. "Do you like it?"

It was a big oblong room with a skylight in the north wall, possibly the handiwork of a dead or bankrupt photographer or maybe a former sculptor or painter tenant, with two cubbyholes for kitchen and bath. *She rented that skylight,* he told himself quietly, thinking how as a rule women rent bathrooms primarily. *It's only incidental that there is a place to sleep and cook food. She chose a place not to hold us but to hold love; she did not just run from one man to another; she did not merely mean to swap one piece of clay she made a bust with for another—* He moved now, and then he thought, *Maybe I'm not embracing her but clinging to her because there is something in me that wont admit it cant swim or cant believe it can.* "It's all right," he said. "It's fine. Nothing can beat us now."

During the next six days he made the rounds of the hospitals, interviewing (or being interviewed by) Residents and Staff Heads. They were brief interviews. He was not particular what he did and he had something to offer—his degree from a good medical school, his twenty months' internship in a hospital which was known, yet always after the first three or four minutes, something began to happen. He knew what it was, though he told himself differently (this sitting after the fifth interview, on a sunny bench in a park among the bums and W.P.A. gardeners and nursemaids and children): *It's because I really dont try hard enough, dont really realise the need for trying because I have accepted com-*

*pletely her ideas about love; I look upon love with the
same boundless faith that it will clothe and feed me as
the Mississippi or Louisiana countryman, converted last
week at a camp-meeting revival, looks upon religion,*
knowing that that was not the reason, that it was the
twenty months of internship instead of twenty-four,
thinking *I have been confounded by numbers,* thinking
how it is apparently more seemly to die in the dulcet
smell than to be saved by an apostate from convention.

At last he found a job. It was not much; it was laboratory work in a charity hospital in the negro tenement
district, where victims of alcohol or pistol- and knife-
wounds were brought, usually by police, and his job
was making routine tests for syphilis. "You dont need a
microscope or Wassermann paper," he told her that
night. "All you need is enough light to tell what race
they belong to." She had set two planks on trestles beneath the skylight which she called her work bench and
at which for some time now she had been puttering with
a package of plaster of paris from the ten cent store,
though he had paid little attention to what she was doing. She now bent over this table with a scrap of paper
and a pencil while he watched the blunt supple hand
make the big sprawling rapid figures.

"You will make this much a month," she said. "And
it costs this much for us to live a month. And we have
this much to draw from to make up the difference." The
figures were cold, incontrovertible, the very pencil marks
had a scornful and impregnable look; incidentally she
now saw to it that he made not only the current weekly

remittances to his sister but that he had also sent to her the equivalent sum of the lunches and the abortive hotel during the six weeks in New Orleans. Then she wrote down a date beside the last figure; it would be in early September. "On that day we wont have any money left."

Then he repeated something he had thought while sitting on the park bench that day: "It will be all right. I've just got to get used to love. I never tried it before; you see, I'm at least ten years behind myself. I'm still free wheeling. But I'll get back into gear soon."

"Yes," she said. Then she crumpled the paper and flipped it aside, turning. "But that's not important. That's just whether it's steak or hamburger. And hunger's not here——" She struck his belly with the flat of her hand. "That's just your old guts growling. Hunger's here." She touched his breast. "Dont you ever forget that."

"I wont. Not now."

"But you may. You've been hungry down here in your guts, so you are afraid of it. Because you are always a little afraid of what you have stood. If you had ever been in love before, you wouldn't have been on that train that afternoon. Would you?"

"Yes," he said. "Yes. Yes."

"So it's more than just training your brain to remember hunger's not in the belly. Your belly, your guts themselves, have got to believe it. Can yours believe it?"

"Yes," he said. *Only she's not so sure of that* he told himself, because three days later when he returned from the hospital he found the work bench littered with twisted bits of wire and bottles of shellac and glue and wood fiber, a few tubes of paint and a pan in which a mass of tissue paper soaked in water, which two afternoons later had become a collection of little figures— deer and wolfhounds and horses and men and women, lean epicene sophisticated and bizarre, with a quality fantastic and perverse; the afternoon after that when he returned she and the figures were gone. She came in an hour later, her yellow eyes like a cat's in the dark, not triumph or exultation but rather fierce affirmation, and with a new ten-dollar bill.

"He took them all," she said, she named a leading department store. "Then he let me dress one of the windows. I have an order for a hundred dollars more—historical figures about Chicago, this part of the West. You know—Mrs. O'Leary with Nero's face and the cow with a ukelele, Kit Carson with legs like Nijinsky and no face, just two eyes and a shelf of forehead to shade them with, buffalo cows with the heads and flanks of Arabian mares. And all the other stores on Michigan Avenue. Here. Take it."

He refused. "It's yours. You earned it." She looked at him—the unwinking yellow stare in which he seemed to blunder and fumble like a moth, a rabbit caught in the glare of a torch; an envelopment almost like a liquid, a chemical precipitant, in which all the dross of small lying and sentimentality dissolved away. "I dont—"

"You dont like the idea of your woman helping to support you, is that it? Listen. Dont you like what we've got?"

"You know I do."

"Then what does it matter what it cost us, what we

pay for it? or how? You stole the money we've got now;
wouldn't you do it again? Isn't it worth it, even if it all
busts tomorrow and we have to spend the rest of our
lives paying interest?"

"Yes. Only it's not going to bust tomorrow. Nor next
month. Nor next year—"

"No. Not as long as we are worthy of keeping of it.
Good enough. Strong enough. Worthy to be allowed to
keep it. To get what you want as decently as you can,
then keep it. Keep it." She came and put her arms
around him, hard, striking her body against him hard,
not in caress but exactly as she would grasp him by the
hair to wake him up from sleep. "That's what I'm going
to do. Try to do. I like bitching, and making things with
my hands. I dont think that's too much to be permitted
to like, to want to have and keep."

She earned that hundred dollars, working at night
now, after he was in bed and sometimes asleep; during
the next five weeks she earned twenty-eight dollars
more, then she filled an order amounting to fifty. Then
the orders stopped; she could get no more. Nevertheless
she continued to work, at night altogether now, since she
was out with her samples, her completed figures all
day, and she worked usually with an audience now, for
now their apartment had become a sort of evening club.
It began with a newspaper man named McCord who had
worked on a New Orleans paper during the brief time
when Charlotte's youngest brother (in a dilettante and
undergraduate heeler manner, Wilbourne gathered)
had cubbed there. She met him on the street; he came

to dinner one evening and took them out to dinner one evening; three nights later he appeared with three men and two women and four bottles of whiskey at their apartment, and after that Wilbourne never knew just whom he would find when he reached home, except that it would not be Charlotte alone and, regardless of who was there, idle, who even after the dearth season of sales had extended into weeks and then a month and summer was almost upon them, still worked in a cheap coverall already filthy as that of any house painter and a glass of whiskey-and-water among the twists of wire and pots of glue and paint and plaster which transformed steadily and endlessly beneath the deft untiring hands into the effigies elegant, bizarre, fantastic and perverse.

Then she made a final sale, a small one, and it was done, finished. It stopped as abruptly and inexplicably as it had begun. The summer season was on now, they told her at the stores, and the tourists and natives too were leaving town to escape the heat. "Except that that's a lie," she said. "It's the saturation point," she told him, told them all: it was at night, she had returned late with the cardboard box containing the figures which had been refused, so the evening's collection of callers had already arrived. "But I expected it. Because these are just fun." She had taken the effigies from the box and set them up on the work bench again. "Like something created to live only in the pitch airless dark, like in a bank vault or maybe a poison swamp, not in the rich normal nourishing air breathed off of guts full of vegetables from Oak Park and Evanston. And so that's

it and that's all. And now I'm not an artist any more and
I'm tired and I'm hungry and I'm going to curl up
with one of our good books and one of our crusts. So let
each and all of you step up to the bench and choose
himself or herself one souvenir and memento of this
occasion, and beat it."

"We can still eat a crust," he told her. *And besides,
she's not done yet,* he thought. *She hasn't quit yet. She
never will,* thinking as he had thought before that there
was a part of her which neither he nor Rittenmeyer had
ever touched, which did not even love love. In less than
a month he believed that he had proof of this; he returned and found her at the bench again, in a profound
excitement which he had never seen before—an excitement without exultation but with a grim and deadly
quality of irresistible driving as she told him about it.
It was one of the men whom McCord had brought, a
photographer. She was to make puppets, marionettes,
and he to photograph them for magazine covers and
advertisements; perhaps later they would use the actual puppets in charades, tableaux—a hired hall, a
rented stable, something, anything. "It's my money,"
she told him. "The hundred and twenty-five dollars I
never could get you to take."

She worked with tense and concentrated fury. She
would be at the bench when he went to sleep, he would
wake at two and three oclock and find the fierce working light above it still burning. Now he would return
(from the hospital at first, then from the park bench
where he spent his days after he lost his job, leaving and

returning home at the usual hours so she would not suspect) and see the actual figures almost as large as small children—a Quixote with a gaunt mad dreamy uncoordinated face, a Falstaff with the worn face of a syphilitic barber and gross with meat (a single figure, yet when he looked at it he seemed to see two: the man and the gross flesh like a huge bear and its fragile consumptive keeper; it seemed to him that he could actually watch the man struggling with the mountain of entrails as the keeper might wrestle with the bear, not to overcome it but to pass it, escape it, as you do with the atavistic beasts in nightmare), Roxane with spit curls and a wad of gum like the sheet music demonstrator in a ten-cent store, Cyrano with the face of a low-comedy Jew in vaudeville, the monstrous flare of whose nostrils ceased exactly on the instant of becoming molluscs, a piece of cheese in one hand and a check book in the other—accumulating about the apartment, filling all available spaces of floor and walls, fragile perverse and disturbing, with incredible rapidity; begun continued and completed in one sustained rush of furious industry—a space of time broken not into successive days and nights but a single interval interrupted only by eating and sleeping.

Then she finished the last one and now she would be gone all day and half the night; he would return in the afternoon and find a scrawled note on a scrap of paper or a margin torn from a newspaper or even the telephone book: *Don't wait for me. Go out and eat*, which he would do and return and go to bed and sometimes to

sleep until she slid naked (she never wore a sleeping
garment, she told him she had never owned one) into
bed to wake him, rouse him to listen with a hard wrestling movement, holding him in her hard arms while she
talked in a grim quiet rapid voice not about money or
its lack, not about the details of the day's progress with
the photographing, but of their present life and situation as though it were a complete whole without past
or future in which themselves as individuals, the need
for money, the figures she had made, were component
parts like the parts of a tableau or a puzzle, none more
important than another; lying still and relaxed in the
darkness while she held him, not even bothering to be
aware whether his eyes were open or not, he seemed to
see their joint life as a fragile globe, a bubble, which
she kept balanced and intact above disaster like a
trained seal does its ball. *She's worse off than I am,* he
thought. *She doesn't even know what it is to hope.*

Then the puppet business ended, as abruptly and completely as the window dressing had. He returned one
evening and she was at home, reading. The filthy overall
in which she had lived for weeks (it was August now)
was gone and then he saw that the work bench was not
only clean of its former litter of wire and paint, it had
been drawn into the center of the room and had become
a table covered with a strip of chintz and stacked with
the magazines and books which formerly had rested
upon the floor and in the unused chairs and such, and,
most surprising of all, a bowl of flowers. "I've got some
things here," she said. "We'll eat at home for a change."

She had chops and such, she prepared the meal in a curiously frivolous apron new too like the chintz on the table; he thought how failure, reacting upon her like on a man by investing her with a sort of dignified humility, had yet brought out in her a quality which he had never seen before, a quality not only female but profoundly feminine. They ate, then she cleared the table. He offered to help but she refused. So he sat with a book beside the lamp, he heard her in the kitchen for a time, then she emerged and entered the bedroom. He did not hear her when she came out of the bedroom at all since her bare feet made no sound on the floor; he just looked up to see her standing beside him—the compactly simple rightness of the body lines, the sober intent yellow stare. She took the book from him and put it on the converted table. "Get your clothes off," she said. "The hell with it. I can still bitch."

But he did not tell her about the job for another two weeks. His reason was no longer concern that the news might destroy her accord with what she was concentrating on, since that was no longer valid now, if it had ever been, and it was no longer the possibility that he might find something else before she would need to know, for that was not valid either now, since he had tried that and failed, nor was it the Micawber-like faith of the inert in tomorrow; it was partly perhaps the knowledge that late enough would be soon enough, but mostly (he did not try to fool himself) it was a profound faith in her. Not in them, in her. *God wont let her starve,* he thought. *She's too valuable. He did too*

*well with her. Even the one who made everything must
fancy some of it enough to want to keep it.* So each day
he would leave the apartment at the usual hour and sit
on his bench in the park until time to go home. And
once each day he would take out the wallet and produce
the slip of paper on which he kept a record of the
dwindling money, as if he expected each time to find that
the amount had changed or that he had misread it the
day before, finding each time that it had not and he had
not—the neat figures, the $182.00 less $5.00 or $10.00,
with the date of each subtraction; by the day it would
be due there would not be enough to pay the quarter's
rent on the first day of September. And then sometimes
he would take out the other paper, the pink cashier's
check with its perforated legend *Only Three Hundred
Dollars.* There would be something almost ceremonial
about it, like the formal preparation by the addict of his
opium pipe, and then for the time he would as completely
renounce reality as the opium smoker himself while he
invented a hundred ways to spend it, shifting the various
components of the sum and their bought equivalents here
and there like a jigsaw puzzle, knowing that this was a
form of masturbation (thinking, *because I am still, and
probably will always be, in the puberty of money),* that
if it were really possible to cash the check and use the
money, he would not even dare to toy with the idea.

Then he returned home one afternoon and found her
at the work bench again. It was still the table, still in
the center of the room; she had merely turned back the
chintz and shoved the books and magazines to one end,

and she wore the apron and not the coverall and she was working now with a kind of idle bemusement like some-one passing time with a deck of cards. The figure was not three inches tall—a little ancient shapeless man with a foolish disorganised face, the face of a harmless im-becile clown. "It's a Bad Smell," she said. Then he understood. "That's all it is, just a bad smell. Not a wolf at the door. Wolves are Things. Keen and ruthless. Strong, even if they are cowards. But this is just a bad smell because hunger is not here—" Again she struck his belly with the back of her hand. "Hunger's up there. It doesn't look like this. It looks like a skyrocket or a roman candle or at least one of those sparkler sticks for little children that sparkle away into a live red coal that's not afraid to die. But this." She looked up at him. Then he knew it was coming. "How much money have we got?"

"A hundred and forty-eight dollars. But it's all right. I—"

"Oh, then you have paid next quarter's rent already." Then it came, it was too late now. *My trouble is, every-time I tell either the truth or a lie I seem to have to sell myself on the idea first.* "Look at me. You mean you haven't been to the hospital in two months?"

"It was the detective. You were busy then, that was the month you forgot to write to New Orleans. He wasn't trying to hur—get me fired. He just hadn't heard from you and he was worried. He was trying to find out if you were all right. It wasn't him, it was the detective who spilled the works. So they let me go. It was funny.

I was fired from a job which existed because of moral turpitude, on the grounds of moral turpitude. Only it wasn't actually that, of course. The job just played out, as I knew in time it would—"

"Well," she said. "And we haven't got a drink in the house. You go down to the store and get a bottle while I—No, wait. We'll go out and eat and drink both. Besides, we'll have to find a dog."

"A dog?" From where he stood he could see her in the kitchen take from the ice box the two chops for supper and wrap them again.

"But certainly, friend," she said. "Get your hat."

It was evening, the hot August, the neon flashed and glared, alternately corpse- and hell-glowing the faces in the street and their own too as they walked, she still carrying the two chops in the thick slick clammy butcher's paper. Within the block they met McCord. "We've lost our job," she told him. "So we're looking for a dog."

Presently it began to seem to Wilbourne that the invisible dog was actually among them. They were in a bar now, one which they frequented, meeting perhaps twice a week by chance or prearrangement the group which McCord had brought into their lives. There were four of these ("We've lost our job," McCord told them. "And now we're waiting for a dog.") present now, the seven of them sitting about a table set for eight, an empty chair, an empty gap, the two chops unwrapped now and on a plate beside a glass of neat whiskey among the highballs. They had not eaten yet; twice Wilbourne leaned to her: "Hadn't we better eat something? It's all right; I can—"

"Yes, it's all right. It's fine." She was not speaking to him. "We've got forty-eight dollars too much; just think of that. Even the Armours haven't got forty-eight dollars too much. Drink up, ye armourous sons. Keep up with the dog."

"Yah," McCord said. "Set, ye armourous sons, in a sea of hemingwaves."

The neon flashed and glared, the traffic lights blinked from green to red and back to green again above the squawking cabs and hearse-like limousines. They had not eaten yet though they had lost two members of the party, they were six in the cab, sitting on each other's knees while Charlotte carried the chops (they had lost the paper now) and McCord held the invisible dog; it was named Moreover now, from the Bible, the poor man's table. "But listen," McCord said. "Just listen a minute. Doc and Gillespie and I own it. Gillespie's up there now, but he will have to be back in town by the first and it will be empty. You could take your hundred bucks—"

"You're impractical," Charlotte said. "You're talking about security. Have you no soul?—How much money have we got now, Harry?"

He looked at the meter. "A hundred and twenty-two dollars."

"But listen," McCord said.

"All right," she said. "But now is no time to talk. You've made your bed; lie in it. And pull the covers

over your head." They were in Evanston now; they had
stopped at a drug store and they had a flashlight now,
the cab crawling along a suburban and opulent curb
while Charlotte, leaning across McCord, played the flashlight upon the passing midnight lawns. "There's one,"
she said.

"I don't see it," McCord said.

"Look at that fence. Did you ever hear of an iron
fence with a wreath of pansies in each panel that didn't
have an iron dog inside of it? The house has got a
mansard roof too."

"I dont see any house," McCord said.

"I dont either. But look at that fence."

The cab stopped, they got out. The torch beam played
on the iron fence with scrolled spear-tipped panels set
in concrete; there was even a hitching-post in the effigy
of a negro boy beside the small scrolled gate. "You're
right," McCord said. "There'll be one here." They did
not use the light now, but even in the faint starlight
they could see it plainly—the cast iron Saint Bernard
with its composite face of the emperor Franz Josef and
a Maine banker in the year 1859. Charlotte placed the
chops upon the iron pediment, between the iron feet;
they returned to the cab. "Listen," McCord said. "It's
completely equipped—three rooms and kitchen, bedding,
cooking things, plenty of wood for the chopping; you
can even bathe if you want to. And all the other cottages
will be empty after the first of September and nobody
to bother you and right on the lake, you can have fish
for a while yet, and with your hundred dollars in grub

and the cold wont come until in October, maybe not until November; you could stay up there until Christmas or even longer than that if you dont mind the cold—"

McCord drove them up to the lake on the Saturday night before Labor Day, the hundred dollars worth of food—the tins, the beans and rice and coffee and salt and sugar and flour—in the rumble. Wilbourne contemplated the equivalent of their last dollar with a certain sobriety. "You dont realise how flexible money is until you exchange it for something," he said. "Maybe this is what the economists mean by a normal diminishing return."

"You dont mean flexible," McCord said. "You mean volatile. That's what Congress means by a fluid currency. If it rains on us before we get this stuff under a roof, you'll see. Those beans and rice and truck will boil us clean out of the car like three matches in a pail of home brew." They had a bottle of whiskey and McCord and Wilbourne took turns driving while Charlotte slept. They reached the cottage just after dawn—a hundred odd acres of water surrounded by second growth spruce, four clearings with a cabin in each (from the chimney of one of them smoke stood. "That's Bradley," McCord said. "I thought he'd be out by now.") and a short pier into the water. There was a narrow finger of beach with a buck standing on it, pink in the Sunday dawn, its head up, watching them for an instant before it whirled, its white scut arcing in long bounds while Charlotte, springing from the car, her face swollen with sleep, ran to the water's edge, squealing. "That's what I was trying to make!" she cried. "Not the animals, the dogs and deer and horses: the motion, the speed."

"Sure," McCord said. "Let's eat." They unloaded the car and carried the things in and started a fire in the stove, then while Charlotte cooked breakfast Wilbourne and McCord carried the bottle down to the water and squatted. They drank from the bottle, saluting one another. Then there was one drink left. "Charlotte's," McCord said. "She can drink to the Wagon, the long drouth."

"I'm happy now," Wilbourne said. "I know exactly where I am going. It's perfectly straight, between two rows of cans and sacks, fifty dollars' worth to a side. Not street, that's houses and people. This is a solitude. Then the water, the solitude wavering slow while you lie and look up at it." Squatting and still holding the almost empty bottle he put his other hand into the water, the still, dawn-breathing liquid with the temperature of the synthetic ice water in hotel rooms, the ripples fanning slowly from his wrist. McCord stared at him. "And then fall will come, the first cold, the first red and yellow leaves drifting down, the double leaves, the reflection rising to meet the falling one until they touch and rock a little, not quite closing. And then you could open your eyes for a minute if you wanted to, remembered to, and watch the shadow of the rocking leaves on the breast beside you."

"For sweet Jesus Schopenhauer," McCord said. "What the bloody hell kind of ninth-rate Teasdale is this? You haven't near done your share of starving yet.

You haven't near served your apprenticeship to destitution. If you're not careful, you'll talk that stuff to some guy who will believe it and'll hand you the pistol and see you use it. Stop thinking about yourself and think about Charlotte for a while."

"That's who I'm talking about. But I wouldn't use the pistol, anyway. Because I started this too late. I still believe in love." Then he told McCord about the cashier's check. "If I didn't believe in it, I'd give you the check and send her back with you tonight."

"And if you believed in it as much as you say you do, you would have torn that check up a long time ago."

"If I tore it up, nobody would ever get the money. He couldn't even get it back from the bank."

"Damn him. You dont owe him anything. Didn't you take his wife off his hands for him? Yah, you're a hell of a guy. You haven't even got the courage of your fornications, have you?" McCord rose. "Come on. I smell coffee."

Wilbourne didn't move, his hand still in the water. "I haven't hurt her." Then he said, "Yes I have. If I hadn't marked her by now, I would—"

"What?"

"Refuse to believe it."

For a full minute McCord stood looking down at the other as he squatted, the bottle in one hand and the other wrist-deep in the water. "Shit!" he said. Then Charlotte called them from the door. Wilbourne rose.

"I wouldn't use the pistol," he said. "I'll still take this."

Charlotte did not take the drink. Instead she set the bottle on the mantel. "To remind us of our lost civilization when our hair begins to spread," she said. They ate. There were two iron cots in each of the two bedrooms, two more on the screened porch. While Wilbourne washed the dishes Charlotte and McCord made up the cots on the porch with bedding from the locker; when Wilbourne came out McCord already lay on one cot, his shoes off, smoking. "Go on," he said. "Take it. Charlotte says she dont want to sleep any more." She came out at that moment, carrying a pad of paper, a tin cup, a new japanned color box.

"We had a dollar and a half left over, even after we bought the whiskey," she said. "Maybe that deer will come back."

"Take some salt to put on his tail," McCord said. "Maybe he will stand still and pose for you."

"I dont want him to pose. That's just what I dont want. I dont want to copy a deer. Anybody can do that." She went on, the screen door slapped behind her. Wilbourne did not look after her. He lay smoking too, his hands beneath his head.

"Listen," McCord said. "You've got a lot of food, there's plenty of wood here and cover when it turns cold, and when things begin to open up in town maybe I can sell some of that junk she made, get orders—"

"I'm not worrying. I told you I am happy. Nothing can take what I have already had away from me."

"Now, aint that just sweet. Listen. Why dont you give me that damn check and send her back with me and you

can eat through your hundred bucks and then move
into the woods and eat ants and play Saint Anthony in
a tree and on Christmas you can take a mussel shell and
make yourself a present of your own oysters. I'm going
to sleep." He turned over and seemed to go to sleep at
once, and soon Wilbourne slept too. He waked once and
knew by the sun that it was past noon and that she was
not in the house. But he was not concerned; lying awake
for a moment it was not the twenty-seven barren years
he looked at, and she would not be far, the path straight
and empty and quiet between the two fifty-dollar rows
of cans and sacks, she would wait for him. *If that is to
be, she will wait,* he thought. *If we are to lie so, it will
be together in the wavering solitude in spite of Mac and
his ninth-rate Teasdale who seems to remember a hell of
a lot of what people read, beneath the red and yellow
drift of the waning year, the myriad kissing of the repeated leaves.*

The sun was just above the trees when she returned.
The top sheet of the pad was still blank, though the paints
had been used. "Were they that bad?" McCord said. He
was busy at the stove with beans and rice and dried
apricots—one of those secret cooking or eating special-
ties such as every bachelor seems to have and which
some can actually produce though, you would have said
at first glance, not McCord.

"Maybe a little bird told her what you were doing
with fifty cents' worth of our grub, so she had to run,"
Wilbourne said. The concoction was ready at last. It was
not so bad, Wilbourne admitted. "Only I dont know

whether it actually is not foul, or if it's something pro-
tective—that what I taste is not this at all but the forty
or fifty cents it represents, if maybe I dont have a gland
for cowardice in my palate or stomach too." He and
Charlotte washed the dishes, McCord went out and returned with an armful of wood and laid a fire. "We wont
need that tonight," Wilbourne said.

"It wont cost you anything but the wood," McCord
said. "And you've got from here to the Canadian line
to get more from. You can run all Northern Wisconsin
up this chimney if you want to." Then they sat before
the fire, smoking and not talking a great deal, until time
for McCord to leave. He would not stay, holiday tomorrow or not. Wilbourne went out to the car with him
and he got into it, looking back at Charlotte in sil-
houette against the fire, in the door. "Yah," he said.
"You dont need to worry, no more than an old lady
being led across the street by a policeman or an eagle
scout. Because when the damned bloody wild drunken
car comes along it wont be the old lady, it will be the
cop or the scout it busts the hell out of. Watch yourself."

"Watch myself?"

"Yah. You cant be even afraid all the time without
taking some pains."

Wilbourne returned to the house. It was late, yet she
had not begun to undress; again he mused, not on the
adaptibility of women to circumstance but on the ability
of women to adapt the illicit, even the criminal, to a
bourgeois standard of respectability as he watched her,
barefoot, moving about the room, making those subtle

alterations in the fixtures of this temporary abode as they even do in hotel rooms rented for but one night, producing from one of the boxes which he had believed to contain only food objects from their apartment in Chicago which he not only did not know she still had but had forgotten they ever owned—the books they had acquired, a copper bowl, even the chintz cover from the ex-work bench, then from a cigarette carton which she had converted into a small receptacle resembling a coffin, the tiny figure of the old man, the Bad Smell; he watched her set it on the mantel and stand looking at it for a time, musing too, then take up the bottle with the drink they had saved her and, with the ritualistic sobriety of a child playing, pour the whiskey onto the hearth. "The lares and penates," she said. "I dont know Latin, but They will know what I mean."

They slept in the two cots on the porch, then, it turning cold just before dawn, in one cot, her bare feet fast on the boards, the hard plunge of elbow and hip waking him as she came into the blankets smelling of bacon and balsam. There was a gray light on the lake and when he heard the loon he knew exactly what it was, he even knew what it would look like, listening to the raucous idiot voice, thinking how man alone of all creatures deliberately atrophies his natural senses and that only at the expense of others; how the four-legged animal gains all its information through smelling and seeing and hearing and distrusts all else while the two-legged one believes only what it reads.

The fire felt good the next morning. While she washed

the breakfast dishes he cut more wood for it behind the
cabin, removing his sweater now, the sun definitely im-
pacting now though he was not fooled, thinking how in
these latitudes Labor Day and not equinox marked the
suspiration of summer, the long sigh toward autumn and
the cold, when she called him from the house. He entered; in the middle of the room stood a stranger carrying balanced on his shoulder a large cardboard box, a
man no older than himself, barefoot, in faded khaki
slacks and a sleeveless singlet, sunbrowned, with blue
eyes and pale sunburned lashes and symmetrical ridges
of straw-colored hair—the perfect reflexive *coiffure*—
who was looking quietly at the effigy on the mantel.
Through the open door behind him Wilbourne saw a
beached canoe. "This is—" Charlotte said. "What did
you say your name was?"

"Bradley," the stranger said. He looked at Wilbourne,
his eyes almost white against his skin like a kodak nega-
tive, balancing the box on his shoulder while he extended
the other hand.

"Wilbourne," Charlotte said. "Bradley's the neighbor. He's leaving today. He brought us what grub they
had left."

"No use lugging it out again," Bradley said. "Your
wife tells me you folks are going to stay on a while, so
I thought—" he gave Wilbourne a brief hard violent
bone-crushing meaningless grip—the broker's front man
two years out of an Eastern college.

"That's decent of you. We'll be glad to have it. Here,
let me—" But the other had already swung the box to

the floor; it was well filled. Charlotte and Wilbourne carefully did not look at it. "Thanks a lot. The more we have in the house, the harder it will be for the wolf to get in."

"Or to crowd us out when he does," Charlotte said. Bradley looked at her. He laughed, that is with his teeth. His eyes did not laugh, the assured, predatory eyes of the still successful prom leader.

"Not bad," he said, "Do you—"

"Thanks," Charlotte said. "Will you have some coffee?"

"Thanks, I've had breakfast. We were up at dawn. Must be back in town tonight." Now he looked at the effigy on the mantel again. "May I?" he said. He approached the mantel. "Do I know him? I seem—"

"I hope not," Charlotte said. Bradley looked at her.

"We hope not yet, she means," Wilbourne said. But Bradley continued to watch Charlotte, the pale brows courteously interrogatory above the predatory eyes which did not smile when the mouth did.

"It's the Bad Smell," Charlotte said.

"Oh. I see." He looked at the effigy. "You made it. I saw you sketching yesterday. Across the lake."

"I know you did."

"Touch," he said. "Can I apologise? I wasn't spying."

"I wasn't hiding." Bradley looked at her and now Wilbourne for the first time saw the eyebrows and mouth in accord, quizzical, sardonic, ruthless, the whole man emanating a sort of crass and insolent confidence.

"Sure?" he said.

"Sufficiently," Charlotte said. She moved to the mantel and took the effigy from it. "It's too bad you are leaving before we can return your call upon your wife. But perhaps you will accept this as a memento of your perspicuity."

"No; really, I—"

"Take it," Charlotte said pleasantly. "You must need it much worse than we do."

"Well, thanks." He took the effigy. "Thanks. We've got to get back to town tonight. But maybe we could look in on the way out. Mrs. Bradley would—"

"Do," Charlotte said.

"Thanks," he said. He turned toward the door. "Thanks again."

"Thanks again too," Charlotte said. He went out; Wilbourne watched him shove the canoe off and step into it. Then Wilbourne went and stooped over the box.

"What are you going to do?" Charlotte said.

"I'm going to carry it back and throw it in his front door."

"Oh, you bloody ass," she said. She came to him. "Stand up. We're going to eat it. Stand up like a man." He rose, she put her hard arms around him, wrestling him against her with restrained savage impatience. "Why dont you grow up, you damned home-wrecking boy scout? Dont you know yet that we just dont look married, thank God, even to brutes?" She held him hard against her, leaning back, her hips against him and moving faintly while she stared at him, the yellow stare inscrutable and derisive and with that quality which he had come to recognise—that ruthless and almost unbearable honesty. "Like a man, I said," holding him hard and derisive against her moving hips though that was not necessary. *She dont need to touch me,* he thought. *Nor the sound of her voice even nor the smell, a slipper will do it, one of those fragile instigations to venery discarded in the floor.* "Come on. That's right. That's better. That's fine now." She freed one hand and began to unfasten his shirt. "Only this is supposed to be bad luck or something in the forenoon, isn't it? Or isn't it?"

"Yes," he said. "Yes." She began to unfasten his belt.

"Or is this just the way you assuage insults to me? Or are you going to bed with me just because somebody happened to remind you I divide at the belly?"

"Yes," he said. "Yes."

Later in the forenoon they heard Bradley's car depart. Face down and half lying across him (She had been asleep, her weight heavy and relaxed, her head beneath his chin, her breath slow and full) she raised up, one elbow in his stomach and the blanket slipping away from her shoulders, while the sound of the car died away. "Well, Adam," she said. But they had always been alone, he told her.

"Ever since that first night. That picture. We couldn't be any more alone, no matter who went away."

"I know it. I mean, I can go swimming now." She slid out from beneath the blanket. He watched her, the grave simple body a little broader, a little solider than

the Hollywood-cod-liver-oil advertisements, the bare feet
padding across the rough boards, toward the screen door.

"There are bathing suits in the locker," he said. She
didn't answer. The screen door slapped. Then he could
not see her any more, or he would have had to raise his
head.

She swam each morning, the three bathing suits still
undisturbed in the locker. He would rise from breakfast
and return to the porch and lie on the cot and hear presently her bare feet cross the room and then the porch;
perhaps he would watch the steadily and smoothly
browning body cross the porch. Then he would sleep
again (this scarcely an hour after he had waked from
slumber, a habit which he formed within the first six
days) to wake later and look out and see her lying on
the pier on stomach or back, her arms folded across or
beneath her face; sometimes he would still be there, not
sleeping now and not even thinking but merely existing
in a drowsy and foetuslike state, passive and almost
unsentient in the womb of solitude and peace, when she
returned, moving then only enough to touch his lips to
the sun-impacted flank as she stopped beside the cot,
tasting the impacted sun. Then one day something happened to him.

September had gone, the nights and mornings were
definitely chilly; she had changed her swim from after
breakfast to after lunch and they were talking about
when they would have to move the bedding in from the
porch to the room with the fireplace. But the days themselves were unchanged—the same stationary recapitula-

tion of golden interval between dawn and sunset, the long quiet identical days, the immaculate monotonous hierarchy of noons filled with the sun's hot honey, through which the waning year drifted in red-and-yellow retrograde of hardwood leaves sourceless and going nowhere. Each day she departed directly after her swim and sunbath, with the pad and color box, leaving him to move about the house empty yet at the same time thunderous with the hard impact of her presence—the few garments she owned, the whisper of her bare feet on the boards—while he believed that he was worrying, not about the inevitable day on which their food would run out, but at the fact that he did not seem to worry about it: a curious state which he had experienced once before when his sister's husband had taken him to task one summer because he refused to exercise his vote. He remembered the exasperation just about to become rage in which he had tried to present his reasons to his brother-in-law, realising at last that he was talking faster and faster not to convince the brother-in-law but to justify his own rage as in a mild nightmare he might be grasping for his falling trousers; that it was not even to the brother-in-law he was talking but to himself.

It became an obsession with him; he realised quite calmly that he had become secretly quietly and decently a little mad; he now thought constantly of the diminishing row of cans and sacks against which he was matching in inverse ratio the accumulating days, yet he would not go to the closet and look at them, count them. He would tell himself how it used to be he would have to steal away to a park bench and take out the wallet and produce the scrap of paper and subtract numbers from one another, while now all he would have to do would be to glance at the row of cans on a shelf; he could count the cans and know exactly how many days more they would have left, he could take a pencil and mark the shelf itself off into days and he would not even have to count cans, he could glance at the shelf and read the position at once, like on a thermometer. But he would not even look into the closet.

He knew that during these hours he was mad and he fought against it sometimes, believing that he had conquered the madness, for in the next succeeding instant the cans, save for a tragic conviction that they did not even matter, were as completely out of his mind as if they had never existed, and he would look about at his familiar surroundings with a sense of profound despair, not even knowing that he was worrying now, worrying so terribly that he did not even know it; he looked about with a kind of aghast amazement at the sunfilled solitude out of which she had walked temporarily yet still remained in and to which she would presently return and re-enter her aura which had remained behind exactly as she might re-enter a garment and find him stretched on the cot, not sleeping now and not even reading, who had lost that habit along with the habit of sleep, and said quietly to himself, *I am bored. I am bored to extinction. There is nothing here that I am needed for. Not even by her. I have already cut enough wood to last until Christmas and there is nothing else for me to do.*

One day he asked her to divide the colors and pad
with him. She did so and found that he was color blind
and didn't even know it. Then each day he would lie
on his back in a small sunny clearing he had found,
surrounded by the fierce astringent smell of balsam,
smoking the cheap pipe (the one provision he had made
before leaving Chicago against the day they would ex-
haust food and money both), his half of the sketch pad
and his converted sardine can color-box intact and pristine beside him. Then one day he decided to make a
calendar, a notion innocently conceived not by mind, out
of a desire for a calendar, but from the sheer boredom
of muscles, and put into effect with the pure quiet sen-
sory pleasure of a man carving a basket from a peach
stone or the Lord's Prayer on a pin head; he drew it
neatly off on the sketch pad, numbering in the days,
planning to use various appropriate colors for Sundays
and the holidays. He discovered at once that he had lost
count of the days, but this only added to the anticipa-
tion, prolonging the work, making more involved the
pleasure, the peach basket to be a double one, the prayer
to be in code. So he went back to that first morning when
he and McCord squatted beside the water, whose name
and number he knew, then he counted forward by re-
constructing from memory the drowsing demarcations
between one dawn and the next, unravelling one by one
out of the wine-sharp and honey-still warp of tideless
solitude the lost Tuesdays and Fridays and Sundays;
when it suddenly occurred to him that he could prove his
figures, establish mathematical truth out of the sunny

and timeless void into which the individual days had
vanished by the dates of and intervals between Charlotte's menstrual periods, he felt as some old crook-
propped contemplator on the ancient sheep-drifted
Syrian hills must have felt after stumbling by accident
on some Alexandrian formula which proved the starry
truths which he had watched nightly all his life and knew
to be true but not how nor why.

That was when the thing happened to him. He sat
looking at what he had made in a gleeful and amazed
amusement at his own cunning in contriving for God, for
Nature the unmathematical, the overfecund, the prime
disorderly and illogical and patternless spendthrift, to
prove his mathematical problem for him, when he discovered that he had given six weeks to the month of October and that the day in which he now stood was November twelfth. It seemed to him that he could see the actual
numeral, incontrovertible and solitary, in the anonymous
identical hierarchy of the lost days; he seemed to see the
row of cans on the shelf a half mile away, the dynamic
torpedolike solid shapes which up to now had merely
dropped one by one, silently and without weight, into
that stagnant time which did not advance and which
would somehow find for its two victims food as it found
them breath, now in reverse to time, time now the mover,
advancing slow and irresistible, blotting the cans one by
one in steady progression as a moving cloud shadow
blots. *Yes,* he thought. *It's the Indian summer that did
it. I have been seduced to an imbecile's paradise by an*

old whore; I have been throttled and sapped of strength and volition by the old weary Lilith of the year.

He burned the calendar and went back to the cabin. She had not returned yet. He went to the closet and counted the cans. It was two hours to sunset yet; when he looked out toward the lake he saw that there was no sun and that a mass of cloud like dirty cotton had crossed from east to north and west and that the feel and taste of the air too had changed. *Yes,* he thought. *The old bitch. She betrayed me and now she doesn't need to pretend.* At last he saw her approaching, circling the lake, in a pair of his trousers and an old sweater they had found in the locker with the blankets. He went to meet her. "Good Lord," she said. "I never saw you look so happy. Have you painted a picture or have you discovered at last that the human race really doesn't have to even try to produce art—" He was moving faster than he knew; when he put his arms around her he jolted her to a stop by physical contact; thrust back, she looked at him with actual and not simulated astonishment now.

"Yes," he said. "How's for a spot of necking?"

"Why, certainly, friend," she said immediately. Then she thrust herself back again to look at him. "What's this? What's going on here?"

"Will you be afraid to stay here alone tonight?" Now she began to free herself.

"Let me go. I cant see you good." He released her, though he did manage to meet the unwinking yellow stare which he had never yet been able to lie to. "Tonight?"

"This is the twelfth of November."

"All right. Then what?" She looked at him. "Come on. Let's go to the house and get to the bottom of this." They returned to the house; again she paused and faced him. "Now let's have it."

"I just counted the cans. Measured the—" She stared at him with that hard, almost grim impersonality. "We can eat for about six days more."

"All right. Then what?"

"It was the mild weather. Like time had stopped and us with it, like two chips on a pond. So I didn't think to worry, to watch. So I'm going to walk to the village. It's only twelve miles. I could be back by noon tomorrow." She stared at him. "A letter. From Mac. It will be there."

"Did you dream it would be there, or did you find it out in the coffee pot when you were measuring the grub?"

"It will be there."

"All right. But wait till tomorrow to go. You cant walk twelve miles before dark." They ate and went to bed. This time she came straight and got into the cot with him, as heedless of the hard and painful elbow which jabbed him as she would have been on her own account if the positions had been reversed, as she was of the painful hand which grasped his hair and shook his head with savage impatience. "My God, I never in my life saw anybody try as hard to be a husband as you do. Listen to me, you lug. If it was just a successful husband and food and a bed I wanted, why the hell do you think I am here instead of back there where I had them?"

"You've got to sleep and eat."

"Certainly we have. So why worry about it? That's like worrying about having to bathe just because the water in the bathroom is about to be cut off." Then she rose, got out of the cot with the same abrupt violence; he watched her cross to the door and open it and look out. He could smell the snow before she spoke. "It's snowing."

"I know it. I knew this afternoon she realised the game was up."

"She?" She closed the door. This time she went to the other cot and got into it. "Try to get to sleep. It'll be a hard walk tomorrow, if it snows much."

"It will be there though."

"Yes," she said. She yawned, her back to him. "It's probably been there a week or two."

He left the cabin shortly after daylight. The snow had ceased and it was quite cold. He reached the village in four hours and found the letter from McCord. It contained a check for twenty-five dollars; he had sold one of the puppets, and he had the promise of a job for Charlotte in a department store during the holiday season. It was well after dark when he reached home. "You can put it all in the pot," he said. "We've got twenty-five dollars. And Mac's got a job for you. He's driving up Saturday night."

"Saturday night?"

"I wired him. I waited for an answer. That's why I'm

late." They ate and this time she got quietly into the
narrow cot with him and this time she even crept close
to him who had never before known her to do such at
any time, to anything.

"I'll be sorry to leave here."

"Will you?" he said quietly, peacefully, lying on his
back, his arms crossed on his chest like a stone effigy on
a tenth-century sepulchre. "You'll probably be glad to
get back, once you are there though. People to see again,
McCord and the others you liked, Christmas and all that.
You can get your hair clean again and your nails mani-
cured—" This time she did not move, whose habit it
was to assault him with that cold and disregardful sav-
ageness, shaking and jerking at him not only for conversation but even for mere emphasis. This time she lay
perfectly still, not even breathing, her voice filled not
with a suspiration but sheer amazed incredulity:

"*You'll* probably. *You* are. *You* can. Harry, what do
you mean?"

"That I wired Mac to come and get you. You'll have
your job; that will keep you until after Christmas all
right. I thought I'd just keep half the twenty-five dollars
and stay on here. Maybe Mac can find something for
me too; if nothing else, maybe a W.P.A. job of some sort.
Then I'd come on back to town and then we could—"

"No!" she cried. "No! No! Jesus God, no! Hold me!
Hold me hard, Harry! This is what it's for, what it all
was for, what we were paying for: so we could be together, sleep together every night: not just to eat and
evacuate and sleep warm so we can get up and eat and

evacuate in order to sleep warm again! Hold me! Hold
me hard! Hard!" He held her, his arms rigid, his face
still turned upward, his lips lifted away from his rigid
teeth.

God, he thought. *God help her. God help her.*

They left snow at the lake, though before they reached
Chicago they had overtaken the end of the south-moving
Indian summer for a little while. But it did not last and
now it was winter in Chicago too; the Canadian wind
made ice in the Lake and blew in the stone canyons holly-
burgeoned with the imminent Christmas, crisping and
frosting the faces of policemen and clerks and pan-
handlers and Red Cross and Salvation Army people
costumed as Santa Claus, the defunctive days dying in
neon upon the fur-framed petal faces of the wives and
daughters of cattle and timber millionaires and the para-
mours of politicians returned from Europe and the dude
ranches to spend the holidays in the air-carved and opulent tenements above the iron lake and the rich sprawling
city before departing for Florida, and of the sons of
London brokers and Midland shoe-peg knights and South
African senators come to look at Chicago because they
had read Whitman and Masters and Sandburg in Oxford
or Cambridge—members of that race which without tact
for exploration and armed with note-books and cameras
and sponge bags elects to pass the season of Christian
holiday in the dark and bitten jungles of savages.

Charlotte's job was in a store which had been one of
her first customers for the first figurines she had made. It
included window- and showcase-dressing, so that her day

sometimes began when the store closed in the afternoon
and that of the other employees ceased. So Wilbourne
and sometimes McCord would wait for her in a bar just
around the corner, where they would eat an early dinner.
Then McCord would depart to begin his upside-down day
at the newspaper and Charlotte and Wilbourne would
return to the store, which would now take on a sort of
bizarre and infernal inverted life—the chromium glass
and synthetic marble cavern which for eight hours had
been filled with the ruthless voracious murmur of furred
shoppers and the fixed regimented grimaces of satin-clad
robot-like saleswomen now empty of uproar, glittering
and quiet and echoed with cavernous silence, dwarfing,
filled now with a grim tense fury like an empty midnight
clinic in which a handful of pygmy-like surgeons and
nurses battle in low-toned decorum for some obscure and
anonymous life, into which Charlotte would vanish too
(not disappear: he would see her from time to time, con-
sulting in pantomime with someone over some object
which one of them held, or entering or leaving a window)
as soon as they entered. He would have an evening
paper and now for the next two or three hours he would
sit on fragile chairs surrounded by jointless figures with
suave organless bodies and serene almost incredible
faces, by draped brocade and sequins or the glitter of
rhinestones, while charwomen appeared on their knees
and pushing pails before them as though they were another species just crawled molelike from some tunnel or
orifice leading from the foundations of the earth itself
and serving some obscure principle of sanitation, not to

the hushed glitter which they did not even look at but
to the subterranean region which they would crawl back
to before light. Then at eleven and midnight and, as
Christmas approached, even later they would go home,
to the apartment which had no work bench and no skylight now but which was new and neat and in a new neat
district near a park (toward which, around ten o'clock
in the morning while lying in bed between his first and
second sleep of the day, he could hear the voices of
nursemaid-harried children moving) where Charlotte
would go to bed and he would sit again at the typewriter
at which he had already spent most of the day, the machine borrowed first from McCord then rented from an
agency then purchased outright from among the firing-
pinless pistols and guitars and gold-filled teeth in a pawnshop, on which he wrote and sold to the confession magazines the stories beginning "I had the body and desires
of a woman yet in knowledge and experience of the
world I was but a child" or "If I had only had a mother's
love to guard me on that fatal day"—stories which he
wrote complete from the first capital to the last period
in one sustained frenzied agonising rush like the half-
back working his way through school who grasps the
ball (his Albatross, his Old Man of the Sea, which, not
the opposing team, not the blank incontrovertible chalk
marks profoundly terrifying and meaningless as an
idiot's nightmare, is his sworn and mortal enemy) and
runs until the play is completed—downed or across the
goal line, it doesn't matter which—then to go to bed himself, with dawn sometimes beyond the open window of

the chill sleeping cubicle, to get into bed beside Charlotte who without waking would sometimes turn to him, murmuring something damp and indistinguishable out of sleep, and to lie again holding her as on that last night at the lake, himself wide awake; carefully rigid and still, knowing no desire to sleep, waiting for the smell and echo of his last batch of moron's pap to breathe out of him.

Thus he was awake mostly while she slept, and vice versa. She would get up and close the window and dress and make coffee (the breakfast which while they were poor, when they did not know for certain where the next measure of coffee to put into the pot was coming from, they would prepare and eat together, the dishes of which they would wash and dry together side by side at the sink) and be gone and he would not know it. Then he in his turn would wake and listen to the passing children while the stale coffee heated, and drink it and sit down to the typewriter, entering without effort and without especial regret the anesthesia of his monotonous inventing. At first he made a kind of ritual of his solitary lunch, fetching in the cans and slices of meat and such the night before, like a little boy with a new Daniel Boone suit hoarding crackers in the improvised forest of a broom closet. But lately, since he had actually bought the typewriter (he had voluntarily relinquished his amateur standing, he told himself then; he no longer had even to pretend to himself it was a lark) he began to dispense with lunch altogether, with the bother of eating, instead writing steadily on, pausing only to sit while his fingers rested, a cigarette scarring slowly into the edge of the rented table, staring at but not seeing the two or three current visible lines of his latest primer-bald moronic fable, his sexual gumdrop, then remembering the cigarette and raising it to rub uselessly at the new scorch before writing again. Then the hour would arrive and with the ink sometimes scarcely dry on the stamped sealed and self-addressed envelope containing the latest story beginning "At sixteen I was an unwed mother" he would leave the apartment and walk through the crowded streets, the steadily shortening afternoons of the dying year, to the bar where he and Charlotte and McCord met.

There was Christmas in the bar too, holly sprigs and mistletoe among the gleaming pyramids of glasses, mirror-repeated, the mirror aping the antic jackets of the barmen, the steaming seasonal bowls of hot rum and whiskey for the patrons to look at and recommend to one another while holding in their hands the same iced cocktails and highballs they had been drinking all summer. Then McCord at their usual table, with what he called breakfast—a quart stein of beer and about another quart of pretzels or salted peanuts or whatever was available, and Wilbourne would have the one drink which he allowed himself before Charlotte came ("I can afford abstemiousness now, sobriety," he told McCord. "I can pay shot for shot and no holds barred with any and all for the privilege of refusing.") and they would wait for the hour when the stores would empty, the glass doors flashing outward to erupt into the tender icy glare of neon the holly-pinned fur-framed faces, the wind-carved canyons merry and crisp with the bright voices speaking the good wishes and good will into intransigeant vapor, the employees' chute too discharging presently the regimented black satin, the feet swollen with the long standing, the faces aching with the sustained long rigid grimacing. Then Charlotte would enter; they would stop talking and watch her approach, shifting and sidling past the throng at the bar and among the waiters and the crowded tables, her coat open above the neat uniform, her hat of the current off-the-face mode thrust further back still as if she had pushed it there herself with a sweep of the forearm in the immemorial female gesture out of the immemorial female weariness, approaching the table, her face pale and tired-looking too though she moved as strongly and surely as ever, the eyes as humorlessly and incorrigibly honest as ever above the blunt strong nose, the broad pale unsubtle mouth. "Rum, men," she would say, then, sinking into the chair which one of them drew for her: "Well, papa." Then they would eat, at the wrong hour, the hour when the rest of the world was just beginning to prime itself for food ("I feel like three bears in a cage on Sunday afternoon," she said.), eating the meal which none of them wanted and then disperse, McCord to the paper, Charlotte and Wilbourne back to the store.

Two days before Christmas when she entered the bar she carried a parcel. It contained Christmas gifts for her children, the two girls. They had no work bench now and no skylight. She unwrapped and rewrapped

them on the bed, the immemorial—the workbench of the
child's unwitting begetting become the altar for the
Child's service, she sitting on the edge of it surrounded
by holly-stippled paper and the fatuous fragile red-and-
green cord and gummed labels, the two gifts she had
chosen reasonably costly but unremarkable, she looking
at them with a sort of grim bemusement above the hands
otherwise and at nearly every other human action un-
hesitating and swift. "They haven't even taught me how
to wrap up packages," she said. "Children," she said.
"It's not a child's function, really. It's for adults: a
week's dispensation to return to childishness, to give
something you dont want yourself to someone who
doesn't want it either, and demand thanks for it. And
the children swap with you. They vacate puerility and
accept the role you abandoned not because they ever had
any particular desire to be grown but just out of that
ruthless piracy of children that will use anything—deception or secrecy or acting—to get anything. Anything,
any bauble will do. Presents dont mean anything to them
until they get big enough to calculate what it probably
cost. That's why little girls are more interested in presents than little boys. So they take what you give them
not because they will accept even that in preference to
nothing but because that's about all they expected anyway from the stupid oxen among whom for some reason
they have to live.—They have offered to keep me on at
the store."

"What?" he said. He had not been listening to her. He
had been hearing but not listening, looking down at the

blunt hands among the tinsel litter, thinking, *Now is the time for me to say, Go home. Be with them tomorrow night.* "What?"

"They are going to keep me on until summer at the store."

He heard this time; he went through the same experience as when he had recognised the number on the calendar he had made, now he knew what the trouble had been all the time, why he would lie rigidly and carefully beside her in the dawn, believing the reason he could not sleep was that he was waiting for the smell of his moron pandering to fade, why he would sit before an unfinished page in the typewriter, believing he was thinking of nothing, believing he was thinking only of the money, how each time they always had the wrong amount of it and that they were about money like some unlucky people were about alcohol: either none or too much. *It was the city I was thinking of,* he thought. *The city and winter together, a combination too strong for us yet, for a time yet—the winter that herds people inside walls wherever they are, but winter and city together, a dungeon; the routine even of sinning, an absolution even for adultery.* "No," he said. "Because we are going to leave Chicago."

"Leave Chicago?"

"Yes. For good. You're not going to work any more just for money. Wait," he said quickly. "I know we have come to live like we had been married five years, but I am not coming the heavy husband on you. I know I catch myself thinking, 'I want my wife to have the best' but I'm not yet saying 'I dont approve of my women working.' It's not that. It's what we have come to work for, got into the habit of working for before we knew it, almost waited too late before we found it out. Do you remember how you said up at the lake when I suggested that you clear out while the clearing was good and you said, 'That's what we bought, what we are paying for: to be together and eat together and sleep together'? And now look at us. When we are together, it's in a saloon or a street car or walking along a crowded street and when we eat together its in a crowded restaurant inside a vacant hour they allow you from the store so you can eat and stay strong so they can get the value of the money they pay you every Saturday and we dont sleep together at all any more, we take turns watching each other sleep; when I touch you I know you are too tired to wake up and you are probably too tired to touch me at all."

Three weeks later, with a scribbled address on a torn newspaper margin folded in his vest pocket, he entered a downtown office building and ascended twenty floors to an opaque glass door lettered *Callaghan Mines* and entered and passed with some difficulty a chromium-finished office girl and faced at last across a desk flat and perfectly bare save for a telephone and a deck of cards laid out for Canfield, a red-faced cold-eyed man of about fifty, with a highwayman's head and the body of a two-hundred-and-twenty-pound college fullback gone to fat, in a suit of expensive tweed which nevertheless looked on him as if he had taken it from a fire sale at

the point of a pistol, to whom Wilbourne essayed to
give a summary of his medical qualifications and experience.

"Never mind that," the other interrupted. "Can you
take care of the ordinary injuries that men working in
a mine shaft might meet?"

"I was just trying to tell you—"

"I heard you. I asked you something else. I said, Take
care of them." Wilbourne looked at him.

"I dont think I—" he began.

"Take care of the mine. Of the people who own it.
Have put money into it. Who will be paying your salary
as long as you earn it. I dont care two damns in hell how
much or how little surgery and pharmacology you know
or dont know or how many degrees you might have from
where to show it. Nobody else out there will; there'll be
no State inspectors out there to ask to see your license.
I want to know if you can be depended on to protect the
mine, the company. Against backfires. Suits from wop
pick-and-shovel men and bohunk powder-monkeys and
chink ore-trammers to whom the notion might occur to
swap the company a hand or a foot for a pension or a
trip back to Canton or Hong Kong."

"Oh," Wilbourne said. "I see. Yes. I can do that."

"All right. You will be given transportation out to the
mine at once. Your pay will be—" he named a sum.

"That's not much," Wilbourne said. The other looked
at him with the cold flesh-bedded eyes. Wilbourne stared
back at him. "I have a degree from a good university, a

recognised medical school. I lacked only a few weeks
of finishing my internship at a hospital which has a—"

"Then you dont want this job. This job is nowhere
near up to your qualifications and, I daresay, your de-
serts. Good day." The cold eyes stared at him; he did
not move. "I said, Good morning."

"I will have to have transportation for my wife," Wilbourne said.

Their train left at three oclock two mornings later.
They waited for McCord at the apartment where they
had lived for two months and left no mark other than
the cigarette scars on the table. "Not even of loving,"
he said. "Not the wild sweet attunement, bare feet hurry-
ing bedward in the half light, covers that wont turn back
fast enough. Just the seminal groaning of box springs,
the preprandial prostate relieving of the ten years' married. We were too busy; we had to rent and support a
room for two robots to live in." McCord came and they
carried down the luggage, the two bags with which they
had left New Orleans, and the typewriter. The manager
shook hands with all three of them and expressed regret
at the dissolution of mutually pleasant domestic bonds.
"Just two of us," Wilbourne said. "None of us are
androgynous." The manager blinked, though just once.

"Ah," he said. "A pleasant journey. You have a cab?"
They had McCord's car; they went out to it in a mild
glitter of minor silver, the final neon and clash and clang
of changing lights; the redcap turned the two bags and
the typewriter over to the porter at the pullman vestibule.

"We've got time for a drink," McCord said.

"You and Harry have one," Charlotte said. "I'm going
to bed." She came and put her arms around McCord,
her face raised. "Good night, Mac." Then McCord
moved and kissed her. She stepped back, turning; they
watched her enter the vestibule and vanish. Then Wilbourne also knew that McCord knew he would never see
her again.

"How about that drink?" McCord said. They went
to the station bar and found a table and then they were
sitting again as they had on so many of the afternoons
while they waited for Charlotte—the same drinking
faces, the same white jackets of waiters and barmen, the
same racked gleaming glasses, only the steaming bowls
and the holly (Christmas, McCord had said, the apotheo-
sis of the bourgeoisie, the season when with shining
fable Heaven and Nature, in accord for once, edict and
postulate us all husbands and fathers under our skins,
when before an altar in the shape of a gold-plated cattle-
trough man may with impunity prostrate himself in an
orgy of unbridled sentimental obeisance to the fairy tale
which conquered the Western world, when for seven days
the rich get richer and the poor get poorer in amnesty:
the whitewashing of a stipulated week leaving the page
blank and pristine again for the chronicling of the fresh
—and for the moment, horselike ("There's the horse,"
McCord said), breathed—revenge and hatred.) missing
now, the waiter coming up as he had used to come—the
same white sleeve, the anonymous featureless waiter-
face you never actually see. "Beer," McCord said.
"What's yours?"

"Ginger ale," Wilbourne said.

"What?"

"I'm on the wagon."

"Since when?"

"Since last night. I cant afford to drink any more."
McCord looked at him.

"Hell," McCord said. "Bring me a double rye then."
The waiter departed. McCord still stared at Wilbourne.
"It seems to agree with you," he said savagely. "Listen,"
he said. "I know this is none of my business. But I wish
I knew what it's all about. Here you were making fair
money, and Charlotte with a good job, you had a nice
place to live in. And then all of a sudden you quit it,
make Charlotte throw up her job to start out in February
to live in a mine shaft in Utah, without a railroad or a
telephone or even a decent can, on a salary of—"

"That was just it. That was why. I had become—" He
ceased. The waiter set the drinks on the table and went
away. Wilbourne raised his ginger ale. "To freedom."

"I would," McCord snarled. "You'll probably be able
to drink to a lot of it before you see any of it again. And
in water too, not even in soda pop. And maybe in a
tighter place than this too. Because that guy is poison.
I know about him. He's wildcat. If the truth was written
about him on a tombstone it wouldn't be an epitaph, it
would be a police record."

"All right," Wilbourne said. "To love, then." There
was a clock above the entrance—the ubiquitous and
synchronised face, oracular admonitory and unsentient:
he had twenty-two minutes yet. *While it will only take*

two minutes to tell Mac what it took me two months to discover, he thought. "I had turned into a husband," he said. "That was all. I didn't even know it until she told me the store had offered to keep her on. At first I used to have to watch myself, rehearse myself each time so I would be sure to say 'my wife' or 'Mrs Wilbourne', then I discovered I had been watching myself for months to keep from saying it; I have even caught myself twice since we came back from the lake thinking 'I want my wife to have the best' exactly like any husband with his Saturday pay envelope and his suburban bungalow full of electric wife-saving gadgets and his table cloth of lawn to sprinkle on Sunday morning that will become his actual own provided he is not fired or run down by a car in the next ten years—the doomed worm blind to all passion and dead to all hope and not even knowing it, oblivious and unaware in the face of all darkness, all unknown, the underlying All-Derisive biding to blast him. I had even stopped being ashamed of the way I earned the money, apologising even to myself for the stories I wrote; I was no more ashamed of them than the city employee buying his own bungalow on the installment plan in which his wife can have the best is ashamed of his badge of office, the rubber plunger for unstopping toilets, which he carries about with him. In fact, I had come to really like to write them, even apart from the money, like the boy who never saw ice before goes bugs about skating right after he learns how. Besides, after I started writing them I learned that I had no idea of the depths of depravity of which the human invention is capable, which is always interesting—"

"You mean, enjoys," McCord said.

"Yes. All right—Respectability. That was what did it. I found out some time back that it's idleness breeds all our virtues, our most bearable qualities—contemplation, equableness, laziness, letting other people alone; good digestion mental and physical: the wisdom to concentrate on fleshly pleasures—eating and evacuating and fornication and sitting in the sun—than which there is nothing better, nothing to match, nothing else in all this world but to live for the short time you are loaned breath, to be alive and know it—oh, yes, she taught me that; she has marked me too forever—nothing, nothing. But it was only recently I have clearly seen, followed out the logical conclusion, that it is one of what we call the prime virtues—thrift, industry, independence—that breeds all the vices—fanaticism, smugness, meddling, fear, and worst of all, respectability. Us, for instance. Because of the fact that for the first time we were solvent, knew for certain where tomorrow's food was coming from (the damned money, too much of it; at night we would lie awake and plan how to get it spent; by spring we would have been carrying steamer folders in our pockets) I had become as completely thrall and slave to respectability as any—"

"But not her," McCord said.

"No. But she's a better man than I am. You said that yourself.—as any man by drink or opium. I had become the Complete Householder. All I lacked was

official sanction in the form of a registered Social Security number as head of a family. We lived in an
apartment that wasn't bohemian, it wasn't even a tabloid
love-nest, it wasn't even in that part of town but in a
neighborhood dedicated by both city ordinance and
architecture to the second year of wedlock among the
five-thousand-a-year bracket. I would be waked in the
mornings by the noise of children passing in the street;
by the time spring came and the windows would have
to stay open I would have been hearing the fretful
cries of Swede nursemaids from the park all day long
and, when the wind was right, smell the smell of infant
urine and animal crackers. I referred to it as home,
there was a corner in it we both called my study; I
had even bought the damn typewriter at last—something I had got along without for twenty-eight years
and so well I didn't even know it, which is too heavy
and unwieldy to carry, yet which I would no more have
dared desert than—"

"You've still got it, I noticed," McCord said.

"—than—Yes. A good portion of any courage is a
sincere disbelief in good luck. It's not courage otherwise—than I would my eyelashes. I had tied myself
hand and foot in a little strip of inked ribbon, daily
I watched myself getting more and more tangled in it
like a roach in a spider web; each morning, so that my
wife could leave on time for her job, I would wash the
coffee pot and the sink and twice a week (for the same
reason) I would buy from the same butcher the gro-
ceries we needed and the chops we would cook ourselves

on Sunday; give us a little more time and we would
have been dressing and undressing inside our kimonas
in one another's presence and turning off the light before we made love. That's it. It's not avocation that
elects our vocations, it's respectability that makes chiro-
practors and clerks and bill posters and motormen and
pulp writers of us." There was a loudspeaker in the bar
too, synchronised too; at this moment a voice cavernous
and sourceless roared deliberately, a sentence in which
could be distinguished a word now and then—"train,"
then others which the mind two or three seconds afterward recognised to be the names of cities far flung
about the continent, cities seen rather than names heard,
as if the listener (so enormous was the voice) were suspended in space watching the globy earth spin slowly
out of its cradling cloud-wisps in fragmentary glimpses
the evocative strange divisions of the sphere, spinning
them on into fog and cloud again before vision and
comprehension could quite grasp them. He looked at
the clock again; he still had fourteen minutes. *Fourteen minutes to try to tell what I have already said in
five words,* he thought.

"And mind, I liked it. I never denied that. I liked it.
I liked the money I made. I even liked the way I made
it, the thing I did, as I told you. It wasn't because of
that that one day I caught myself back from thinking
'My wife must have the best.' It was because I found
out one day that I was afraid. And I found out at the
same time that I will still be afraid, no matter what I

do, that I will still be afraid as long as she lives or I live."

"You are still afraid now?"

"Yes. And not about money. Damn money. I can make all the money we will need; certainly there seems to be no limit to what I can invent on the theme of female sex troubles. I dont mean that, nor Utah either. I mean us. Love, if you will. Because it cant last. There is no place for it in the world today, not even in Utah. We have eliminated it. It took us a long time, but man is resourceful and limitless in inventing too, and so we have got rid of love at last just as we have got rid of Christ. We have radio in the place of God's voice and instead of having to save emotional currency for months and years to deserve one chance spend it all for love we can now spread it thin into coppers and titillate ourselves at any newsstand, two to the block like sticks of chewing gum or chocolate from the automatic machines. If Jesus returned today we would have to crucify him quick in our own defense, to justify and preserve the civilization we have worked and suffered and died shrieking and cursing in rage and impotence and terror for two thousand years to create and perfect in man's own image; if Venus returned she would be a soiled man in a subway lavatory with a palm full of French post-cards—" McCord turned in his chair and beckoned, a single repressed violent gesture. The waiter appeared, McCord pointed to his glass. Presently the waiter's hand set the refilled glass on the table and withdrew.

"All right," McCord said. "So what?"

"I was in eclipse. It began that night in New Orleans when I told her I had twelve hundred dollars and it lasted until that night she told me the store would keep her on. I was outside of time. I was still attached to it, supported by it in space as you have been ever since there was a not-you to become you, and will be until there is an end to the not-you by means of which alone you could once have been—that's the immortality—supported by it but that's all, just on it, non-conductive, like the sparrow insulated by its own hard non-conductive dead feet from the high-tension line, the current of time that runs through remembering, that exists only in relation to what little of reality (I have learned that too) we know, else there is no such thing as time. You know: *I was not*. Then *I am*, and time begins, retroactive, is was and will be. Then *I was* and so I am not and so time never existed. It was like the instant of virginity, it was the instant of virginity: that condition, fact, that does not actually exist except during the instant you know you are losing it; it lasted as long as it did because I was too old, I waited too long; twenty-seven is too long to wait to get out of your system what you should have rid yourself of at fourteen or fifteen or maybe even younger—the messy wild hurried fumbling of two panting amateurs beneath the front steps or in an afternoon hayloft. You remember: the precipice, the dark precipice; all mankind before you went over it and lived and all after you will but that means nothing to you because they cant tell you, forewarn you, what to do in order to survive. It's the solitude, you see.

You must do it in solitude and you can bear just so much solitude and still live, like electricity. And for this one or two seconds you will be absolutely alone: not before you were and not after you are not, because you are never alone then; in either case you are secure and companioned in a myriad and inextricable anonymity: in the one, dust from dust; in the other, seething worms to seething worms. But now you are going to be alone, you must, you know it, it must be, so be it; you herd the beast you have ridden all your life, the old familiar well-broken nag, up to the precipice—"

"There's the damned horse," McCord said. "I've been waiting for it. After ten minutes we sound like *Bit and Spur*. We dont talk, we moralise at each other like two circuit-riding parsons travelling the same country lane."

"—Maybe you thought all the time that when the moment came you could rein back, save something, maybe not, the instant comes and you know you cannot, know you knew all the time you could not, and you cannot; you are one single abnegant affirmation, one single fluxive Yes out of the terror in which you surrender volition, hope, all—the darkness, the falling, the thunder of solitude, the shock, the death, the moment when, stopped physically by the ponderable clay, you yet feel all your life rush out of you into the pervading immemorial blind receptive matrix, the hot fluid blind foundation—grave-womb or womb-grave, it's all one. But you return; maybe you knew that all the time, but you return, maybe you even live out your three score and ten or whatever it is but forever afterward you will know that forever more you have lost some of it, that for that one second or two seconds you were present in space but not in time, that you are not the three score and ten they have credited you with and that you will have to discharge someday to make the books balance, but three score and nine and three hundred and sixty-four and twenty-three and fifty-eight—"

"Sweet Jesus," McCord said. "Holy choriated cherubim. If I am ever unlucky enough to have a son, I'm going to take him to a nice clean whore-house myself on his tenth birthday."

"So that's what happened to me," Wilbourne said. "I waited too long. What would have been two seconds at fourteen or fifteen was eight months at twenty-seven. I was in eclipse, and we almost scraped bottom on that snow-bound Wisconsin lake with nine dollars and twenty cents' worth of food between us and starving. I beat that, I thought I did. I believed I waked up in time and beat that; we came back here and I thought we were going great guns, until that night before Christmas when she told me about the store and I realised what we had got into, that the starving was nothing, it could have done nothing but kill us, while this was worse than death or division even: it was the mausoleum of love, it was the stinking catafalque of the dead corpse borne between the olfactoryless walking shapes of the immortal unsentient demanding ancient meat." The loudspeaker spoke again; they made to rise at the same time; at the same moment the waiter materialised and McCord paid him. "So I am afraid," Wilbourne said.

"I wasn't afraid then because I was in eclipse but I am awake now and I can be afraid now, thank God. Because this Anno Domini 1938 has no place in it for love. They used money against me while I was asleep because I was vulnerable in money. Then I waked up and rectified the money and I thought I had beat Them until that night when I found out They had used respectability on me and that it was harder to beat than money. So I am vulnerable in neither money nor respectability now and so They will have to find something else to force us to conform to the pattern of human life which has now evolved to do without love—to conform, or die." They entered the train shed—the cavernous gloom in which the constant electricity which knew no day from night burned wanly on toward the iron winter dawn among wisps of steam, in which the long motionless line of darkened Pullmans seemed to stand knee-deep, bedded and fixed forever in concrete. They passed the soot-dulled steel walls, the serried cubicles filled with snoring, to the open vestibule. "So I am afraid. Because They are smart, shrewd, They will have to be; if They were to let us beat Them, it would be like unchecked murder and robbery. Of course we cant beat Them; we are doomed of course; that's why I am afraid. And not for me: do you remember that night at the lake when you said I was an old woman being led across the street by a policeman or a boy scout, and that when the drunken car came it would not be the old lady, it would—"

"But why go to Utah in February to beat it? And if you cant beat it, why in hell go to Utah?"

"Because I—" Steam, air, hissed behind them in a long sigh; the porter appeared suddenly from nowhere as the waiter had done.

"All right, gentlemen," he said. "We're going."

Wilbourne and McCord shook hands. "Maybe I'll write you," Wilbourne said. "Charlotte probably will, anyway. She's a better gentleman than I am, too." He stepped into the vestibule and turned, the porter behind him, his hand on the door knob, waiting; he and McCord looked at each other, the two speeches unspoken between them, each knowing they would not be spoken: *I wont see you again* and *No. You wont see us again.* "Because crows and sparrows get shot out of trees or drowned by floods or killed by hurricanes and fires, but not hawks. And maybe I can be the consort of a falcon, even if I am a sparrow." The train gathered itself, the first, the beginning of motion, departure came back car by car and passed under his feet. "And something I told myself up there at the lake," he said. "That there is something in me she is not mistress to but mother. Well, I have gone a step farther." The train moved, he leaned out, McCord moving too to keep pace with him. "That there is something in me you and she parented between you, that you are father of. Give me your blessing."

"Take my curse," McCord said.

Old Man

As the short convict had testified, the tall one, when he returned to the surface, still retained what the short one called the paddle. He clung to it, not instinctively against the time when he would be back inside the boat and would need it, because for a time he did not believe he would ever regain the skiff or anything else that would support him, but because he did not have time to think about turning it loose. Things had moved too fast for him. He had not been warned, he had felt the first snatching tug of the current, he had seen the skiff begin to spin and his companion vanish violently upward like in a translation out of Isaiah, then he himself was in the water, struggling against the drag of the paddle which he did not know he still held each time he fought back to the surface and grasped at the spinning skiff which at one instant was ten feet away and the next poised above his head as though about to brain him, until at last he grasped the stern, the drag of his body becoming a rudder to the skiff, the two of them, man and boat and with the paddle perpendicular above them like a jackstaff, vanishing from the view of the short convict (who had vanished from that of the tall one with the same celerity though in a vertical direction) like a tableau snatched offstage intact with violent and incredible speed.

He was now in the channel of a slough, a bayou, in which until today no current had run probably since the old subterranean outrage which had created the country. There was plenty of current in it now though; from his trough behind the stern he seemed to see the trees and sky rushing past with vertiginous speed, looking down at him between the gouts of cold yellow in lugubrious and mournful amazement. But they were fixed and secure in something; he thought of that, he remembered in an instant of despairing rage the firm earth fixed and founded strong and cemented fast and stable forever by the generations of laborious sweat, somewhere beneath him, beyond the reach of his feet, when, and again without warning, the stern of the skiff struck him a stunning blow across the bridge of his nose. The instinct which had caused him to cling to it now caused him to fling the paddle into the boat in order to grasp the gunwale with both hands just as the skiff pivoted and spun away again. With both hands free he now dragged himself over the stern and lay prone on his face, streaming with blood and water and panting, not with exhaustion but with that furious rage which is terror's aftermath.

But he had to get up at once because he believed he had come much faster (and so farther) than he had. So he rose, out of the watery scarlet puddle in which he had lain, streaming, the soaked denim heavy as iron on his limbs, the black hair plastered to his skull, the blood-infused water streaking his jumper, and dragged his forearm gingerly and hurriedly across his lower face

and glanced at it then grasped the paddle and began to
try to swing the skiff back upstream. It did not even
occur to him that he did not know where his companion
was, in which tree among all which he had passed or
might pass. He did not even speculate on that for the
reason that he knew so incontestably that the other was
upstream from him, and after his recent experience the
mere connotation of the term upstream carried a sense
of such violence and force and speed that the concep-
tion of it as other than a straight line was something
which the intelligence, reason, simply refused to harbor,
like the notion of a rifle bullet the width of a cotton
field.

The bow began to swing back upstream. It turned
readily, it outpaced the aghast and outraged instant in
which he realised it was swinging far too easily, it had
swung on over the arc and lay broadside to the current
and began again that vicious spinning while he sat, his
teeth bared in his bloody streaming face while his spent
arms flailed the impotent paddle at the water, that
innocent-appearing medium which at one time had held
him in iron-like and shifting convolutions like an ana-
conda yet which now seemed to offer no more resistance
to the thrust of his urge and need than so much air, like
air; the boat which had threatened him and at last
actually struck him in the face with the shocking violence of a mule's hoof now seemed to poise weightless
upon it like a thistle bloom, spinning like a wind vane
while he flailed at the water and thought of, envisioned,
his companion safe, inactive and at ease in the tree with

nothing to do but wait, musing with impotent and terrified fury upon that arbitrariness of human affairs which
had abrogated to the one the secure tree and to the other
the hysterical and unmanageable boat for the very reason that it knew that he alone of the two of them would
make any attempt to return and rescue his companion.

The skiff had paid off and now ran with the current
again. It seemed again to spring from immobility into
incredible speed, and he thought he must already be
miles away from where his companion had quitted him,
though actually he had merely described a big circle
since getting back into the skiff, and the object (a clump
of cypress trees choked by floating logs and debris)
which the skiff was now about to strike was the same
one it had careened into before when the stern had
struck him. He didn't know this because he had not yet
ever looked higher than the bow of the boat. He didn't
look higher now, he just saw that he was going to strike;
he seemed to feel run through the very insentient fabric
of the skiff a current of eager gleeful vicious incorrigible wilfulness; and he who had never ceased to flail
at the bland treacherous water with what he had believed to be the limit of his strength now from somewhere, some ultimate absolute reserve, produced a final
measure of endurance, will to endure which adumbrated
mere muscle and nerves, continuing to flail the paddle
right up to the instant of striking, completing one last
reach thrust and recover out of pure desperate reflex, as
a man slipping on ice reaches for his hat and money-

pocket, as the skiff struck and hurled him once more flat on his face in the bottom of it.

This time he did not get up at once. He lay flat on his face, slightly spread-eagled and in an attitude almost peaceful, a kind of abject meditation. He would have to get up sometime, he knew that, just as all life consists of having to get up sooner or later and then having to lie down again sooner or later after a while. And he was not exactly exhausted and he was not particularly without hope and he did not especially dread getting up. It merely seemed to him that he had accidentally been caught in a situation in which time and environment, not himself, was mesmerised; he was being toyed with by a current of water going nowhere, beneath a day which would wane toward no evening; when it was done with him it would spew him back into the comparatively safe world he had been snatched violently out of and in the meantime it did not much matter just what he did or did not do. So he lay on his face, now not only feeling but hearing the strong quiet rustling of the current on the underside of the planks, for a while longer. Then he raised his head and this time touched his palm gingerly to his face and looked at the blood again, then he sat up onto his heels and leaning over the gunwale he pinched his nostrils between thumb and finger and expelled a gout of blood and was in the act of wiping his fingers on his thigh when a voice slightly above his line of sight said quietly, "It's taken you a while," and he who up to this moment had had neither reason nor time to raise his eyes higher than the bows looked up and saw, sitting in a tree and looking at him, a woman. She was not ten feet away. She sat on the lowest limb of one of the trees holding the jam he had grounded on, in a calico wrapper and an army private's tunic and a sunbonnet, a woman whom he did not even bother to examine since that first startled glance had been ample to reveal to him all the generations of her life and background, who could have been his sister if he had a sister, his wife if he had not entered the penitentiary at an age scarcely out of adolescence and some years younger than that at which even his prolific and monogamous kind married—a woman who sat clutching the trunk of the tree, her stockingless feet in a pair of man's unlaced brogans less than a yard from the water, who was very probably somebody's sister and quite certainly (or certainly should have been) somebody's wife, though this too he had entered the penitentiary too young to have had more than mere theoretical female experience to discover yet. "I thought for a minute you wasn't aiming to come back."

"Come back?"

"After the first time. After you run into this brush pile the first time and got into the boat and went on." He looked about, touching his face tenderly again; it could very well be the same place where the boat had hit him in the face.

"Yah," he said. "I'm here now though."

"Could you maybe get the boat a little closer? I taken a right sharp strain getting up here; maybe I better . . ." He was not listening; he had just discovered

that the paddle was gone; this time when the skiff hurled
him forward he had flung the paddle not into it but
beyond it. "It's right there in them brush tops," the
woman said. "You can get it. Here. Catch a holt of
this." It was a grapevine. It had grown up into the tree
and the flood had torn the roots loose. She had taken a
turn with it about her upper body; she now loosed it and
swung it out until he could grasp it. Holding to the end
of the vine he warped the skiff around the end of the
jam, picking up the paddle, and warped the skiff on beneath the limb and held it and now he watched her
move, gather herself heavily and carefully to descend—
that heaviness which was not painful but just excruciat-
ingly careful, that profound and almost lethargic awk-
wardness which added nothing to the sum of that first
aghast amazement which had served already for the
catafalque of invincible dream since even in durance
he had continued (and even with the old avidity, even
though they had caused his downfall) to consume the
impossible pulp-printed fables carefully censored and
as carefully smuggled into the penitentiary; and who to
say what Helen, what living Garbo, he had not dreamed
of rescuing from what craggy pinnacle or dragoned
keep when he and his companion embarked in the skiff.
He watched her, he made no further effort to help her
beyond holding the skiff savagely steady while she lowered herself from the limb—the entire body, the de-
formed swell of belly bulging the calico, suspended by
its arms, thinking, *And this is what I get. This, out of*

*all the female meat that walks, is what I have to be
caught in a runaway boat with.*

"Where's that cottonhouse?" he said.

"Cottonhouse?"

"With that fellow on it. The other one."

"I dont know. It's a right smart of cottonhouses around
here. With folks on them too, I reckon." She was examining him. "You're bloody as a hog," she said. "You
look like a convict."

"Yah," he said, snarled. "I feel like I done already
been hung. Well, I got to pick up my pardner and then
find that cottonhouse." He cast off. That is, he released
his hold on the vine. That was all he had to do, for even
while the bow of the skiff hung high on the log jam and
even while he held it by the vine in the comparatively
dead water behind the jam, he felt steadily and constantly the whisper, the strong purring power of the
water just one inch beyond the frail planks on which
he squatted and which, as soon as he released the vine,
took charge of the skiff not with one powerful clutch but
in a series of touches light, tentative, and catlike; he
realised now that he had entertained a sort of foundationless hope that the added weight might make the
skiff more controllable. During the first moment or two
he had a wild (and still foundationless) belief that it
had; he had got the head upstream and managed to
hold it so by terrific exertion continued even after he
discovered that they were travelling straight enough
but stern-first and continued somehow even after the
bow began to wear away and swing: the old irresistible

movement which he knew well by now, too well to fight
against it, so that he let the bow swing on downstream
with the hope of utilising the skiff's own momentum to
bring it through the full circle and so upstream again,
the skiff travelling broadside then bow-first then broadside again, diagonally across the channel, toward the
other wall of submerged trees; it began to flee beneath
him with terrific speed, they were in an eddy but did not
know it; he had no time to draw conclusions or even
wonder; he crouched, his teeth bared in his blood-caked
and swollen face, his lungs bursting, flailing at the
water while the trees stooped hugely down at him. The
skiff struck, spun, struck again; the woman half lay in
the bow, clutching the gunwales, as if she were trying
to crouch behind her own pregnancy; he banged now
not at the water but at the living sapblooded wood with
the paddle, his desire now not to go anywhere, reach
any destination, but just to keep the skiff from beating
itself to fragments against the tree trunks. Then something exploded, this time against the back of his head,
and stooping trees and dizzy water, the woman's face
and all, fled together and vanished in bright soundless
flash and glare.

An hour later the skiff came slowly up an old logging
road and so out of the bottom, the forest, and into (or
onto) a cottonfield—a gray and limitless desolation now
free of turmoil, broken only by a thin line of telephone
poles like a wading millipede. The woman was now
paddling, steadily and deliberately, with that curious
lethargic care, while the convict squatted, his head be-

tween his knees, trying to stanch the fresh and apparently inexhaustible flow of blood from his nose with handfuls of water. The woman ceased paddling, the skiff drifted on, slowing, while she looked about. "We're done out," she said.

The convict raised his head and also looked about. "Out where?"

"I thought maybe you might know."

"I dont even know where I used to be. Even if I knowed which way was north, I wouldn't know if that was where I wanted to go." He cupped another handful of water to his face and lowered his hand and regarded the resulting crimson marbling on his palm, not with dejection, not with concern, but with a kind of sardonic and vicious bemusement. The woman watched the back of his head.

"We got to get somewhere."

"Dont I know it? A fellow on a cottonhouse. Another in a tree. And now that thing in your lap."

"It wasn't due yet. Maybe it was having to climb that tree quick yesterday, and having to set in it all night. I'm doing the best I can. But we better get somewhere soon."

"Yah," the convict said. "I thought I wanted to get somewhere too and I aint had no luck at it. You pick out a place to get to now and we'll try yours. Gimme that oar." The woman passed him the paddle. The boat was a double-ender; he had only to turn around.

"Which way you fixing to go?" the woman said.

"Never you mind that. You just keep on holding on."

He began to paddle, on across the cottonfield. It began
to rain again, though not hard at first. "Yah," he said.
"Ask the boat. I been in it since breakfast and I aint
never knowed, where I aimed to go or where I was
going either."

That was about one oclock. Toward the end of the
afternoon the skiff (they were in a channel of some sort
again, they had been in it for some time; they had got
into it before they knew it and too late to get out again,
granted there had been any reason to get out, as, to the
convict anyway, there was certainly none and the fact
that their speed had increased again was reason enough
to stay in it) shot out upon a broad expanse of debris-
filled water which the convict recognised as a river and,
from its size, the Yazoo River though it was little
enough he had seen of this country which he had not
quitted for so much as one single day in the last seven
years of his life. What he did not know was that it was
now running backward. So as soon as the drift of the
skiff indicated the set of the current, he began to paddle
in that direction which he believed to be downstream,
where he knew there were towns—Yazoo City, and as
a last resort, Vicksburg, if his luck was that bad, if not,
smaller towns whose names he did not know but where
there would be people, houses, something, anything he
might reach and surrender his charge to and turn his
back on her forever, on all pregnant and female life
forever and return to that monastic existence of shotguns and shackles where he would be secure from it.
Now, with the imminence of habitations, release from

her, he did not even hate her. When he looked upon the swelling and unmanageable body before him it seemed to him that it was not the woman at all but rather a separate demanding threatening inert yet living mass of which both he and she were equally victims; thinking, as he had been for the last three or four hours, of that minute's—nay, second's—aberration of eye or hand which would suffice to precipitate her into the water to be dragged down to death by that senseless millstone which in its turn would not even have to feel agony, he no longer felt any glow of revenge toward her as its custodian, he felt sorry for her as he would for the living timber in a barn which had to be burned to rid itself of vermin.

He paddled on, helping the current, steadily and strongly, with a calculated husbandry of effort, toward what he believed was downstream, towns, people, something to stand upon, while from time to time the woman raised herself to bail the accumulated rain from the skiff. It was raining steadily now though still not hard, still without passion, the sky, the day itself dissolving without grief; the skiff moved in a nimbus, an aura of gray gauze which merged almost without demarcation with the roiling spittle-frothed debris-choked water. Now the day, the light, definitely began to end and the convict permitted himself an extra notch or two of effort because it suddenly seemed to him that the speed of the skiff had lessened. This was actually the case though the convict did not know it. He merely took it as a phe nomenon of the increasing obfuscation, or at most as a result of the long day's continuous effort with no food, complicated by the ebbing and fluxing phases of anxiety and impotent rage at his absolutely gratuitous predicament. So he stepped up his stroke a beat or so, not from alarm but on the contrary, since he too had received that lift from the mere presence of a known stream, a river known by its ineradicable name to generations of men who had been drawn to live beside it as man always has been drawn to dwell beside water, even before he had a name for water and fire, drawn to the living water, the course of his destiny and his actual physical appearance rigidly coerced and postulated by it. So he was not alarmed. He paddled on, upstream without knowing it, unaware that all the water which for forty hours now had been pouring through the levee break to the north was somewhere ahead of him, on its way back to the River.

It was full dark now. That is, night had completely come, the gray dissolving sky had vanished, yet as though in perverse ratio surface visibility had sharpened, as though the light which the rain of the afternoon had washed out of the air had gathered upon the water as the rain itself had done, so that the yellow flood spread on before him now with a quality almost phosphorescent, right up to the instant where vision ceased. The darkness in fact had its advantages; he could now stop seeing the rain. He and his garments had been wet for more than twenty-four hours now so he had long since stopped feeling it, and now that he could no longer see it either it had in a certain sense ceased for him.

Also, he now had to make no effort even not to see the swell of his passenger's belly. So he was paddling on, strongly and steadily, not alarmed and not concerned but just exasperated because he had not yet begun to see any reflection on the clouds which would indicate the city or cities which he believed he was approaching but which were actually now miles behind him, when he heard a sound. He did not know what it was because he had never heard it before and he would never be expected to hear such again since it is not given to every man to hear such at all and to none to hear it more than once in his life. And he was not alarmed now either because there was not time, for although the visibility ahead, for all its clarity, did not extend very far, yet in the next instant to the hearing he was also seeing something such as he had never seen before. This was that the sharp line where the phosphorescent water met the darkness was now about ten feet higher than it had been an instant before and that it was curled forward upon itself like a sheet of dough being rolled out for a pudding. It reared, stooping; the crest of it swirled like the mane of a galloping horse and, phosphorescent too, fretted and flickered like fire. And while the woman huddled in the bows, aware or not aware the convict did not know which, he (the convict), his swollen and blood-streaked face gaped in an expression of aghast and incredulous amazement, continued to paddle directly into it. Again he simply had not had time to order his rhythm-hypnotised muscles to cease. He continued to paddle though the skiff had ceased to move forward at all but seemed to be hanging in space while the paddle still reached thrust recovered and reached again; now instead of space the skiff became abruptly surrounded by a welter of fleeing debris—planks, small buildings, the bodies of drowned yet antic animals, entire trees leaping and diving like porpoises above which the skiff seemed to hover in weightless and airy indecision like a bird above a fleeing countryside, undecided where to light or whether to light at all, while the convict squatted in it still going through the motions of paddling, waiting for an opportunity to scream. He never found it. For an instant the skiff seemed to stand erect on its stern and then shoot scrabbling and scrambling up the curling wall of water like a cat, and soared on above the licking crest itself and hung cradled into the high actual air in the limbs of a tree, from which bower of new-leafed boughs and branches the convict, like a bird in its nest and still waiting his chance to scream and still going through the motions of paddling though he no longer even had the paddle now, looked down upon a world turned to furious motion and in incredible retrograde.

Some time about midnight, accompanied by a rolling cannonade of thunder and lightning like a battery going into action, as though some forty hours' constipation of the elements, the firmament itself, were discharging in clapping and glaring salute to the ultimate acquiescence to desperate and furious motion, and still leading its charging welter of dead cows and mules and outhouses and cabins and hencoops, the skiff passed Vicksburg. The convict didn't know it. He wasn't looking high

enough above the water; he still squatted, clutching
the gunwales and glaring at the yellow turmoil about
him out of which entire trees, the sharp gables of houses,
the long mournful heads of mules which he fended off
with a splintered length of plank snatched from he knew
not where in passing (and which seemed to glare re-
proachfully back at him with sightless eyes, in limber-
lipped and incredulous amazement) rolled up and then
down again, the skiff now travelling forward now sideways now sternward, sometimes in the water, sometimes
riding for yards upon the roofs of houses and trees and
even upon the backs of the mules as though even in death
they were not to escape that burden-bearing doom with
which their eunuch race was cursed. But he didn't see
Vicksburg; the skiff, travelling at express speed, was in
a seething gut between soaring and dizzy banks with a
glare of light above them but he did not see it; he saw
the flotsam ahead of him divide violently and begin to
climb upon itself, mounting, and he was sucked through
the resulting gap too fast to recognise it as the trestling
of a railroad bridge; for a horrible moment the skiff
seemed to hang in static indecision before the looming
flank of a steamboat as though undecided whether to
climb over it or dive under it, then a hard icy wind
filled with the smell and taste and sense of wet and
boundless desolation blew upon him; the skiff made one
long bounding lunge as the convict's native state, in a
final paroxysm, regurgitated him onto the wild bosom
of the Father of Waters.

This is how he told about it seven weeks later, sitting

in new bedticking garments, shaved and with his hair
cut again, on his bunk in the barracks:

During the next three or four hours after the thunder
and lightning had spent itself the skiff ran in pitch
streaming darkness upon a roiling expanse which, even
if he could have seen, apparently had no boundaries.
Wild and invisible, it tossed and heaved about and beneath the boat, ridged with dirty phosphorescent foam
and filled with a debris of destruction—objects nameless and enormous and invisible which struck and
slashed at the skiff and whirled on. He did not know he
was now upon the River. At that time he would have
refused to believe it, even if he had known. Yesterday
he had known he was in a channel by the regularity of
the spacing between the bordering trees. Now, since even
by daylight he could have seen no boundaries, the last
place under the sun (or the streaming sky rather) he
would have suspected himself to be would have been a
river; if he had pondered at all about his present where-
abouts, about the geography beneath him, he would
merely have taken himself to be travelling at dizzy and
inexplicable speed above the largest cottonfield in the
world; if he who yesterday had known he was in a river,
had accepted that fact in good faith and earnest, then
had seen that river turn without warning and rush back
upon him with furious and deadly intent like a frenzied
stallion in a lane—if he had suspected for one second
that the wild and limitless expanse on which he now
found himself was a river, consciousness would simply
have refused; he would have fainted.

When daylight—a gray and ragged dawn filled with driving scud between icy rain-squalls—came and he could see again, he knew he was in no cottonfield. He knew that the wild water on which the skiff tossed and fled flowed above no soil tamely trod by man, behind the straining and surging buttocks of a mule. That was when it occurred to him that its present condition was no phenomenon of a decade, but that the intervening years during which it consented to bear upon its placid and sleepy bosom the frail mechanicals of man's clumsy contriving was the phenomenon and this the norm and the river was now doing what it liked to do, had waited patiently the ten years in order to do, as a mule will work for you ten years for the privilege of kicking you once. And he also learned something else about fear too, something he had even failed to discover on that other occasion when he was really afraid—that three or four seconds of that night in his youth while he looked down the twice-flashing pistol barrel of the terrified mail clerk before the clerk could be persuaded that his (the convict's) pistol would not shoot: that if you just held on long enough a time would come in fear after which it would no longer be agony at all but merely a kind of horrible outrageous itching, as after you have been burned bad.

He did not have to paddle now, he just steered (who had been without food for twenty-four hours now and without any sleep to speak of for fifty) while the skiff sped on across that boiling desolation where he had long since begun to not dare believe he could possibly be

where he could not doubt he was, trying with his fragment of splintered plank merely to keep the skiff intact
and afloat among the houses and trees and dead animals
(the entire towns, stores, residences, parks and farm-
yards, which leaped and played about him like fish),
not trying to reach any destination, just trying to keep
the skiff afloat until he did. He wanted so little. He
wanted nothing for himself. He just wanted to get rid
of the woman, the belly, and he was trying to do that in
the right way, not for himself, but for her. He could
have put her back into another tree at any time—

"Or you could have jumped out of the boat and let
her and it drown," the plump convict said. "Then they
could have given you the ten years for escaping and
then hung you for the murder and charged the boat to
your folks."

"Yah," the tall convict said.—But he had not done
that. He wanted to do it the right way, find somebody,
anybody he could surrender her to, something solid he
could set her down on and then jump back into the
river, if that would please anyone. That was all he
wanted—just to come to something, anything. That
didn't seem like a great deal to ask. And he couldn't do
it. He told how the skiff fled on—

"Didn't you pass nobody?" the plump convict said.
"No steamboat, nothing?"

"I dont know," the tall one said.—while he tried
merely to keep it afloat, until the darkness thinned and
lifted and revealed—

"Darkness?" the plump convict said. "I thought you said it was already daylight."

"Yah," the tall one said. He was rolling a cigarette, pouring the tobacco carefully from a new sack, into the creased paper. "This was another one. They had several while I was gone."—the skiff to be moving still rapidly up a winding corridor bordered by drowned trees which the convict recognised again to be a river running again in the direction that, until two days ago, had been upstream. He was not exactly warned through instinct that this one, like that of two days ago, was in reverse. He would not say that he now believed himself to be in the same river, though he would not have been surprised to find that he did believe this, existing now, as he did and had and apparently was to continue for an unnamed period, in a state in which he was toy and pawn on a vicious and inflammable geography. He merely realised that he was in a river again, with all the subsequent inferences of a comprehensible, even if not familiar, portion of the earth's surface. Now he believed that all he had to do would be to paddle far enough and he would come to something horizontal and above water even if not dry and perhaps even populated; and, if fast enough, in time, and that his only other crying urgency was to refrain from looking at the woman who, as vision, the incontrovertible and apparently inescapable presence of his passenger, returned with dawn, had ceased to be a human being and (you could add twenty-four more hours to the first twenty-four and the first fifty now, even counting the hen. It was dead, drowned, caught by one

wing under a shingle on a roof which had rolled momentarily up beside the skiff yesterday and he had eaten
some of it raw though the woman would not) had become
instead one single inert monstrous sentient womb from
which, he now believed, if he could only turn his gaze
away and keep it away, would disappear, and if he could
only keep his gaze from pausing again at the spot it
had occupied, would not return. That's what he was
doing this time when he discovered the wave was coming.

He didn't know how he discovered it was coming
back. He heard no sound, it was nothing felt nor seen.
He did not even believe that finding the skiff to be now
in slack water—that is, that the motion of the current
which, whether right or wrong, had at least been horizontal, had now stopped that and assumed a vertical
direction—was sufficient to warn him. Perhaps it was
just an invincible and almost fanatic faith in the in-
ventiveness and innate viciousness of that medium on
which his destiny was now cast, apparently forever; a
sudden conviction far beyond either horror or surprise
that now was none too soon for it to prepare to do whatever it was it intended doing. So he whirled the skiff,
spun it on its heel like a running horse, whereupon,
reversed, he could not even distinguish the very channel
he had come up. He did not know whether he simply
could not see it or if it had vanished some time ago and
he not aware at the time; whether the river had become
lost in a drowned world or if the world had become
drowned in one limitless river. So now he could not tell
if he were running directly before the wave or quarter-

ing across its line of charge; all he could do was keep
that sense of swiftly accumulating ferocity behind him
and paddle as fast as his spent and now numb muscles
could be driven, and try not to look at the woman, to
wrench his gaze from her and keep it away until he
reached something flat and above water. So, gaunt,
hollow-eyed, striving and wrenching almost physically
at his eyes as if they were two of those suction-tipped
rubber arrows shot from the toy gun of a child, his spent
muscles obeying not will now but that attenuation beyond mere exhaustion which, mesmeric, can continue
easier than cease, he once more drove the skiff full tilt
into something it could not pass and, once more hurled
violently forward onto his hands and knees, crouching,
he glared with his wild swollen face up at the man with
the shotgun and said in a harsh, croaking voice: "Vicksburg? Where's Vicksburg?"

Even when he tried to tell it, even after the seven
weeks and he safe, secure, riveted warranted and doubly
guaranteed by the ten years they had added to his sentence for attempted escape, something of the old hysteric
incredulous outrage came back into his face, his voice,
his speech. He never did even get on the other boat. He
told how he clung to a strake (it was a dirty unpainted
shanty boat with a drunken rake of tin stove pipe, it had
been moving when he struck it and apparently it had
not even changed course even though the three people on
it must have been watching him all the while—a second
man, barefoot and with matted hair and beard also at
the steering sweep, and then—he did not know how

long—a woman leaning in the door, in a filthy assort-
ment of men's garments, watching him too with the
same cold speculation) being dragged violently along,
trying to state and explain his simple (and to him at
least) reasonable desire and need; telling it, trying to
tell it, he could feel again the old unforgettable affronting like an ague fit as he watched the abortive tobacco
rain steadily and faintly from between his shaking hands
and then the paper itself part with a thin dry snapping
report:

"Burn my clothes?" the convict cried. "Burn them?"

"How in hell do you expect to escape in them bill-
boards?" the man with the shotgun said. He (the convict) tried to tell it, tried to explain as he had tried to
explain not to the three people on the boat alone but to
the entire circumambience—desolate water and forlorn
trees and sky—not for justification because he needed
none and knew that his hearers, the other convicts, required none from him, but rather as, on the point of
exhaustion, he might have picked dreamily and in-
credulously at a suffocation. He told the man with the
gun how he and his partner had been given the boat and
told to pick up a man and a woman, how he had lost his
partner and failed to find the man, and now all in the
world he wanted was something flat to leave the woman
on until he could find an officer, a sheriff. He thought of
home, the place where he had lived almost since childhood, his friends of years whose ways he knew and who
knew his ways, the familiar fields where he did work he
had learned to do well and to like, the mules with char-

acters he knew and respected as he knew and respected
the characters of certain men; he thought of the barracks at night, with screens against the bugs in summer
and good stoves in winter and someone to supply the
fuel and the food too; the Sunday ball games and the
picture shows—things which, with the exception of the
ball games, he had never known before. But most of
all, his own character (Two years ago they had offered
to make a trusty of him. He would no longer need to
plow or feed stock, he would only follow those who did
with a loaded gun, but he declined. "I reckon I'll stick
to plowing," he said, absolutely without humor. "I done
already tried to use a gun one time too many.") his
good name, his responsibility not only toward those
who were responsible toward him but to himself, his own
honor in the doing of what was asked of him, his pride
in being able to do it, no matter what it was. He thought
of this and listened to the man with the gun talking about
escape and it seemed to him that, hanging there, being
dragged violently along (it was here he said that he first
noticed the goats' beards of moss in the trees, though it
could have been there for several days so far as he knew.
It just happened that he first noticed it here.) that he
would simply burst.

"Cant you get it into your head that the last thing I
want to do is run away?" he cried. "You can set there
with that gun and watch me; I give you fair lief. All I
want is to put this woman—"

"And I told you she could come aboard," the man
with the gun said in his level voice. "But there aint no

room on no boat of mine for nobody hunting a sheriff in no kind of clothes, let alone a penitentiary suit."

"When he steps aboard, knock him in the head with the gun barrel," the man at the sweep said. "He's drunk."

"He aint coming aboard," the man with the gun said. "He's crazy."

Then the woman spoke. She didn't move, leaning in the door, in a pair of faded and patched and filthy overalls like the two men: "Give them some grub and tell them to get out of here." She moved, she crossed the deck and looked down at the convict's companion with her cold sullen face. "How much more time have you got?"

"It wasn't due till next month," the woman in the boat said. "But I—" The woman in overalls turned to the man with the gun.

"Give them some grub," she said. But the man with the gun was still looking down at the woman in the boat.

"Come on," he said to the convict. "Put her aboard, and beat it."

"And what'll happen to you," the woman in overalls said, "when you try to turn her over to an officer. When you lay alongside a sheriff and the sheriff asks you who you are?" Still the man with the gun didn't even look at her. He hardly even shifted the gun across his arm as he struck the woman across the face with the back of his other hand, hard. "You son of a bitch," she said. Still the man with the gun did not even look at her.

"Well?" he said to the convict.

"Dont you see I cant?" the convict cried. "Cant you see that?"

Now, he said, he gave up. He was doomed. That is, he knew now that he had been doomed from the very start never to get rid of her, just as the ones who sent him out with the skiff knew that he never would actually give up; when he recognised one of the objects which the woman in overalls was hurling into the skiff to be a can of condensed milk, he believed it to be a presage, gratuitous and irrevocable as a death-notice over the telegraph, that he was not even to find a flat stationary surface in time for the child to be born on it. So he told how he held the skiff alongside the shanty-boat while the first tentative toying of the second wave made up beneath him, while the woman in overalls passed back and forth between house and rail, flinging the food—the hunk of salt meat, the ragged and filthy quilt, the scorched lumps of cold bread which she poured into the skiff from a heaped dishpan like so much garbage—while he clung to the strake against the mounting pull of the current, the new wave which for the moment he had forgotten because he was still trying to state the incredible simplicity of his desire and need until the man with the gun (the only one of the three who wore shoes) began to stamp at his hands, he snatching his hands away one at a time to avoid the heavy shoes, then grasping the rail again until the man with the gun kicked at his face, he flinging himself sideways to avoid the shoe and so breaking his hold on the rail, his weight canting the skiff off at a tangent on the increasing current so that it began to leave the shanty boat behind and he paddling again now, violently, as a man hurries toward the precipice for which he knows at last he is doomed, looking back at the other boat, the three faces sullen derisive and grim and rapidly diminishing across the widening water and at last, apoplectic, suffocating with the intolerable fact not that he had been refused but that he had been refused so little, had wanted so little, asked for so little, yet there had been demanded of him in return the one price out of all breath which (they must have known) if he could have paid it, he would not have been where he was, asking what he asked, raising the paddle and shaking it and screaming curses back at them even after the shotgun flashed and the charge went scuttering past along the water to one side.

So he hung there, he said, shaking the paddle and howling, when suddenly he remembered that other wave, the second wall of water full of houses and dead mules building up behind him back in the swamp. So he quit yelling then and went back to paddling. He was not trying to outrun it. He just knew from experience that when it overtook him, he would have to travel in the same direction it was moving in anyway, whether he wanted to or not, and when it did overtake him, he would begin to move too fast to stop, no matter what places he might come to where he could leave the woman, land her in time. Time: that was his itch now, so his only chance was to stay ahead of it as long as he could and hope to reach something before it struck. So he went on, driving the skiff with muscles which had been too tired so long they had quit feeling it, as when a man has had bad luck for so long that he ceases to believe it is even bad, let alone luck. Even when he ate —the scorched lumps the size of baseballs and the weight and durability of cannel coal even after having lain in the skiff's bilge where the shanty boat woman had thrown them—the iron-like lead-heavy objects which no man would have called bread outside of the crusted and scorched pan in which they had cooked—it was with one hand, begrudging even that from the paddle.

He tried to tell that too—that day while the skiff fled on among the bearded trees while every now and then small quiet tentative exploratory feelers would come up from the wave behind and toy for a moment at the skiff, light and curious, then go on with a faint hissing sighing, almost a chuckling, sound, the skiff going on, driving on with nothing to see but trees and water and solitude: until after a while it no longer seemed to him that he was trying to put space and distance behind him or shorten space and distance ahead but that both he and the wave were now hanging suspended simultaneous and unprogressing in pure time, upon a dreamy desolation in which he paddled on not from any hope even to reach anything at all but merely to keep intact what little of distance the length of the skiff provided between himself and the inert and inescapable mass of female meat before him; then night and the skiff rushing on, fast since any speed over anything unknown and

invisible is too fast, with nothing before him and behind
him the outrageous idea of a volume of moving water
toppling forward, its crest frothed and shredded like
fangs, and then dawn again (another of those dreamlike
alterations day to dark then back to day again with that
quality truncated, anachronic and unreal as the waxing
and waning of lights in a theatre scene) and the skiff
emerging now with the woman no longer supine beneath
the shrunken soaked private's coat but sitting bolt upright, gripping the gunwales with both hands, her eyes
closed and her lower lip caught between her teeth and
he driving the splintered board furiously now, glaring
at her out of his wild swollen sleepless face and crying,
croaking, "Hold on! For God's sake hold on!"

"I'm trying to," she said. "But hurry! Hurry!" He
told it, the unbelievable: hurry, hasten: the man falling
from a cliff being told to catch onto something and save
himself; the very telling of it emerging shadowy and
burlesque, ludicrous, comic and mad, from the ague of
unbearable forgetting with a quality more dreamily
furious than any fable behind proscenium lights:

He was in a basin now— "A basin?" the plump convict said. "That's what you wash in."

"All right," the tall one said, harshly, above his
hands. "I did." With a supreme effort he stilled them
long enough to release the two bits of cigarette paper
and watched them waft in light fluttering indecision to
the floor between his feet, holding his hands motionless
even for a moment longer—a basin, a broad peaceful
yellow sea which had an abruptly and curiously ordered

air, giving him, even at that moment, the impression
that it was accustomed to water even if not total sub-
mersion; he even remembered the name of it, told to
him two or three weeks later by someone: Atchafalaya—

"Louisiana?" the plump convict said. "You mean
you were clean out of Mississippi? Hell fire." He stared
at the tall one. "Shucks," he said. "That aint but just
across from Vicksburg."

"They never named any Vicksburg across from where
I was," the tall one said. "It was Baton Rouge they
named." And now he began to talk about a town, a little
neat white portrait town nestling among enormous very
green trees, appearing suddenly in the telling as it probably appeared in actuality, abrupt and airy and miragelike and incredibly serene before him behind a scattering of boats moored to a line of freight cars standing
flush to the doors in water. And now he tried to tell that
too: how he stood waist-deep in water for a moment
looking back and down at the skiff in which the woman
half lay, her eyes still closed, her knuckles white on the
gunwales and a tiny thread of blood creeping down her
chin from her chewed lip, and he looking down at her
in a kind of furious desperation.

"How far will I have to walk?" she said.

"I dont know, I tell you!" he cried. "But it's land
somewhere yonder! It's land, houses."

"If I try to move, it wont even be born inside a boat,"
she said. "You'll have to get closer."

"Yes," he cried, wild, desperate, incredulous. "Wait.
I'll go and surrender, then they will have—" He didn't

finish, wait to finish; he told that too: himself splashing,
stumbling, trying to run, sobbing and gasping; now he
saw it—another loading platform standing above the
yellow flood, the khaki figures on it as before, identical,
the same; he said how the intervening days since that
first innocent morning telescoped, vanished as if they
had never been, the two contiguous succeeding instants
(succeeding? simultaneous) and he transported across
no intervening space but merely turned in his own footsteps, plunging, splashing, his arms raised, croaking
harshly. He heard the startled shout, "There's one of
them!", the command, the clash of equipment, the
alarmed cry: "There he goes! There he goes!"

"Yes!" he cried, running, plunging, "here I am!
Here! Here!" running on, into the first scattered volley,
stopping among the bullets, waving his arms, shrieking,
"I want to surrender! I want to surrender!" watching
not in terror but in amazed and absolutely unbearable
outrage as a squatting clump of the khaki figures parted
and he saw the machine gun, the blunt thick muzzle slant
and drop and probe toward him and he still screaming
in his hoarse crow's voice, "I want to surrender! Cant
you hear me?" continuing to scream even as he whirled
and plunged splashing, ducking, went completely under
and heard the bullets going thuck-thuck-thuck on the
water above him and he scrabbling still on the bottom,
still trying to scream even before he regained his feet
and still all submerged save his plunging unmistakable
buttocks, the outraged screaming bubbling from his
mouth and about his face since he merely wanted to sur-

render. Then he was comparatively screened, out of range, though not for long. That is (he didn't tell how nor where) there was a moment in which he paused, breathed for a second before running again, the course back to the skiff open for the time being though he could still hear the shouts behind him and now and then a shot, and he panting, sobbing, a long savage tear in the flesh of one hand, got when and how he did not know, and he wasting precious breath, speaking to no one now any more than the scream of the dying rabbit is addressed to any mortal ear but rather an indictment of all breath and its folly and suffering, its infinite capacity for folly and pain, which seems to be its only immortality: "All in the world I want is just to surrender."

He returned to the skiff and got in and took up his splintered plank. And now when he told this, despite the fury of element which climaxed it, it (the telling) became quite simple; he now even creased another cigarette paper between fingers which did not tremble at all and filled the paper from the tobacco sack without spilling a flake, as though he had passed from the machine-gun's barrage into a bourne beyond any more amazement: so that the subsequent part of his narrative seemed to reach his listeners as though from beyond a sheet of slightly milky though still transparent glass, as something not heard but seen—a series of shadows, edgeless yet distinct, and smoothly flowing, logical and unfrantic and making no sound: They were in the skiff, in the center of the broad placid trough which had no boundaries and down which the tiny forlorn skiff flew to

the irresistible coercion of a current going once more he
knew not where, the neat small liveoak-bowered towns
unattainable and miragelike and apparently attached to
nothing upon the airy and unchanging horizon. He did
not believe them, they did not matter, he was doomed;
they were less than the figments of smoke or of delirium,
and he driving his unceasing paddle without destination
or even hope now, looking now and then at the woman
sitting with her knees drawn up and locked and her
entire body one terrific clench while the threads of
bloody saliva crept from her teeth-clenched lower lip.
He was going nowhere and fleeing from nothing, he
merely continued to paddle because he had paddled so
long now that he believed if he stopped his muscles
would scream in agony. So when it happened he was not
surprised. He heard the sound which he knew well (he
had heard it but once before, true enough, but no man
needed hear it but once) and he had been expecting it;
he looked back, still driving the paddle, and saw it,
curled, crested with its strawlike flotsam of trees and
debris and dead beasts and he glared over his shoulder
at it for a full minute out of that attenuation far beyond
the point of outragement where even suffering, the
capability of being further affronted, had ceased, from
which he now contemplated with savage and invulnerable
curiosity the further extent to which his now anesthetised
nerves could bear, what next could be invented for them
to bear, until the wave actually began to rear above his
head into its thunderous climax. Then only did he turn
his head. His stroke did not falter, it neither slowed nor

increased; still paddling with that spent hypnotic steadiness, he saw the swimming deer. He did not know what it was nor that he had altered the skiff's course to follow it, he just watched the swimming head before him as the wave boiled down and the skiff rose bodily in the old familiar fashion on a welter of tossing trees and houses and bridges and fences, he still paddling even while the paddle found no purchase save air and still paddled even as he and the deer shot forward side by side at arm's length, he watching the deer now, watching the deer begin to rise out of the water bodily until it was actually running along upon the surface, rising still, soaring clear of the water altogether, vanishing upward in a dying crescendo of splashings and snapping branches, its damp scut flashing upward, the entire animal vanishing upward as smoke vanishes. And now the skiff struck and canted and he was out of it too, standing knee-deep, springing out and falling to his knees, scrambling up, glaring after the vanished deer. "Land!" he croaked. "Land! Hold on! Just hold on!" He caught the woman beneath the arms, dragging her out of the boat, plunging and panting after the vanished deer. Now earth actually appeared—an acclivity smooth and swift and steep, bizarre, solid and unbelievable; an Indian mound, and he plunging at the muddy slope, slipping back, the woman struggling in his muddy hands.

"Let me down!" she cried. "Let me down!" But he held her, panting, sobbing, and rushed again at the muddy slope; he had almost reached the flat crest with

his now violently unmanageable burden when a stick
under his foot gathered itself with thick convulsive
speed. *It was a snake*, he thought as his feet fled beneath
him and with the indubitable last of his strength he half
pushed and half flung the woman up the bank as he
shot feet first and face down back into that medium
upon which he had lived for more days and nights than
he could remember and from which he himself had never
completely emerged, as if his own failed and spent flesh
were attempting to carry out his furious unflagging will
for severance at any price, even that of drowning, from
the burden with which, unwitting and without choice,
he had been doomed. Later it seemed to him that he had
carried back beneath the surface with him the sound of
the infant's first mewling cry.

Wild Palms

NEITHER THE MANAGER OF THE MINE NOR HIS WIFE MET them—a couple even less old though considerably harder, in the face at least, than Charlotte and Wilbourne. Their name was Buckner, they called each other Buck and Bill. "Only the name is Billie, i.e.," Mrs Buckner said in a harsh Western voice. "I'm from Colorado" (she pronounced the a like in radish). "Buck's from Wyoming."

"It's a perfect whore's name, isn't it?" Charlotte said pleasantly.

"Just what do you mean by that?"

"That's all. I didn't mean to offend. It would be a good whore. That's what I would try to be."

Mrs Buckner looked at her. (This was while Buckner and Wilbourne were up at the commissary, getting the blankets and the sheep coats and woollen underwear and socks.) "You and him aint married, are you?"

"What made you think that?"

"I dont know. You can just tell somehow."

"No, we're not. I hope you dont mind, since we're going to live in the same house together."

"Why should I? Me and Buck wasn't married for a while either. But we are now all right." Her voice was not triumphant, it was smug. "And I've got it put away good too. Even Buck dont know where. Not that that

179

would make any difference. Buck's all right. But it dont
do a girl any harm to be safe."

"What put away?"

"The paper. The license." Later (she was cooking the
evening meal now and Wilbourne and Buckner were still
across the canyon at the mine) she said, "Make him
marry you."

"Maybe I will," Charlotte said.

"You make him. It's better that way. Especially
when you get jammed."

"Are you jammed?"

"Yes. About a month."

In fact, when the ore train—a dummy engine with
neither head nor rear and three cars and a cubicle of
caboose containing mostly stove—reached the snow-
choked railhead there was no one in sight at all save a
grimed giant upon whom they had apparently come by
complete surprise, in a grimed sheep-lined coat, with
pale eyes which looked as if he had not slept much lately
in a grimed face which obviously had not been shaved
and doubtless not been washed in some time—a Pole,
with an air fierce proud and wild and a little hysterical,
who spoke no English, jabbering, gesturing violently
toward the opposite wall of the canyon where a half
dozen houses made mostly of sheet iron and window-
deep in drifts, clung. The canyon was not wide, it was a
ditch, a gutter, it soared, swooping, the pristine snow
scarred and blemished by and dwarfing the shaft entrance, the refuse dump, the few buildings; beyond the
canyon rims the actual unassailable peaks rose, cloud-

ravelled in some incredible wind, on the dirty sky. "It will be beautiful in the spring," Charlotte said.

"It had better be," Wilbourne said.

"It will be. It is now. But let's go somewhere. I'm going to freeze in a minute."

Again Wilbourne tried the Pole. "Manager," he said. "Which house?"

"Yah; boss," the Pole said. He flung his hand again toward the opposite canyon wall, he moved with incredible speed for all his size and, Charlotte starting momentarily back before she caught herself, he pointed at her thin slippers in the trodden ankle-deep snow then took both lapels of her coat in his grimed hands and drew them about her throat and face with almost a woman's gentleness, the pale eyes stooping at her with an expression at once fierce, wild and tender; he shoved her forward, patting her back, he actually gave her a definite hard slap on the bottom. "Ron," he said. "Ron."

Then they saw and entered the path crossing the narrow valley. That is, it was not exactly a path free of snow or snow-packed by feet, it was merely that here the snow level was lower, the width of a single man between the two snow banks and so protected somewhat from the wind. "Maybe he lives in the mine and only comes home over the week-end," Charlotte said.

"But he's got a wife, they told me. What would she do?"

"Maybe the ore train just comes once a week too."

"You must not have seen the engineer."

"We haven't seen his wife, either," she said. She made

a sound of disgust. "That wasn't even funny. Excuse me, Wilbourne."

"I do."

"Excuse me, mountains. Excuse me, snow. I think I'm going to freeze."

"She wasn't there this morning, anyway," Wilbourne said. Nor was the manager at the mine. They chose a house, not at random and not because it was the largest, which it was not, and not even because there was a thermometer (it registered fourteen degrees above zero) beside the door, but simply because it was the first house they came to and now they had both become profoundly and ineradicably intimate with cold for the first time in their lives, a cold which left an ineffaceable and unforgettable mark somewhere on the spirit and memory like first sex experience or the experience of taking human life. Wilbourne knocked once at this door with a hand which could not even feel the wood and did not wait for an answer, opening it and thrusting Charlotte ahead of him into a single room where a man and a woman, sitting identical in woolen shirts and jeans pants and shoeless woollen socks on either side of a dog-eared pack of cards laid out for a game of some sort on a plank across a nail keg, looked up at them in amazement.

"You mean *he* sent you out here? Callaghan himself?" Buckner said.

"Yes," Wilbourne said. He could hear Charlotte and Mrs. Buckner where Charlotte stood over the heater about ten feet away (it burned gasoline; when a match

was struck to it, which happened only when they had to
turn it off to refill the tank, since it burned otherwise
all the time, night and day, it took fire with a bang and
glare which after a while even Wilbourne got used to
and no longer clapped his mouth shut just before his
heart jumped out) talking: "Is them all the clothes you
brought out here? You'll freeze. Buck'll have to go to
the commissary."—"Yes," Wilbourne said. "Why? Who
else would send me?"

"You—ah—you didn't bring anything? Letter or
nothing?"

"No. He said I wouldn't—"

"Oh, I see. You paid your own way. Railroad fare."

"No. He paid it."

"Well, I'll be damned," Buckner said. He turned his
head toward his wife. "You hear that, Bill?"

"What?" Wilbourne said. "What's wrong?"

"Never mind now," Buckner said. "We'll go up to
the commissary and get you fixed up for sleeping, and
some warmer clothes than them you've got. He didn't
even tell you to buy yourself a couple of Roebuck sheep
coats, did he?"

"No," Wilbourne said. "But let me get warm first."

"You wont never get warm out here," Buckner said.
"If you sit over a stove trying to, waiting to, you wont
ever move. You'll starve, you wont even get up to fill
the stove tank when it burns out. The thing is, to make
up your mind you will always be a little cold even in
bed and just go on about your business and after a while
you will get used to it and forget it and then you wont

even notice you are cold because you will have forgotten
what being warm was ever like. So come on now. You
can take my coat."

"What will you do?"

"It aint far. I have a sweater. Carrying the stuff will
warm us up some."

The commissary was another iron single room filled
with the iron cold and lighted by the hushed iron glare
of the snow beyond a single window. The cold in it was
a dead cold. It was like aspic, almost solid to move
through, the body reluctant as though, and with justice,
more than to breathe, live, was too much to ask of it.
On either side rose wooden shelves, gloomy and barren
save for the lower ones, as if this room too were a
thermometer not to measure cold but moribundity, an
incontrovertible centigrade (*We should have brought the
Bad Smell*, Wilbourne was already thinking), a con-
tracting mercury of sham which was not even grandiose.
They hauled down the blankets, the sheep coats and
woollens and galoshes; they felt like ice, like iron, stiff;
carrying them back to the cabin Wilbourne's lungs (he
had forgot the altitude) labored at the rigid air which
felt like fire in them.

"So you're a doctor," Buckner said.

"I'm the doctor," Wilbourne said. They were outside
now. Buckner locked the door again. Wilbourne looked
out across the canyon, toward the opposite wall with its
tiny lifeless scar of mine entrance and refuse dump.
"Just what's wrong here?"

"I'll show you after a while. Are you a doctor?"

Now Wilbourne looked at him. "I just told you I was. What do you mean?"

"Then I guess you've got something to show it. Degree: what do they call them?"

Wilbourne looked at him. "Just what are you getting at? Am I to be responsible to you for my capabilities, or to the man who is paying my salary?"

"Salary?" Buckner laughed harshly. Then he stopped. "I guess I am going about this wrong. I never aimed to rub your fur crossways. When a man comes into my country and you offer him a job and he claims he can ride, we want proof that he can and he wouldn't get mad when we asked him for it. We would even furnish him a horse to prove it on, only it wouldn't be the best horse we had and if we never had but one horse and it would be a good horse, it wouldn't be that one. So we wouldn't have a horse for him to prove it on and we would have to ask him. That's what I'm doing now." He looked at Wilbourne, sober and intent, out of hazel eyes in a gaunt face like raw beef muscle.

"Oh," Wilbourne said. "I see. I have a degree from a pretty fair medical school. I had almost finished my course in a well-known hospital. Then I would have been—known, anyway; that is, they would have admitted publicly that I knew—about what any doctor knows, and more than some probably. Or at least I hope so. Does that satisfy you?"

"Yes," Buckner said. "That's all right." He turned and went on. "You wanted to know what's wrong here. We'll leave these things at the cabin and go over to the

shaft and I'll show you." They left the blankets and
woollens at the cabin and crossed the canyon, the path
which was no path just as the commissary had not been
a commissary but a sort of inscrutable signpost like a
code word set beside a road.

"That ore train we came up on," Wilbourne said.
"What was in it when it went down to the valley?"

"Oh, it was loaded," Buckner said. "It has to get there
loaded. Leave here loaded, anyway. I see to that. I dont
want my throat cut until I know it."

"Loaded with what?"

"Ah," Buckner said. The mine was not a shaft, it was
a gallery pitching at once straight back into the bowels
of the rock—a round tube like the muzzle of a howitzer,
shored with timbers and filled with the dying snow-glare
as they advanced, and the same dead aspic-like cold
that was in the commissary and lined by two light-gauge
rails along which as they entered (they stepped quickly
aside for it or they would have been run down) came a
filled ore tram pushed by a running man whom Wilbourne recognised also to be a Pole though shorter,
thicker, squatter (he was to realise later that none of
them were the giants they seemed, that the illusion of
size was an aura, an emanation of that wild childlike
innocence and credulity which they possessed in common)—the same pale eyes, the same grimed unshaven
face above the same filthy sheep-lined coat.

"I thought—" Wilbourne began. But he did not say
it. They went on; the last glare of the snow faded and
now they entered a scene like something out of an

Eisenstein Dante. The gallery became a small amphi-
theatre, branching off in smaller galleries like the spread
fingers from a palm, lighted by an incredible extravagance of electricity as though for a festival—an extravagance of dirty bulbs which had, though in inverse ratio,
that same air of sham and moribundity which the big,
almost barren building labeled *Commissary* in tremendous new letters had—in the light from which still
more of the grimed, giant-seeming men in sheep coats
and with eyes which had not slept much lately worked
with picks and shovels with that same frenzy of the man
running behind the loaded tram, with shouts and ejaculations in that tongue which Wilbourne could not understand almost exactly like a college baseball team cheer-
ing one another on, while from the smaller galleries
which they had not penetrated yet and where still more
electric bulbs glared in the dust-laden and icy air came
either echoes or the cries of still other men, meaningless
and weird, filling the heavy air like blind erratic birds.
"He told me you had Chinese and Italians too," Wilbourne said.

"Yah," Buckner said. "They left. The chinks left in
October. I waked up one morning and they were gone.
All of them. They walked down, I guess. With their
shirt tails hanging out and in them straw slippers. But
then there wasn't much snow in October. Not all the
way down, anyhow. They smelled it. The wops—"

"Smelled it?"

"There hasn't been a payroll in here since September."

"Oh," Wilbourne said. "I see now. Yes. So they smelled it. Like niggers do."

"I dont know. I never had any smokes here. The wops made a little more noise. They struck, all proper. Threw down their picks and shovels and walked out. There was a—what do you call it? deputation?—waited on me. Considerable talk, all pretty loud, and a lot of hands, the women standing outside in the snow, holding up the babies for me to look at. So I opened the commissary and gave them all a woollen shirt apiece, men, women and children (you should have seen them, the kids in a man's shirt, the ones that were just big enough to walk I mean. They wore them outside like overcoats.) and a can of beans apiece and sent them out on the ore train. There was still a considerable hands, fists now, and I could hear them for a good while after the train was out of sight. Going down Hogben (he runs the ore train; the railroad pays him) just uses the engine to brake with, so it dont make much fuss. Not as much as they did, anyway. But the hunkies stayed."

"Why? Didn't they—"

"Find out that everything had blew? They dont understand good. Oh, they could hear all right; the wops could talk to them: one of the wops was the interpreter for them. But they are queer people; they dont understand dishonesty. I guess when the wops tried to tell them, it just didn't make sense, that a man could let folks keep on working without intending to pay them. So now they think they are making overtime. Doing all the work. They are not trammers or miners either, they

are blasters. There's something about a hunky that likes
dynamite. Maybe it's the noise. But now they are doing
it all. They wanted to put their women in here too. I
understood that after a while and stopped it. That's why
they dont sleep much. They think that when the money
comes tomorrow, they'll get all of it. They probably
think now you brought it and that Saturday night they'll
all get thousands of dollars apiece. They're like kids.
They will believe anything. That's why when they find
out you have kidded them, they kill you. Oh, not with a
knife in the back and not even with a knife, they walk
right up to you and stick the stick of dynamite into your
pocket and hold you with one hand while they strike the
match to the fuse with the other."

"And you haven't told them?"

"Told them how? I cant talk to them; the interpreter
was one of the wops. Besides, he's got to keep his mine
looking like it's running and that's what I am supposed
to do. So he can keep on selling the stock. That's why
you are here—a doctor. When he told you there wouldn't
be any medical inspectors out here to worry you about
a license, he told you the truth. But there are mining
inspectors out here, laws and regulations for running
mines that say there must be a doctor. That's why he
paid you and your wife's fare out here. Besides, the
money might come in. When I saw you this morning I
thought you had brought it too. Well? Seen enough?"

"Yes," Wilbourne said. They returned toward the
entrance; once more they stepped quickly aside to let a
filled ore tram pass, pushed at a run by another grimed

and frantic Pole. They emerged into the living cold of
the immaculate snow, the fading day. "I dont believe it,"
Wilbourne said.

"You saw, didn't you?"

"I mean the reason you are still here. You were not
expecting any money."

"Maybe I'm waiting for a chance to slip away. And
these bastards wont even go to sleep at night and give me
one.—Hell," he said. "That's a lie too. I waited here
because it's winter and I might as well be here as any
where else, long as there is enough grub in the commissary and I can keep warm. And because I knew he
would have to send another doctor soon or come here
himself and tell me and them wild bastards in there the
mine is closed."

"Well, here I am," Wilbourne said. "He sent another
doctor. What is it you want of a doctor?"

For a long moment Buckner looked at him—the hard
little eyes which would have had to be good at measuring and commanding men of a sort, a class, a type, or
he would not be where he now was; the hard eyes which
perhaps never before, Wilbourne told himself, had been
faced with the need of measuring a man who merely
claimed to be a doctor. "Listen," he said. "I've got a
good job, only I haven't had any pay since September.
We've saved about three hundred bucks, to get out of
here with when this does blow, and to live on until I
can find something else. And now Bill turns up a month
gone with a kid and we cant afford a kid. And you claim
to be a doctor and I believe you are. How about it?"

"No," Wilbourne said.

"It's my risk. I'll see you are clear."

"No," Wilbourne said.

"You mean you dont know how?"

"I know how. It's simple enough. One of the men in the hospital did it once—emergency patient—maybe to show us what never to do. He didn't need to show me."

"I'll give you a hundred bucks."

"I've got a hundred bucks," Wilbourne said.

"A hundred and fifty bucks. That's half of it. You see I cant do more."

"I've got a hundred and fifty bucks too. I've got a hundred and eighty-five bucks. And even if I didn't have but ten bucks—"

Buckner turned away. "You're lucky. Let's go eat."

He told Charlotte about it. Not in bed, as they had used to talk, because they all slept in the same room— the cabin had but one, with a lean-to for what privacy was absolutely required—but outside the cabin where, knee-deep in snow, in the galoshes now, they could see the opposite canyon wall and the serrated cloud-ravelled peaks beyond, where Charlotte said again, indomitable: "It will be beautiful in the spring."

"And you said no," she said. "Why? Was it the hundred dollars?"

"You know better than that. It was a hundred and fifty, incidentally."

"Low I may be, but not that low?"

"No. It was because I—"

"You are afraid?"

"No. It's nothing. Simple enough. A touch with the blade to let the air in. It's because I—"

"Women do die of it though."

"Because the operator was no good. Maybe one in ten thousand. Of course there are no records. It's because I—"

"It's all right. It's not because the price was too low, nor because you are afraid. That's all I wanted to know. You dont have to. Nobody can make you. Kiss me. We cant even kiss inside, let alone—"

The four of them (Charlotte now slept in the woollen underwear like the others) slept in the one room, not in beds but on mattresses on the floor ("It's warmer that way," Buckner explained. "Cold comes from underneath.") and the gasoline stove burned constantly. They had opposite corners but even at that the two mattresses were not fifteen feet apart, so Wilbourne and Charlotte could not even talk, whisper. It meant less to the Buckners though, even though they seemed to have little enough of preliminary talking and whispering to do; at times and with the lamp not five minutes dark Wilbourne and Charlotte would hear the abrupt stallion-like surge from the other bed, the violent blanket-muffled motion ceasing into the woman's panting moans and at times a series of pure screams tumbling over one another, though such was not for them. Then one day the thermometer reversed itself from fourteen below to forty-one below and they moved the two mattresses together and slept as a unit, the two women in the middle, and still sometimes before the light was scarcely out (or perhaps they would be wakened by it) there would come the ruthless stallion crash with no word spoken, as if they had been drawn violently and savagely to one another out of pure slumber like steel and magnet, the fierce breathing, the panting and shuddering woman-moans, and Charlotte saying, "Cant you all do that without pulling the covers loose?" and still it was not for them.

They had been there a month, it was almost March now and the spring for which Charlotte waited that much nearer, when one afternoon Wilbourne returned from the mine where the dirty and unsleeping Poles still labored in that fierce deluded frenzy and the blind birdlike incomprehensible voices still flew back and forth among the dusty extravagant electric bulbs, and found Charlotte and Mrs Buckner watching the cabin door as he entered. And he knew what was coming and perhaps even that he was already done for. "Listen, Harry," she said. "They are going to leave. They've got to. It's all up here and they have only three hundred dollars, to get where they are going and to live on until he can find work. So they've got to do something before it's too late."

"So have we," he said. "And we haven't got three hundred dollars."

"We haven't got a baby either. We haven't had bad luck. You said it's simple, that only one in ten thousand die, that you know how to do it, that you are not afraid. And they want to take the risk."

"Do you want a hundred dollars that bad?"

"Have I ever? Ever talked about money, except the hundred and twenty-five of mine you wouldn't take? You know that. Just as I know you wouldn't take their money."

"I'm sorry. I didn't mean that. It's because I—"

"It's because they are in trouble. Suppose it was us. I know you will have to throw away something. But we have thrown away a lot, threw it away for love and we're not sorry."

"No," he said. "Not sorry. Never."

"This is for love too. Not ours maybe. But love." She went to the shelf on which they kept their personal effects and took down the meager case of instruments with which he had been equipped before he left Chicago, along with the two railroad tickets. "This would be good for him to know, if he could know it: that the only time you ever used them was to amputate his manager from the mine. What else do you need?"

Buckner came up beside Wilbourne. "All right?" he said. "I'm not afraid and she aint. Because you're all right. I aint watched you for a month for nothing. Maybe if you had agreed quick, right off, that first day, I wouldn't let you, I'd be afraid. But not now. I'll take all the risk and I'll remember my promise: I'll see you are clear. And it aint a hundred, it's still a hundred and fifty."

He tried to say No, he tried hard. *Yes,* he thought quietly, *I have thrown away lots, but apparently not this. Honesty about money, security, degree,* and then for a terrible moment he thought, *Maybe I would have thrown away love first too* but he stopped this in time; he said, "You haven't got enough money, even if your name were Callaghan. I'll just take all the risk instead."

Three days later they who had not been met walked with the Buckners across the canyon to the waiting ore train. Wilbourne had steadily refused even the hundred dollars, accepting at last and instead of it a hundred dollar assignment on Buckner's back pay which they both knew would never be paid, this to be expended against its equivalent in food from the commissary, whose key Buckner had surrendered to him. "It sounds damn foolish to me," Buckner said. "The commissary is yours anyway."

"It will keep the books balanced," Wilbourne said. They followed the path which was no path, to the train, the engine with neither head nor tail, the three ore cars, the toy caboose. Buckner looked up at the mine, the gaping orifice, the refuse dump scarring the pristine snow. It was clear now, the sun low and thin above the serrated rosy peaks in a sky of incredible blue. "What will they think when they find you are gone?"

"Maybe they will think I have gone after the money myself. I hope they do, for your sake." Then he said, "They are better off here. No worries about rent and such and getting drunk and then getting sober again, enough food to keep you all until spring. And they have something to do, keep the days filled, and nights to lie in bed and count up that overtime. A man can go a long way on what he thinks he's going to get. And he may send some money yet."

"Do you believe that?"

"No," Buckner said. "Dont you believe it either."

"I dont think I ever have," Wilbourne said. "Not even that day in his office. Maybe even less then than at any time." They were standing a little aside from the two women. "Look, when you get out and find a chance, have her see a doctor. A good one. Tell him the truth."

"What for?" Buckner said.

"I'd rather you would. I'd feel easier."

"Nah," the other said. "She's all right. Because you're all right. If I hadn't known that, do you think I'd a let you do it?" Now it was time; the locomotive blew a shrill peanut-whistle blast, the Buckners got into the caboose and it began to move. Charlotte and Wilbourne looked after it for only a moment, then Charlotte turned, already running. The sun was almost down, the peaks ineffable and tender, the sky amber and azure; for an instant Wilbourne heard the voices from the mine, wild faint and incomprehensible.

"Oh, God," Charlotte said. "Let's dont even eat to-night. Hurry. Run." She ran on, then she stopped and turned, the broad blunt face rosy in the reflected pink, the eyes now green with it above the shapeless sheep collar of the shapeless coat. "No," she said. "You run in front, so I can be undressing us both in the snow. But run." But he did not go ahead, he did not even run, he walked so he could watch her diminishing ahead of him along the path which was no path, then mounting the other wall toward the cabin, who, save for the fact that

she wore them with the same abrupt obliviousness with
which she wore dresses, should never have worn pants
at all, and entered the cabin and found her now stripping
off even the wollen underwear. "Hurry," she said.
"Hurry. Six weeks. I have almost forgotten how. No,"
she said, "I'll never forget that. You never forget that,
thank you sweet God." Then she said, holding him, the
hard arms and thighs: "I guess I am a sissy about love.
I never could, even with just one other person in the
bed with us."

They didn't get up to prepare or eat supper. After a
time they slept; Wilbourne waked somewhere in the
rigid night to find the stove had gone out and the room
freezing cold. He thought of Charlotte's undergarment
where she had flung it away onto the floor; she would
need it, she should have it on now. But it too would be
like iron ice and he thought for a while about getting
up and fetching it into the bed and thawing it, warming
it beneath his body until she could put it on and at last
he found will power to begin to move but at once she
clutched him. "Where you going?" He told her. She
clutched him, hard. "When I get cold, you can always
cover me."

Each day he would visit the mine, where the frenzied
and unabated work continued. On the first visit the men
looked at him not with curiosity or surprise but merely
with interrogation, obviously looking for Buckner too.
But nothing else happened and he realised that they
did not even know probably that he was merely the mine's
official doctor, that they recognised in him only another

American (he almost said white man), another repre-
sentative of that remote golden unchallengeable Power
in which they held blind faith and trust. He and Charlotte began to discuss the question of telling them, trying
to. "Only what good would it do?" he said. "Buckner
was right. Where would they go, and what would they
do when they got there? There's plenty of food for them
here to last out the winter, and they probably haven't
saved any money (granted they ever got square with the
commissary even when they were being paid enough
wages to save) and as Buckner said, you can live pretty
happy a long time on illusion. Maybe you aren't happy
any other time. I mean, if you are a hunky that never
learned anything else but how to time a dynamite fuse
five hundred feet underground. And another thing.
We've still got three-quarters of the hundred dollars in
grub ourselves, and if everybody left here, somebody
would hear about it and he might even send a man in
here to pick up the other three cans of beans."

"And something else too," Charlotte said. "They cant
go now. They cant walk out in this snow. Hadn't you
noticed?"

"Noticed what?"

"That little toy train hasn't been back since it took
the Buckners out. That's two weeks ago."

He hadn't noticed this, he did not know if it would
come back again, so they agreed that the next time it
appeared they would wait no longer, they would tell (or
try to tell) the men in the mine. Then two weeks later the
train did return. They crossed the canyon to where the

wild filthy jabbering men were already beginning to load the cars. "Now what?" Wilbourne said. "I cant talk to them."

"Yes, you can. Some way. They believe you are the boss now and nobody yet ever failed to understand the man he believes is his boss. Try to get them over to the commissary."

Wilbourne moved forward, over to the loading chute in which the first tram of ore was already rattling, and raised his hand. "Wait," he said loudly. The men paused. looking at him out of the gaunt pale-eyed faces. "Commissary," he shouted. "Store!" jerking his arm toward the opposite canyon wall; now he recalled the word which the first one, the one who drew up Charlotte's coat for her that first day, had used. "Ron," he said. "Ron." They looked at him a moment longer, silently, the eyes round beneath the brute-like and terrific arching of pale brows, the expressions eager, puzzled, and wild. Then they looked at one another, they huddled, jabbering in that harsh incomprehensible tongue. Then they moved toward him in a body. "No, no," he said. "All." He gestured toward the mine shaft. "All of you." Someone comprehended quickly this time, almost at once the short one whom Wilbourne had seen behind the galloping ore tram on his first visit to the mine dashed out of the group and up the snowy slope on his short strong thick piston-like legs and vanished into the orifice and reappeared, followed by the rest of the endless shift. These mingled with the first group, jabbering and gesticulating. Then they all ceased and looked at Wilbourne, obedient and subdued. "Look at their faces," he said. "God, I hate to be the one to have to do this. Damn Buckner anyway."

"Come on," Charlotte said. "Let's get it over." They crossed the valley, the miners following, incredibly dirty against the snow—the faces of a poorly made-up and starving black-face minstrel troupe—to the commissary. Wilbourne unlocked the door. Then he saw at the rear of the group five women. He and Charlotte had never seen them before; they seemed to have sprung from the snow itself, shawled; two of them carried infants, one of which could not have been a month old.

"My God," Wilbourne said. "They dont even know I'm a doctor. They dont even know they are supposed to have a doctor, that the law requires that they have one." He and Charlotte entered. In the gloom after the snow-glare the faces vanished and only the eyes watched him out of nothing, subdued, patient, obedient, trusting and wild. "Now what?" he said again. Then he began to watch Charlotte and now they all watched her, the five women pushing forward also to see, as she fastened with four tacks produced from somewhere a sheet of wrapping paper to the end of a section of shelves where the light from the single window fell on it and began to draw swiftly with one of the scraps of charcoal she had brought from Chicago—the elevation of a wall in cross section with a grilled window in it unmistakably a pay window and as unmistakably shut, on one side of the window a number of people unmistakably miners (she had even included the woman with the baby); on the other side

of the window an enormous man (she had never seen
Callaghan, he had merely described him to her, yet the
man was Callaghan) sitting behind a table heaped with
glittering coins which the man was shovelling into a sack
with a huge hand on which glittered a diamond the size
of a ping-pong ball. The she stepped aside. For a moment longer there was no sound. Then an indescribable
cry rose, fierce but not loud, only the shrill voices of the
women much more than a whisper, wailing, and they
turned as one upon Wilbourne, the wild pale frenzied
eyes glaring at him with at once incredulous ferocity and
profound reproach.

"Wait!" Charlotte cried. "Wait!" They paused; they
watched her once more as the crayon moved, and now,
at the rear of the throng waiting outside the closed
window Wilbourne saw his own face emerge from beneath the flying chalk; anyone would have recognised
him: they did at once. The sound ceased, they looked
at Wilbourne then at one another in bewilderment. Then
they looked at Charlotte again as she ripped the paper
from the wall and began to attach a fresh sheet; this
time one of them stepped forward and helped her, Wilbourne too watching the flying crayon again. This time
it was himself, indubitably himself and indubitably a
doctor, anyone would have known it—the horn glasses,
the hospital tunic every charity patient, every hunky
gutted by flying rock or steel or premature dynamite
and coming to in company emergency stations, has seen,
a bottle which was indubitably medicine in one hand, a
spoonful of which he was offering to a man who was com-

positely all of them, every man who ever labored in the
bowels of earth—the same wild unshaven look, even the
sheepskin collar, and behind the doctor the same huge
hand with its huge diamond in the act of extracting from
the doctor's pocket a wallet thin as paper. Again the
eyes turned toward Wilbourne, the reproach gone now
and only the ferocity remaining and that not at him. He
gestured toward the remaining laden shelves. Presently
he was able to reach Charlotte in the pandemonium and
take her arm.

"Come on," he said. "Let's get out of here." Later
(he had returned to the ore train, where Hogben, its
entire crew, sat over the red hot stove in the caboose
not much larger than a broom closet. "You'll be back in
thirty days then," Wilbourne said. "I have to make a trip
every thirty days for us to hold the franchise," Hogben
said. "You better bring your wife on out now."—"We'll
wait," Wilbourne said. Then he returned to the cabin and
he and Charlotte stood in the door and watched the
crowd emerge from the commissary with its pitiful loot
and later cross the canyon and board the ore train, filling
the three open cars. The temperature was not forty-one
now, neither was it back up to fourteen. The train moved;
they could see the tiny faces looking back at the mine
entrance, the refuse dump, with incredulous bewilderment, a kind of shocked and unbelieving sorrow; as the
train moved a burst of voices reached across the canyon
to them, faint with distance, forlorn, grieving, and wild)
he said to Charlotte, "Thank God we got our grub out
first."

"Maybe it wasn't ours," she said soberly.

"Buckner's then. They hadn't paid him either."

"But he ran away. They didn't."

It was still nearer spring then; by the time the ore train made its next ritualistic and empty visitation perhaps they would see the beginning of the mountain spring which neither of them had seen and did not know would not appear until that time which in their experience was the beginning of summer. They talked of this at night now, with the thermometer again sometimes at forty-one. But they could at least talk in bed now, in the dark where beneath the blankets Charlotte would, after an amount of savage heaving and twisting (this too ritualistic) emerge from the woollen undergarment to sleep in the old fashion. She would not fling it out from beneath the blankets but would keep it inside, a massy wad upon and beneath and around which they slept, so it would be warm for the morning. One night she said, "You haven't heard from Buckner yet. But of course you haven't; how could you have."

"No," he said, suddenly sober. "And I wish I would. I told him to take her to a doctor soon as they got out. But he probably— He promised to write me."

"I wish you would too."

"We may have a letter when the ore train comes back for us."

"If it comes back." But he suspected nothing, though later it seemed incredible to him that he had not, even though at the time he could not have said why he should have suspected, on what evidence. But he did not. Then one day about a week before the ore train was due there was a knock and he opened the door upon a man with a mountain face and a pack and a pair of slung snow shoes on his back.

"You Wilbourne?" he said. "Got a letter for you." He produced it—a pencilled envelope smudged with handling and three weeks old.

"Thanks," Wilbourne said. "Come in and eat."

But the other declined. "One of them big airplanes fell somewhere back in yonder just before Christmas. You hear or see anything about that time?"

"I wasn't here then," Wilbourne said. "You better eat first."

"There's a reward for it. I guess I wont stop."

The letter was from Buckner. It said *Everything O K Buck.* Charlotte took it from him and stood looking at it. "That's what you said. You said it was simple, didn't you. Now you feel all right about it."

"Yes," Wilbourne said. "I am relieved."

Charlotte looked at the letter, the four words, counting O and K as two. "Just one in ten thousand. All you have to do is be reasonably careful, isn't it? Boil the tools and so forth. Does it matter who you do it on?"

"They have to be fe—" Then he stopped. He looked at her, he thought swiftly, *Something is about to happen to me. Wait. Wait.* "Do it on?"

She looked at the letter. "That was foolish, wasn't it. Maybe I was mixed up with incest." Now it did happen to him. He began to tremble, he was trembling even before he grasped her shoulder and jerked her about to face him.

"Do it on?"

She looked at him, still holding the cheap ruled sheet with its heavy pencilling—the sober intent gaze with that greenish cast which the snow gave her eyes. She spoke in short brutal sentences like out of a primer. "That night. That first night alone. When we couldn't wait to cook supper. When the stove went out my douche bag was hanging behind it. It froze and when we lit the stove again I forgot it and it burst."

"And every time since then you didn't—"

"I should have known better. I always did take it easy. Too easy. I remember somebody telling me once, I was young then, that when people loved, hard, really loved each other, they didn't have children, the seed got burned up in the love, the passion. Maybe I believed it. Wanted to believe it because I didn't have a douche bag any more. Or maybe I just hoped. Anyway it's done."

"When?" he said, shaking her, trembling. "How long since you missed? Are you sure?"

"Sure that I missed? Yes. Sixteen days."

"But you're not sure," he said, rapidly, knowing he was talking only to himself: "You cant be sure yet. Sometimes they miss, any woman. You can never be sure until two—"

"Do you believe that?" she said quietly. "That's just when you want a child. And I dont and you dont because we cant. I can starve and you can starve but not it. So we must, Harry."

"No!" he cried. "No!"

"You said it was simple. We have proof it is, that it's nothing, no more than clipping an ingrowing toenail. I'm strong and healthy as she is. Dont you believe that?"

"Ah," he cried, "So you tried it on her first. That was it. You wanted to see if she would die or not. That's why you were so bent on selling me the idea when I had already said no—"

"The stove went out the night after they left, Harry. But yes, I did wait to hear from her first. She would have done the same if it had been me first. I would have wanted her to. I would have wanted her to live whether I did or not just as she would want me to live whether she did or not, just as I want to live."

"Yes," he said. "I know. I didn't mean that. But you— you—"

"So it's all right. It's simple. You know that now by your own hand."

"No! No!"

"All right," she said quietly. "Maybe we can find a doctor to do it when we go out next week."

"No!" he cried, shouted, gripping her shoulder, shaking her. "Do you hear me?"

"You mean no one else shall do it, and you wont?"

"Yes! That's what I mean! That's exactly what I mean!"

"Are you that afraid?"

"Yes!" he said. "Yes!"

The next week passed. He took to walking, slogging

and plunging in the waist-deep drifts, *not to not see her;
it's because I cant breathe in there,* he told himself;
once he went up to the mine even, the deserted gallery
dark now of the extravagant and unneeded bulbs though
it still seemed to him that he could hear the voices, the
blind birds, the echoes of that frenzied and incomprehensible human speech which still remained, hanging batlike and perhaps head-down about the dead
corridors until his presence startled them into flight. But
sooner or later the cold—something—would drive him
back to the cabin and they did not quarrel simply because she refused to be drawn into one and again he
would think, *She is not only a better man and a better
gentleman than I am, she is a better everything than I
will ever be.* They ate together, went through the day's
routine, they slept together to keep from freezing; now
and then he took her (and she accepted him) in a kind
of frenzy of immolation, saying, crying, "At least it
doesn't matter now; at least you wont have to get up in
the cold." Then it would be day again; he would refill
the tank when the stove burned out; he would carry out
and throw into the snow the cans which they had opened
for the last meal, and there would be nothing else for
him to do, nothing else under the sun for him to do.
So he would walk (there was a pair of snow shoes in
the cabin but he never tried to use them) among but
mostly into the drifts which he had not yet learned to
distinguish in time to avoid, wallowing and plunging,
thinking, talking to himself aloud, weighing a thousand
expedients: *A kind of pill,* he thought—this, a trained

doctor: *whores use them, they are supposed to work,
they must work, something must; it cant be this difficult,
this much of a price,* and not believing it, knowing that
he would never be able to make himself believe it, thinking, *And this is the price of the twenty-six years, the two
thousand dollars I stretched over four of them by not
smoking, by keeping my virginity until it damn near
spoiled on me, the dollar and two dollars a week or a
month my sister could not afford to send: that I should
have deprived myself of all hope forever of anesthesia
from either pills or pamphlets. And now anything else
is completely out.* "So there's just one thing left," he
said, aloud, in a kind of calm like that which follows
the deliberate ridding of the stomach of a source of
nausea. "Just one thing left. We'll go where it is warm,
where it wont cost so much to live, where I can find work
and we can afford a baby and if no work, charity wards,
orphanages, doorsteps anyway. No, no, not orphanage;
not doorstep. We can do it, we must do it; I will find
something, anything.—Yes!" he thought, cried aloud
into the immaculate desolation, with harsh and terrible
sardonicism, "I will set up as a professional abortion-
ist." Then he would return to the cabin and still they
did not quarrel simply because she would not, this not
through any forbearance feigned or real nor because
she herself was subdued and afraid but simply because
(and he knew this too and he cursed himself for this too
in the snow) she knew that one of them must keep some
sort of head and she knew beforehand it would not be
he.

Then the ore train came. He had packed the remaining provisions out of Buckner's theoretical hundred dollars into a box. They loaded this and the two bags with which they had left New Orleans· almost exactly a year ago and themselves into the toy caboose. At the mainline junction he sold the cans of beans and salmon and lard, the sacks of sugar and coffee and flour, to a small storekeeper for twenty-one dollars. They rode two nights and a day in day coaches and left the snow behind and found buses now, cheaper now, her head tilted back against the machine-made doily, her face in profile against the dark fleeing snow-free countryside and the little lost towns, the neon, the lunch rooms with broad strong Western girls got up out of Hollywood magazines (Hollywood which is no longer in Hollywood but is stippled by a billion feet of burning colored gas across the face of the American earth) to resemble Joan Crawford, asleep or not he could not tell.

They reached San Antonio, Texas, with a hundred and fifty-two dollars and a few cents. It was warm here, it was almost like New Orleans; the pepper trees had been green all winter and the oleander and mimosa and lantana were already in bloom and cabbage palms exploded shabbily in the mild air as in Louisiana. They had a single room with a decrepit gas plate, reached by an outside gallery in a shabby wooden house. And now they did quarrel. "Cant you see?" she said. "My period would come now, tomorrow. Now is the time, the simple time to do it. Like you did with her—what's her name? the whore's name? Bill. Billie, i,e. You shouldn't have let me learn so much about it. I wouldn't know how to pick my time to worry you then."

"Apparently you learned about it without any help from me," he said, trying to restrain himself, cursing himself: *You bastard, she's the one that's in trouble; it's not you.* "I had settled it. I had said no. You were the one who—" Now he did stop himself, rein himself in. "Listen. There's a pill of some sort. You take it when your time is due. I'll try to get some of them."

"Try where?"

"Where would I try? Who would ever need such? At a brothel. Oh, God, Charlotte! Charlotte!"

"I know," she said. "We cant help it. It's not us now. That's why: dont you see? I want it to be us again, quick, quick. We have so little time. In twenty years I cant any more and in fifty years we'll both be dead. So hurry. Hurry."

He had never been in a brothel in his life and had never even sought one before. So now he discovered what a lot of people have: how difficult it is to find one; how you lived in the duplex for ten years before you discovered that the late-sleeping ladies next door were not night-shift telephone girls. At last that occurred to him which the veriest yokel seems to inherit with breath: he asked a taxi-driver and was presently set down before a house a good deal like the one he lived in and pressed a button which made no audible response though presently a curtain over the narrow window beside the door fell a second before he could have sworn someone had looked out at him. Then the door opened, a negro maid conducted him down a dim hallway and into a room containing a bare veneered dining-table bearing an imitation cut-glass punch bowl and scarred by the white rings from damp glass-bottoms, a pianola slotted for coins, and twelve chairs ranged along the four walls in orderly sequence like tombstones in a military graveyard, where the maid left him to sit and look at a lithograph of the Saint Bernard dog saving the child from the snow and another of President Roosevelt, until there entered a double-chinned woman of no especial age more than forty, with blondined hair and a lilac satin gown not quite clean. "Good evening," she said. "Stranger in town?"

"Yes," he told her. "I asked a taxi-driver. He—"

"Dont apologise," she said. "The drivers is all my friends here."

He remembered the driver's parting advice: "The first white person you see, buy them some beer. You'll be jake then."—"Wont you have some beer?" he said.

"Why, I dont mind if I do," the woman said. "It might refresh us." Immediately (she had rung no bell that Wilbourne could see) the maid entered. "Two beers, Louisa," the woman said. The maid went out. The woman sat down too. "So you're a stranger in San Tone. Well, some of the sweetest friendships I ever seen was made in one night or even after one session between two folks that never even seen one another an hour ago. I got American girls here or Spanish (strangers like Spanish girls, once, anyway. It's the influence of the moving pictures, I always say) and one little Eyetalian that just—" The maid entered with two tankards of beer. It could not have been much farther away than wherever it was she had been standing when the woman in purple had rung no bell that Wilbourne could see. The maid went out.

"No, he said. "I dont want—I came here—I—" The woman was watching him; she had started to raise her mug. Instead she set it back on the table, watching him. "I'm in trouble," he said quietly. "I hoped you could help me."

Now the woman even withdrew her hand from the tankard and he saw now that her eyes, even if they were no less muddy, were also no less cold than the big diamond at her breast. "And just what made you think I could or would help you out of whatever your trouble is? The driver tell you that too? What'd he look like? You take his number?"

"No," Wilbourne said. "I—"

"Never mind that now. What kind of trouble are you in?" He told her, simply and quietly, while she watched him. "H'm," she said. "And so you, a stranger here, found right off a taxi-driver that brought you straight to me to find a doctor to do your business. Well, well." Now she did ring the bell, not violently, just hard.

"No, no, I dont—" *She even keeps a doctor in the house,* he thought. "I dont—"

"Undoubtless," the woman said. "It's all a mistake. You'll get back to the hotel or wherever it is and find you just drempt your wife was knocked up or even that you had a wife."

"I wish I would," Wilbourne said. "But I—" The door opened and a man entered, a biggish man, fairly young, bulging his clothes a little, who gave Wilbourne a hot, embracing, almost loverlike glare out of hot brown flesh-bedded eyes beneath the straight innocently parted hair of a little boy and continued to look at him from then on. His neck was shaved.

"Thatim?" he said over his shoulder to the woman in purple, in a voice husky with prolonged whiskey begun at too early an age yet withal the voice of a disposition cheerful, happy, even joyous. He did not even wait for an answer, he came straight to Wilbourne and before the other could move plucked him from the chair with one hamlike hand. "Whadya mean, you sonafabitch, coming into a respectable house and acting like a sonafabitch? hah?" He glared at Wilbourne happily. "Out?" he said.

"Yah," the woman in purple said. "Then I want to find that taxi-driver." Wilbourne began to struggle. At once the young man turned upon him with loverlike joy, beaming. "Not in here," the woman said sharply. "Out, like I told you, you ape."

"I'll go," Wilbourne said. "You can turn me loose."

"Yah; sure, you sonafabitch," the young man said. "I'll just help you. You got helped in, see. This way." They were in the hall again, now there was a small slight black-haired dark-faced man also, in dingy trousers and a tieless blue shirt: a Mexican servant of some sort. They went on to the door, the back of Wilbourne's coat bunched in the young man's huge hand. The young man opened it. *The brute will have to hit me once,* Wilbourne thought. *Or he will burst, suffocate. But all right. All right.*

"Maybe you could tell me," he said. "All I want is—"

"Yah; sure," the young man said. "Maybe I awda sockm, Pete. Whadya think?"

"Sockm," the Mexican said.

He did not even feel the fist. He felt the low stoop strike him across the back, then the grass already damp with dew, before he began to feel his face at all. "Maybe you could tell me—" he said.

"Yah; sure," the young man said in his hoarse happy voice, "ask me another." The door slammed. After a while Wilbourne got up. Now he could feel his eye, the whole side of his face, his whole head, the slow painful pounding of the blood, though in the drugstore mirror presently (it was on the first corner he came to, he entered it; he was indeed learning fast the things he should have known before he was nineteen years old) he could see no discoloration yet. But the mark was apparent, something was, because the clerk said.

"What happened to your face, mister?"

"Fight," he said. "I knocked up my girl. I want something for it."

For a moment the clerk looked at him, hard. Then he said, "Cost you five bucks."

"Do you guarantee it?"

"Nah."

"All right. I'll take it."

It was a small tin box, unlettered. It contained five objects which might have been coffee beans. "He said whiskey would help, and moving around. He said to take two of them tonight and go somewhere and dance." She took all five of them, they went out and got two pints of whiskey and found at last a dance hall full of cheap colored bulbs and khaki uniforms and rentable partners or hostesses.

"Drink some of it too," she said. "Does your face hurt very bad now?"

"No," he said. "Drink it. Drink all you can."

"God," she said. "You cant dance, can you?"

"No," he said. "Yes. Yes, I can dance." They moved about the floor, bumped and shoved and bumping and shoving, somnambulistic and sometimes in step, during each short phase of hysterical music. By eleven oclock she had drunk almost half of one of the bottles but it only made her sick. He waited until she emerged from the washroom, her face the color of putty, the eyes indomitable and yellow. "You lost the pills too," he said.

"Two of them. I was afraid of that so I used the basin and washed them off and took them again. Where's the bottle?"

They had to go out for her to drink, then they returned. At twelve she had almost finished the first bottle and the lights were turned off save for a spotlight which played on a revolving globe of colored glass, so that the dancers moved with the faces of corpses in a wheeling of colored mote-beams resembling a marine nightmare. There was a man with a megaphone; it was a dancing contest and they did not even know it; the music crashed and ceased, the lights flared on, the air was filled by the bellowing megaphone and the winning couple moved forward. "I'm sick again," she said. Once more he waited for her—the putty face, the indomitable eyes. "I washed them off again," she said. "But I cant drink any more. Come on. They close at one oclock."

Perhaps they were coffee beans because after three days nothing had happened and after five days even he admitted that the time had passed. Now they did quarrel, he cursing himself for it as he sat on his park benches reading the help wanted columns in newspapers grubbed out of trash bins while he waited for his black eye, his shiner, to disappear so he could apply decently for work, cursing himself because she had borne up for so long and would and could continue to bear up save that he had worn her out at last, knowing he had done this, swearing he would change, stop it. But when he returned to the room (she was thinner now and there was something in her eyes; all the pills and whiskey had done was to put something in her eyes that had not been there before) it would be as if his promises had never been made, she cursing him now and striking at him with her hard fists then catching herself, clinging to him, crying, "Oh, God, Harry, make me stop! Make me hush! Bust the hell out of me!" Then they would lie holding one another, fully dressed now, in a sort of peace for a time.

"It'll be all right," he said. "A lot of people have to do it these days. Charity wards are not bad. Then we can find someone to take the baby until I can—"

"No. It wont do, Harry. It wont do."

"I know it sounds bad at first. Charity. But charity isn't—"

"Damn charity. Have I ever cared where money comes from, where or how we lived, had to live? It's not that. They hurt too much."

"I know that too. But women have been bearing children—You have borne two yourself—"

"Damn pain too. I take easy and breed hard but damn that, I'm used to that, I don't mind that. I said they hurt too much. Too damned much." Then he understood, knew what she meant; he thought quietly, as he had thought before, that she had already and scarcely knowing him given up more than he would ever possess to relinquish, remembering the old tried true incontrovertible words: *Bone of my bone, blood and flesh and even memory of my blood and flesh and memory.* You dont beat it, he told himself. You dont beat it that easy. He was about to say, "But this will be ours," when he realised that this was it, this was exactly it.

But still he could not say yes, could not say "All right." He could say it to himself on the park benches, he could hold his hand out and it would not shake. But he could not say the word to her; he would lie beside her, holding her while she slept, and he would watch the ultimate last of his courage and manhood leave him. "That's right," he would whisper to himself, "stall. Stall. She will be in the fourth month soon, then I can tell myself I know it is too late to risk it; even she will believe then." Then she would wake and it would start all over—the reasoning which got nowhere becoming the

quarreling and then the cursing until she would catch
herself and cling to him, crying in frantic despair:
"Harry! Harry! What are we doing? We, we, *us!* Make
me hush! Bust me! Knock me cold!" This last time he
held her until she was quiet. "Harry, will you make a
compact with me?"

"Yes," he said wearily. "Anything."

"A compact. And then until it's up, we will never
mention pregnancy again." She named the date when her
next period would have come; it was thirteen days
away. "That's the best time, and after that it will be
four months and it will be too late to risk it. So from
now until then we wont even talk about it; I will try
to make things as easy as possible while you look for
a job, a good job that will support three of us—"

"No," he said. "No! No!"

"Wait," she said. "You promised.—Then if you
haven't found a job by that time, you will do it, take
it away from me."

"No!" he cried. "I wont! Never!"

"But you promised," she said, quietly, gently, slowly,
as if he were a child just learning English. "Dont
you see there is nothing else?"

"I promised; yes. But I didn't mean—"

"I told you once how I believe it isn't love that dies,
it's the man and the woman, something in the man and
the woman that dies, doesn't deserve the chance any
more to love. And look at us now. We have the child,
only we both know we cant have it, cant afford to
have it. And they hurt too bad, Harry. Too damned bad.

I'm going to hold you to the promise, Harry. And so from now until that day comes, we wont even have to mention it, think about it again. Kiss me." After a moment he leaned to her. Not touching otherwise, they kissed, as brother and sister might.

Now it was like Chicago again, the first weeks there while he went from hospital to hospital, the interviews which seemed to die, to begin to wilt and fade tranquilly at a given identical instant, he already foreknowing this and expecting it and so meeting the obsequy decently. But not now, not this time. In Chicago he would think, *I imagine I am going to fail* and he would fail; now he knew he was going to fail and he refused to believe it, refused to accept no for an answer until threatened almost with physical violence. He was not trying hospitals alone, he was trying anyone, anything. He told lies, any lie; he approached appointments with a frantic cold maniacal determination which was inherent with its own negation; he promised anyone that he could and would do anything; walking along the street one afternoon he glanced up by sheer chance and saw a doctor's sign and entered and actually offered to perform any abortions thrown his way for half the fee, stated his experience and (he realised later when comparatively sane again) only his ejection by force forestalled his showing Buckner's letter as a testimonial to his ability.

Then one day he returned home in the middle of the afternoon. He stood outside his own door for a long time before he opened it. And even then he did not

enter but stood instead in the opening with on his head
a cheap white bellows-topped peaked cap with a yellow
band—the solitary insignia of a rankless W.P.A. school-
crossing guard—and his heart cold and still with a
grief and despair that was almost peaceful. "I get ten
dollars a week," he said.

"Oh, you monkey!" she said, then for the last time
in his life he saw her cry. "You bastard! You damned
bastard! So you can rape little girls in parks on Saturday afternoons!" She came and snatched the cap from
his head and hurled it into the fireplace (a broken grate
hanging by one side and stuffed with faded frilled paper
which had once been either red or purple) and then
clung to him, crying hard, the hard tears springing
and streaming. "You bastard, you damned bastard, you
damned damned damned—"

She boiled the water herself and fetched out the
meager instruments they had supplied him with in
Chicago and which he had used but once, then lying on
the bed she looked up at him. "It's all right. It's simple. You know that; you did it before."

"Yes," he said. "Simple. You just have to let the
air in. All you have to do is let the air—" Then he
began to tremble again. "Charlotte. Charlotte."

"That's all. Just a touch. Then the air gets in and
tomorrow it will be all over and I will be all right and
it will be us again forever and ever."

"Yes. Ever and ever. But I'll have to wait a minute,
until my hand—Look. It wont stop. I cant make it
stop."

"All right. We'll wait a minute. It's simple. It's funny. New, I mean. We've done this lots of ways but not with knives, have we? There. Now your hand has stopped."

"Charlotte," he said. "Charlotte."

"It's all right. We know how. What was it you told me nigger women say? Ride me down, Harry."

And now, sitting on his bench in Audubon Park lush green and bright with the Louisiana summer already fully accomplished although it was not yet June, and filled with the cries of children and the sound of pram wheels like the Chicago apartment had been, he watched against his eyelids the cab (it had been told to wait) stopping before the neat and unremarkable though absolutely unimpugnable door and she getting out of the cab in the dark dress carried a full year and better, for three thousand miles and better, in the bag from last spring and mounting the steps. Now the bell, perhaps the same negro maid: "Why, Miss—" then nothing, remembering who paid the wages, though probably not since by ordinary negroes quit an employment following death or division. And now the room, as he had first seen it, the room in which she said, "Harry—do they call you Harry?—what are we going to do?" *(Well, I did it,* he thought. *She will have to admit that.)* He could see them, the two of them, Rittenmeyer in the double-breasted suit (it might be flannel now but it would be dark flannel, obtruding smoothly its unobtrusive cut and cost); the four of them, Charlotte here and the three others yonder, the two children who were unremarkable, the daughters, the one with the mother's hair but nothing else, the other, the younger one, with nothing, the younger sitting perhaps on the father's knee, the other, the older, leaning against him; the three faces, the one impeccable, the two of them invincible and irrevocable, the second cold and unwinking, the third merely unwinking; he could see them, he could hear them:

'Go speak to your mother, Charlotte. Take Ann with you.'

'I dont want to.'

'Go. Take Ann's hand.' He could hear, see them: Rittenmeyer setting the little one onto the floor, the older one takes her hand and they approach. *And now she will take the little one onto her lap, it staring at her still with that intent absolutely blank detachment of infants, the older one leans to her, obedient, cold, suffering the caress, already withdrawing before the kiss is completed, and returns to her father; an instant later Charlotte sees her beckoning, gesturing in violent surreptitious pantomime to the little one. So Charlotte sets the little one onto the floor again and it returns to the father, turning against his knee and already hunching one buttock toward its father's lap as children do, still staring at Charlotte with that detachment empty even of curiosity.*

'Let them go,' Charlotte says.

'You want them sent away?'

'Yes. They want to go.' The children depart. And now he hears her; it is not Charlotte; he knows that as Rittenmeyer never will: *'So that's what you have taught them.'*

'I? I taught them? I taught them nothing!' he cries. *'Nothing! It wasn't me who—'*

'I know. I'm sorry. I didn't mean that. I have not— Have they been well?'

'Yes. As I wrote you. If you will recall, for several months I had no address. The letters were returned. You may have them when and if you like. You dont look well yourself. Is that why you came back home? Or have you come back home?'

'To see the children. And to give you this.' She produces the check, double-signed and perforated against any tampering, the slip of paper more than a year old, creased and intact and only a little worn.

'You came home on his money then. Then it belongs to him.'

'No. It's yours.'

'I refuse to accept it.'

'So would he.'

'Then burn it. Destroy it.'

'Why? Why do you wish to hurt yourself? Why do you like suffering, when there is so much of it that has to be done, so damned much? Give it to the children. A bequest. If not from me, from Ralph then. He is still their uncle. He has not harmed you.'

'A bequest?' he says. Then she tells him. Oh, yes, Wilbourne told himself, she will tell him; he could see it, hear it—the two people between whom something like love must have existed once, or who at least had

known together the physical striving with which alone
the flesh can try to capture what little it is ever to
know of love. Oh, she will tell him; he could see and
hear her as she lays the check upon the table at her hand
and tells him:

'*It was a month ago. It was all right, only I kept on
losing blood and it got to be pretty bad. Then all of a
sudden two days ago the blood stopped and so there is
something wrong, which might be something badder
still—what do they call it? toxemia, septicemia? It
doesn't matter—that we are watching for. Waiting for.*'

The men who passed the bench he sat on walked in
linen suits, and now he began to notice a general exodus
from the park—the negro nursemaids who managed to
lend a quality bizarre and dazzling even to their starched
white-crossed blue, the children moving with thin cries
in bright random like blown petals, across the green.
It was near noon; Charlotte would have been in the
house more than half an hour. *Because it will take that
long,* he thought seeing and hearing them: *He is trying to persuade her to go to a hospital at once, the
best, the best doctors; he will assume all blame, tell
all the lies; he insists, calm, not at all importunate and
not to be denied.*

'*No. H— he knows a place. On the Mississippi coast.
We are going there. We will get a doctor there if necessary.*'

'*The Mississippi coast? Why in God's name the Mississippi coast? A country doctor in a little lost Missis-*

*sippi shrimping village when in New Orleans there
are the best, the very best—'*

'We may not need a doctor after all. And we can
live cheaper there until we find out.'

'You have money for coast vacations then.'

'We have money.' It was dead noon now; the air
fell still, the stippled shadows unmoving upon his lap,
upon the six bills in his hand, the two twenties, the five,
the three ones, hearing them, seeing them:

'Take up the check again. It is not mine.'

'Nor mine. Let me go my way, Francis. A year ago
you let me choose and I chose. I will stick to it. I wont
have you retract, break your oath to yourself. But I
want to ask one thing of you.'

'Of me? A favor?'

'If you like. I dont ask a promise. Maybe what I
am trying to express is just a wish. Not hope; wish. If
anything happens to me.'

'If anything happens to you. What am I to do?'

'Nothing.'

'Nothing?'

'Yes. Against him. I dont ask it for his sake nor even
for mine. I ask it for the sake of—of—I dont even
know what I am trying to say. For the sake of all the
men and women who ever lived and blundered but
meant the best and all that ever will live and blunder
but mean the best. For your sake maybe, since yours
is suffering too—if there is any such thing as suffering, if any of us ever did, if any of us were ever born
strong enough and good enough to be worthy to love*

or suffer either. Maybe what I am trying to say is justice.'

'*Justice?*' And now he could hear Rittenmeyer laughing, who had never laughed since laughter is the yesterday's slight beard, the negligee among emotions. '*Justice? This, to me? Justice?*' *Now she rises; he too: they face one another.*

'*I didn't ask a promise,*' *she says.* '*That would have been too much to ask.*'

'*Of me.*'

'*Of anyone. Any man or woman. Not only you.*'

'*But it is I who give none. Remember. Remember. I said you could come back home when you wished, and I would take you back, into my house at least. But can you expect that again? from any man? Tell me; you spoke once of justice; tell me that.*'

'*I don't expect it. I told you before that maybe what I was trying to say was hope.*' *She will turn now, he told himself, approaching the door, and they will stand looking at one another and maybe it will be like Mc-Cord and me in the Chicago station that night last*—He stopped. He was about to say 'last year' and he ceased and sat perfectly still and said aloud in quiet amazement, "That night was not five months ago."—*And they will both know they will never see one another again and neither of them will say it.* '*Good-bye, Rat,*' *she says. And he will not answer,* he thought. *No. He will not answer, this man of ultimatums, upon whom for the rest of his life will yearly devolve the necessity for decrees which he knows beforehand he cannot sup-*

*port, who would have denied the promise she did not
ask yet would perform the act and she to know this
well, too well, too well—this face impeccable and invincible upon which all existing light in the room will
have seemed to gather as though in benediction, affirmation not of righteousness but rightness, having been
consistently and incontrovertibly right; and withal tragic
too since in the being right there was nothing of con-
solation nor of peace.*

Now it would be time. He rose from the bench and
followed the curve of blanched oyster shells between the
massy bloom of oleander and wygelia, jasmine japonica
and orange, toward the exit and the street, beneath the
noon. The cab came up, slowing into the curb; the driver
opened the door. "Station," Wilbourne said.

"Union Station?"

"No. The one for Mobile. The coast." He got in.
The door closed, the cab went on; the scaling palm
trunks began to flee past. "They were both well?" he
said.

"Listen," she said. "If we're going to get it."

"Get it?"

"You'll know in time, won't you?"

"We're not going to get anything. I'm going to hold
you. Haven't I held you so far?"

"Dont be a fool now. There's no time now. You'll
know in time. Get to hell out, do you hear?"

"Out?"

"Promise me. Dont you know what they'll do to
you? You cant lie to anybody, even if you would. And

you couldn't help me. But you'll know in time. Just telephone an ambulance or the police or something and wire Rat and get to hell out fast. Promise me."

"I'm going to hold you," he said. "That's what I'll promise you. They were both well?"

"Yes," she said; the scaling palm trunks fled constantly past. "They were all right."

Old Man

WHEN THE WOMAN ASKED HIM IF HE HAD A KNIFE, standing there in the streaming bedticking garments which had got him shot at, the second time by a machine gun, on the two occasions when he had seen any human life after leaving the levee four days ago, the convict felt exactly as he had in the fleeing skiff when the woman suggested that they had better hurry. He felt the same outrageous affronting of a condition purely moral, the same raging impotence to find any answer to it; so that, standing above her, spent suffocating and inarticulate, it was a full minute before he comprehended that she was now crying, "The can! The can in the boat!" He did not anticipate what she could want with it; he did not even wonder nor stop to ask. He turned running; this time he thought, *It's another moccasin* as the thick body truncated in that awkward reflex which had nothing of alarm in it but only alertness, he not even shifting his stride though he knew his running foot would fall within a yard of the flat head. The bow of the skiff was well up the slope now where the wave had set it and there was another snake just crawling over the stern into it and as he stooped for the bailing can he saw something else swimming toward the mound, he didn't know what—a head, a face at the apex of a vee of ripples. He snatched up the can; by pure juxtaposition of it and water he scooped it full, already turning. He saw the deer again, or another one. That is, he saw a deer—a side glance, the light smoke-colored phantom in a cypress vista then gone, vanished, he not pausing to look after it, galloping back to the woman and kneeling with the can to her lips until she told him better.

It had contained a pint of beans or tomatoes, something, hermetically sealed and opened by four blows of an axe heel, the metal flap turned back, the jagged edges razor-sharp. She told him how, and he used this in lieu of a knife, he removed one of his shoelaces and cut it in two with the sharp tin. Then she wanted warm water—"If I just had a little hot water," she said in a weak serene voice without particular hope; only when he thought of matches it was again a good deal like when she had asked him if he had a knife, until she fumbled in the pocket of the shrunken tunic (it had a darker double vee on one cuff and a darker blotch on the shoulder where service stripes and a divisional emblem had been ripped off but this meant nothing to him) and produced a match-box contrived by telescoping two shotgun shells. So he drew her back a little from the water and went to hunt wood dry enough to burn, thinking this time, *It's just another snake*, only, he said, he should have thought *ten thousand other snakes*: and now he knew it was not the same deer because he saw three at one time, does or bucks he did not know which since they were all antlerless in May and besides he had never seen one of any kind anywhere before except on a Christmas card; and then the rabbit, drowned, dead anyway, already torn open, the bird, the hawk, standing upon it—the erected crest, the hard vicious patrician nose, the intolerant omnivorous yellow eye—and he kicking at it, kicking it lurching and broadwinged into the actual air.

When he returned with the wood and the dead rabbit, the baby, wrapped in the tunic, lay wedged between two cypress-knees and the woman was not in sight, though while the convict knelt in the mud, blowing and nursing his meagre flame, she came slowly and weakly from the direction of the water. Then, the water heated at last and there produced from some where he was never to know, she herself perhaps never to know until the need comes, no woman perhaps ever to know, only no woman will even wonder, that square of something somewhere between sackcloth and silk—squatting, his own wet garments steaming in the fire's heat, he watched her bathe the child with a savage curiosity and interest that became amazed unbelief, so that at last he stood above them both, looking down at the tiny terra-cotta colored creature resembling nothing, and thought, *And this is all. This is what severed me violently from all I ever knew and did not wish to leave and cast me upon a medium I was born to fear, to fetch up at last in a place I never saw before and where I do not even know where I am.*

Then he returned to the water and refilled the bailing can. It was drawing toward sunset now (or what would have been sunset save for the high prevailing

overcast) of this day whose beginning he could not
even remember; when he returned to where the fire
burned in the interlaced gloom of the cypresses, even
after this short absence, evening had definitely come,
as though darkness too had taken refuge upon that
quarter-acre mound, that earthen Ark out of Genesis,
that dim wet cypress-choked life-teeming constricted
desolation in what direction and how far from what
and where he had no more idea than of the day of the
month, and had now with the setting of the sun crept
forth again to spread upon the waters. He stewed the
rabbit in sections while the fire burned redder and redder in the darkness where the shy wild eyes of small
animals—once the tall mild almost plate-sized stare of
one of the deer—glowed and vanished and glowed
again, the broth hot and rank after the four days; he
seemed to hear the roar of his own saliva as he watched
the woman sip the first canful. Then he drank too; they
ate the other fragments which had been charring and
scorching on willow twigs; it was full night now. "You
and him better sleep in the boat," the convict said. "We
want to get an early start tomorrow." He shoved the
bow of the skiff off the land so it would lie level, he
lengthened the painter with a piece of grapevine and returned to the fire and tied the grapevine about his wrist
and lay down. It was mud he lay upon, but it was solid
underneath, it was earth, it did not move; if you fell
upon it you broke your bones against its incontrovertible passivity sometimes but it did not accept you substanceless and enveloping and suffocating, down and

down and down; it was hard at times to drive a plow through, it sent you spent, weary, and cursing its light-long insatiable demands back to your bunk at sunset at times but it did not snatch you violently out of all familiar knowing and sweep you thrall and impotent for days against any returning. *I dont know where I am and I dont reckon I know the way back to where I want to go,* he thought. *But at least the boat has stopped long enough to give me a chance to turn it around.*

He waked at dawn, the light faint, the sky jonquil-colored; the day would be fine. The fire had burned out; on the opposite side of the cold ashes lay three snakes motionless and parallel as underscoring, and in the swiftly making light others seemed to materialise: earth which an instant before had been mere earth broke up into motionless coils and loops, branches which a moment before had been mere branches now become immobile ophidian festoons even as the convict stood thinking about food, about something hot before they started. But he decided against this, against wasting this much time, since there still remained in the skiff quite a few of the rocklike objects which the shanty woman had flung into it, besides (thinking this) no matter how fast nor successfully he hunted, he would never be able to lay up enough food to get them back to where they wanted to go. So he returned to the skiff, paying himself back to it by his vine-spliced painter, back to the water on which a low mist thick as cotton batting (though apparently not very tall, deep) lay, into which the stern of the skiff was already beginning to disappear although it lay with its prow almost touching the mound. The woman waked, stirred. "We fixing to start now?" she said.

"Yah," the convict said. "You aint aiming to have another one this morning, are you?" He got in and shoved the skiff clear of the land, which immediately began to dissolve into the mist. "Hand me the oar," he said over his shoulder, not turning yet.

"The oar?"

He turned his head. "The oar. You're laying on it." But she was not, and for an instant during which the mound, the island continued to fade slowly into the mist which seemed to enclose the skiff in weightless and impalpable wool like a precious or fragile bauble or jewel, the convict squatted not in dismay but in that frantic and astonished outrage of a man who, having just escaped a falling safe, is struck by the following two-ounce paper weight which was sitting on it: this the more unbearable because he knew that never in his life had he less time to give way to it. He did not hesitate. Grasping the grapevine end he sprang into the water, vanishing in the violent action of climbing and reappeared still climbing and (who had never learned to swim) plunged and threshed on toward the almost-vanished mound, moving through the water then upon it as the deer had done yesterday and scrabbled up the muddy slope and lay gasping and panting, still clutching the grapevine end.

Now the first thing he did was to choose what he believed to be the most suitable tree (for an instant in

which he knew he was insane he thought of trying to
saw it down with the flange of the bailing can) and build
a fire against the butt of it. Then he went to seek food.
He spent the next six days seeking it while the tree
burned through and fell and burned through again at
the proper length and he nursing little constant cunning flames along the flanks of the log to make it pad-
dle-shaped, nursing them at night too while the woman
and baby (it was eating, nursing now, he turning his
back or even returning into the woods each time she
prepared to open the faded tunic) slept in the skiff. He
learned to watch for stooping hawks and so found more
rabbits and twice possums; they ate some drowned fish
which gave them both a rash and then a violent flux and
one snake which the woman thought was turtle and
which did them no harm, and one night it rained and
he got up and dragged brush, shaking the snakes (he
no longer thought, *It aint nothing but another moccasin*,
he just stepped aside for them as they, when there was
time, telescoped sullenly aside for him) out of it with
the old former feeling of personal invulnerability and
built a shelter and the rain stopped at once and did not
recommence and the woman went back to the skiff.

Then one night—the slow tedious charring log was
almost a paddle now—one night and he was in bed, in
his bed in the bunkhouse and it was cold, he was trying
to pull the covers up only his mule wouldn't let him,
prodding and bumping heavily at him, trying to get
into the narrow bed with him and now the bed was cold
too and wet and he was trying to get out of it only the

mule would not let him, holding him by his belt in its
teeth, jerking and bumping him back into the cold wet
bed and, leaning, gave him a long swipe across the face
with its cold limber musculated tongue and he waked to
no fire, no coal even beneath where the almost-finished
paddle had been charring and something else prolonged
and coldly limber passed swiftly across his body where
he lay in four inches of water while the nose of the
skiff alternately tugged at the grapevine tied about his
waist and bumped and shoved him back into the water
again. Then something else came up and began to nudge
at his ankle (the log, the oar, it was) even as he groped
frantically for the skiff, hearing the swift rustling going
to and fro inside the hull as the woman began to thrash
about and scream. "Rats!" she cried. "It's full of rats!"

"Lay still!" he cried. "It's just snakes. Cant you hold
still long enough for me to find the boat?" Then he
found it, he got into it with the unfinished paddle; again
the thick muscular body convulsed under his foot; it
did not strike; he would not have cared, glaring astern
where he could see a little—the faint outer luminosity
of the open water. He poled toward it, thrusting aside
the snake-looped branches, the bottom of the skiff re-
sounding faintly to thick solid plops, the woman shrieking steadily. Then the skiff was clear of the trees, the
mound, and now he could feel the bodies whipping
about his ankles and hear the rasp of them as they
went over the gunwale. He drew the log in and scooped
it forward along the bottom of the boat and up and out;
against the pallid water he could see three more of them

in lashing convolutions before they vanished. "Shut up!" he cried. "Hush! I wish I was a snake so I could get out too!"

When once more the pale and heatless wafer disc of the early sun stared down at the skiff (whether they were moving or not the convict did not know) in its nimbus of fine cotton batting, the convict was hearing again that sound which he had heard twice before and would never forget—that sound of deliberate and irresistible and monstrously disturbed water. But this time he could not tell from what direction it came. It seemed to be everywhere, waxing and fading; it was like a phantom behind the mist, at one instant miles away, the next on the point of overwhelming the skiff within the next second; suddenly, in the instant he would believe (his whole weary body would spring and scream) that he was about to drive the skiff point-blank into it and with the unfinished paddle of the color and texture of sooty bricks, like something gnawed out of an old chimney by beavers and weighing twenty-five pounds, he would whirl the skiff frantically and find the sound dead ahead of him again. Then something bellowed tremendously above his head, he heard human voices, a bell jangled and the sound ceased and the mist vanished as when you draw your hand across a frosted pane, and the skiff now lay upon a sunny glitter of brown water flank to flank with, and about thirty yards away from, a steamboat. The decks were crowded and packed with men women and children sitting or standing beside and among a homely conglomeration of hur-

ried furniture, who looked mournfully and silently down
into the skiff while the convict and the man with a megaphone in the pilot house talked to each other in alternate puny shouts and roars above the chuffing of the
reversed engines:

"What in hell are you trying to do? Commit sui-
cide?"

"Which is the way to Vicksburg?"

"Vicksburg? Vicksburg? Lay alongside and come
aboard."

"Will you take the boat too?"

"Boat? Boat?" Now the megaphone cursed, the roaring waves of blasphemy and biological supposition
empty cavernous and bodiless in turn, as if the water,
the air, the mist had spoken it, roaring the words then
taking them back to itself and no harm done, no scar,
no insult left anywhere. "If I took aboard every floating sardine can you sonabitchin mushrats want me to
I wouldn't even have room forrard for a leadsman.
Come aboard! Do you expect me to hang here on stern
engines till hell freezes?"

"I aint coming without the boat," the convict said.
Now another voice spoke, so calm and mild and sensible
that for a moment it sounded more foreign and out of
place than even the megaphone's bellowing and bodiless profanity:

"Where is it you are trying to go?"

"I aint trying," the convict said. "I'm going. Parchman." The man who had spoken last turned and ap-

peared to converse with a third man in the pilot house.
Then he looked down at the skiff again.

"Carnarvon?"

"What?" the convict said. "Parchman?"

"All right. We're going that way. We'll put you off
where you can get home. Come aboard."

"The boat too?"

"Yes, yes. Come along. We're burning coal just to
talk to you." So the convict came alongside then and
watched them help the woman and baby over the rail
and he came aboard himself, though he still held to the
end of the vine-spliced painter until the skiff was hoisted
onto the boiler deck. "My God," the man, the gentle one,
said, "is that what you have been using for a paddle?"

"Yah," the convict said. "I lost the plank."

"The plank," the mild man (the convict told how
he seemed to whisper it), "the plank. Well. Come along
and get something to eat. Your boat is all right now."

"I reckon I'll wait here," the convict said. Because
now, he told them, he began to notice for the first time
that the other people, the other refugees who crowded
the deck, who had gathered in a quiet circle about the
upturned skiff on which he and the woman sat, the
grapevine painter wrapped several times about his
wrist and clutched in his hand, staring at him and the
woman with queer hot mournful intensity, were not
white people—

"You mean niggers?" the plump convict said.

"No. Not Americans."

"Not Americans? You was clean out of *America* even?"

"I dont know," the tall one said. "They called it Atchafalaya."—Because after a while he said, "What?" to the man and the man did it again, gobble-gobble—

"Gobble-gobble?" the plump convict said.

"That's the way they talked," the tall one said. "Gobble-gobble, whang, caw-caw-to-to."—And he sat there and watched them gobbling at one another and then looking at him again, then they fell back and the mild man (he wore a Red Cross brassard) entered, followed by a waiter with a tray of food. The mild man carried two glasses of whiskey.

"Drink this," the mild man said. "This will warm you." The woman took hers and drank it but the convict told how he looked at his and thought, *I aint tasted whiskey in seven years*. He had not tasted it but once before that; it was at the still itself back in a pine hollow; he was seventeen, he had gone there with four companions, two of whom were grown men, one of twenty-two or -three, the other about forty; he remembered it. That is, he remembered perhaps a third of that evening—a fierce turmoil in the hell-colored firelight, the shock and shock of blows about his head (and likewise of his own fists on other hard bone), then the waking to a splitting and blinding sun in a place, a cowshed, he had never seen before and which later turned out to be twenty miles from his home. He said he thought of this and he looked about at the faces watching him and he said,

"I reckon not."

"Come, come," the mild man said. "Drink it."

"I dont want it."

"Nonsense," the mild man said. "I'm a doctor. Here. Then you can eat." So he took the glass and even then he hesitated but again the mild man said, "Come along, down with it; you're still holding us up," in that voice still calm and sensible but a little sharp too—the voice of a man who could keep calm and affable because he wasn't used to being crossed—and he drank the whiskey and even in the second between the sweet full fire in his belly and when it began to happen he was trying to say, "I tried to tell you! I tried to!" But it was too late now in the pallid sun-glare of the tenth day of terror and hopelessness and despair and impotence and rage and outrage and it was himself and the mule, his mule (they had let him name it—John Henry) which no man save he had plowed for five years now and whose ways and habits he knew and respected and who knew his ways and habits so well that each of them could anticipate the other's very movements and intentions; it was himself and the mule, the little gobbling faces flying before them, the familiar hard skull-bones shocking against his fists, his voice shouting, "Come on, John Henry! Plow them down! Gobble them down, boy!" even as the bright hot red wave turned back, meeting it joyously, happily, lifted, poised, then hurling through space, triumphant and yelling, then again the old shocking blow at the back of his head: he lay on the deck, flat on his back and pinned arm and leg and cold sober again, his nostrils gushing again, the mild man stooping over him with behind the thin rimless glasses the coldest eyes the convict had ever seen—eyes which the convict said were not looking at him but at the gushing blood with nothing in the world in them but complete impersonal interest.

"Good man," the mild man said. "Plenty of life in the old carcass yet, eh? Plenty of good red blood too. Anyone ever suggest to you that you were hemophilic?" ("What?" the plump convict said. "Hemophilic? You know what that means?" The tall convict had his cigarette going now, his body jackknifed backward into the coffinlike space between the upper and lower bunks, lean, clean, motionless, the blue smoke wreathing across his lean dark aquiline shaven face. "That's a calf that's a bull and a cow at the same time."

"No, it aint," a third convict said. "It's a calf or a colt that aint neither one."

"Hell fire," the plump one said. "He's got to be one or the other to keep from drounding." He had never ceased to look at the tall one in the bunk; now he spoke to him again: "You let him call you that?") The tall one had done so. He did not answer the doctor (this was where he stopped thinking of him as the mild man) at all. He could not move either, though he felt fine, he felt better than he had in ten days. So they helped him to his feet and steadied him over and lowered him onto the upturned skiff beside the woman, where he sat bent forward, elbows on knees in the immemorial attitude, watching his own bright crimson staining the mud-trodden deck, until the doctor's clean clipped hand appeared under his nose with a phial.

"Smell," the doctor said. "Deep." The convict inhaled, the sharp ammoniac sensation burned up his nostrils and into his throat. "Again," the doctor said. The convict inhaled obediently. This time he choked and spat a gout of blood, his nose now had no more feeling than a toenail, other than it felt about the size of a ten-inch shovel, and as cold.

"I ask you to excuse me," he said. "I never meant—"

"Why?" the doctor said. "You put up as pretty a scrap against forty or fifty men as I ever saw. You lasted a good two seconds. Now you can eat something. Or do you think that will send you haywire again?"

They both ate, sitting on the skiff, the gobbling faces no longer watching them now, the convict gnawing slowly and painfully at the thick sandwich, hunched, his face laid sideways to the food and parallel to the earth as a dog chews; the steamboat went on. At noon there were bowls of hot soup and bread and more coffee; they ate this too, sitting side by side on the skiff, the grape vine still wrapped about the convict's wrist. The baby waked and nursed and slept again and they talked quietly:

"Was it Parchman he said he was going to take us?"

"That's where I told him I wanted to go."

"It never sounded exactly like Parchman to me. It sounded like he said something else." The convict had thought that too. He had been thinking about that fairly soberly ever since they boarded the steamboat and soberly indeed ever since he had remarked the nature of the other passengers, those men and women definitely a little shorter than he and with skin a little different in pigmentation from any sunburn, even though the eyes were sometimes blue or gray, who talked to one another in a tongue he had never heard before and who apparently did not understand his own, people the like of whom he had never seen about Parchman nor anywhere else and whom he did not believe were going there or beyond there either. But after his hill-billy country fashion and kind he would not ask, because to his raising asking information was asking a favor and you did not ask favors of strangers; if they offered them perhaps you accepted and you expressed gratitude almost tediously recapitulant, but you did not ask. So he would watch and wait, as he had done before, and do or try to do to the best of his ability what the best of his judgment dictated.

So he waited, and in midafternoon the steamboat chuffed and thrust through a willow-choked gorge and emerged from it, and now the convict knew it was the River. He could believe it now—the tremendous reach, yellow and sleepy in the afternoon—("Because it's too big," he told them soberly. "Aint no flood in the world big enough to make it do more than stand a little higher so it can look back and see just where the flea is, just exactly where to scratch. It's the little ones, the little piddling creeks that run backward one day and forward the next and come busting down on a man full of dead mules and hen houses.")—and the steamboat moving up this now (*like a ant crossing a plate*, the convict thought, sitting beside the woman on the upturned skiff, the baby nursing again, apparently looking too out across the water where, a mile away on either hand, the twin lines of levee resembled parallel unbroken floating thread) and then it was nearing sunset and he began to hear, to notice, the voices of the doctor and of the man who had first bawled at him through the megaphone now bawling again from the pilot house overhead:

"Stop? Stop? Am I running a street car?"

"Stop for the novelty then," the doctor's pleasant voice said. "I dont know how many trips back and forth you have made in yonder nor how many of what you call mushrats you have fetched out. But this is the first time you ever had two people—no, three—who not only knew the name of some place they wished to go to but were actually trying to go there." So the convict waited while the sun slanted more and more and the steamboat-ant crawled steadily on across its vacant and gigantic plate turning more and more to copper. But he did not ask, he just waited. *Maybe it was Carrollton he said*, he thought. *It begun with a C.* But he did not believe that either. He did not know where he was, but he did know that this was not anywhere near the Carrollton he remembered from that day seven years ago when, shackled wrist to wrist with the deputy sheriff, he had passed through it on the train—the slow spaced repeated shattering banging of trucks where two railroads crossed, a random scattering of white houses tranquil among trees on green hills lush with summer, a

pointing spire, the finger of the hand of God. But there
was no river there. *And you aint never close to this
river without knowing it,* he thought. *I dont care who
you are nor where you have been all your life.* Then
the head of the steamboat began to swing across the
stream, its shadow swinging too, travelling long before
it across the water, toward the vacant ridge of willow-
massed earth empty of all life. There was nothing there
at all, the convict could not even see either earth or
water beyond it; it was as though the steamboat were
about to crash slowly through the thin low frail willow
barrier and embark into space, or lacking this, slow and
back and fill and disembark him into space, granted it
was about to disembark him, granted this was that place
which was not near Parchman and was not Carrollton
either, even though it did begin with c. Then he turned
his head and saw the doctor stooping over the woman,
pushing the baby's eyelid up with his forefinger, peer-
ing at it.

"Who else was there when he came?" the doctor said.

"Nobody," the convict said.

"Did it all yourselves, eh?"

"Yes," the convict said. Now the doctor stood up and
looked at the convict.

"This is Carnarvon," he said.

"Carnarvon?" the convict said. "That aint—" Then
he stopped, ceased. And now he told about that—the
intent eyes as dispassionate as ice behind the rimless
glasses, the clipped quick-tempered face that was not
accustomed to being crossed or lied to either. ("Yes,"

the plump convict said. "That's what I was aiming to
ask. Them clothes. Anybody would know them. How if
this doctor was as smart as you claim he was—"

"I had slept in them for ten nights, mostly in the
mud," the tall one said. "I had been rowing since midnight with that sapling oar I had tried to burn out that
I never had time to scrape the soot off. But it's being
scared and worried and then scared and then worried
again in clothes for days and days and days that
changes the way they look. I dont mean just your pants."
He did not laugh. "Your face too. That doctor knowed."

"All right," the plump one said. "Go on.")

"I know it," the doctor said. "I discovered that while
you were lying on the deck yonder sobering up again.
Now dont lie to me. I dont like lying. This boat is
going to New Orleans."

"No," the convict said immediately, quietly, with
absolute finality. He could hear them again—the thuck-
thuck-thuck on the water where an instant before he had
been. But he was not thinking of the bullets. He had
forgotten them, forgiven them. He was thinking of himself crouching, sobbing, panting before running again
—the voice, the indictment, the cry of final and irrevocable repudiation of the old primal faithless Manipu-
lator of all the lust and folly and injustice: *All in the
world I wanted was just to surrender*; thinking of it,
remembering it but without heat now, without passion
now and briefer than an epitaph: *No. I tried that once.
They shot at me.*

"So you dont want to go to New Orleans. And you

didn't exactly plan to go to Carnarvon. But you will take Carnarvon in preference to New Orleans." The convict said nothing. The doctor looked at him, the magnified pupils like the heads of two bridge nails. "What were you in for? Hit him harder than you thought, eh?"

"No. I tried to rob a train."

"Say that again." The convict said it again. "Well? Go on. You dont say that in the year 1927 and just stop, man." So the convict told it, dispassionately too —about the magazines, the pistol which would not shoot, the mask and the dark lantern in which no draft had been arranged to keep the candle burning so that it died almost with the match but even then left the metal too hot to carry, won with subscriptions. *Only it aint my eyes or my mouth either he's watching*, he thought. *It's like he is watching the way my hair grows on my head.* "I see," the doctor said. "But something went wrong. But you've had plenty of time to think about it since. To decide what was wrong, what you failed to do."

"Yes," the convict said. "I've thought about it a right smart since."

"So next time you are not going to make that mistake."

"I don't know," the convict said. "There aint going to be a next time."

"Why? If you know what you did wrong, they wont catch you next time."

The convict looked at the doctor steadily. They looked

at each other steadily; the two sets of eyes were not so different after all. "I reckon I see what you mean," the convict said presently. "I was eighteen then. I'm twenty-five now."

"Oh," the doctor said. Now (the convict tried to tell it) the doctor did not move, he just simply quit looking at the convict. He produced a pack of cheap cigarettes from his coat. "Smoke?" he said.

"I wouldn't care for none," the convict said.

"Quite," the doctor said in that affable clipped voice. He put the cigarettes away. "There has been conferred upon my race (the Medical race) also the power to bind and to loose, if not by Jehovah perhaps, certainly by the American Medical Association—on which incidentally, in this day of Our Lord, I would put my money, at any odds, at any amount, at any time. I dont know just how far out of bounds I am on this specific occasion but I think we'll put it to the touch." He cupped his hands to his mouth, toward the pilot house overhead. "Captain!" he shouted. "We'll put these three passengers ashore here." He turned to the convict again. "Yes," he said, "I think I shall let your native State lick its own vomit. Here." Again his hand emerged from his pocket, this time with a bill in it.

"No," the convict said.

"Come, come; I dont like to be disputed either."

"No," the convict said. "I aint got any way to pay it back."

"Did I ask you to pay it back?"

"No," the convict said. "I never asked to borrow it either."

So once more he stood on dry land, who had already been toyed with twice by that risible and concentrated power of water, once more than should have fallen to the lot of any one man, any one lifetime, yet for whom there was reserved still another unbelievable recapitulation, he and the woman standing on the empty levee, the sleeping child wrapped in the faded tunic and the grape vine painter still wrapped about the convict's wrist, watching the steamboat back away and turn and once more crawl onward up the platter-like reach of vacant water burnished more and more to copper, its trailing smoke roiling in slow copper-edged gouts, thinning out along the water, fading, stinking away across the vast serene desolation, the boat growing smaller and smaller until it did not seem to crawl at all but to hang stationary in the airy substanceless sunset, dissolving into nothing like a pellet of floating mud.

Then he turned and for the first time looked about him, behind him, recoiling, not through fear but through pure reflex and not physically but the soul, the spirit, that profound sober alert attentiveness of the hillman who will not ask anything of strangers, not even information, thinking quietly, *No. This aint Carrollton neither.* Because he now looked down the almost perpendicular landward slope of the levee through sixty feet of absolute space, upon a surface, a terrain flat as a waffle and of the color of a waffle or perhaps of the summer coat of a claybank horse and possessing that

same piled density of a rug or peltry, spreading away
without undulation yet with that curious appearance of
imponderable solidity like fluid, broken here and there
by thick humps of arsenical green which nevertheless
still seemed to possess no height and by writhen veins
of the color of ink which he began to suspect to be actual
water but with judgment reserved, with judgment still
reserved even when presently he was walking in it.
That's what he said, told: So they went on. He didn't
tell how he got the skiff singlehanded up the revetment
and across the crown and down the opposite sixty foot
drop, he just said he went on, in a swirling cloud of
mosquitoes like hot cinders, thrusting and plunging
through the saw-edged grass which grew taller than his
head and which whipped back at his arms and face like
limber knives, dragging by the vine-spliced painter the
skiff in which the woman sat, slogging and stumbling
knee-deep in something less of earth than water, along
one of those black winding channels less of water than
earth: and then (he was in the skiff too now, paddling
with the charred log, what footing there had been having given away beneath him without warning thirty minutes ago, leaving only the air-filled bubble of his jumper-
back ballooning lightly on the twilit water until he rose
to the surface and scrambled into the skiff) the house,
the cabin a little larger than a horse-box, of cypress
boards and an iron roof, rising on ten-foot stilts slender
as spiders' legs, like a shabby and death-stricken (and
probably poisonous) wading creature which had got that
far into that flat waste and died with nothing nowhere

in reach or sight to lie down upon, a pirogue tied to the
foot of a crude ladder, a man standing in the open door
holding a lantern (it was that dark now) above his
head, gobbling down at them.

He told it—of the next eight or nine or ten days,
he did not remember which, while the four of them
—himself and the woman and baby and the little wiry
man with rotting teeth and soft wild bright eyes like a
rat or a chipmunk, whose language neither of them
could understand—lived in the room and a half. He did
not tell it that way, just as he apparently did not consider it worth the breath to tell how he had got the
hundred-and-sixty-pound skiff singlehanded up and
across and down the sixty-foot levee. He just said, "After
a while we come to a house and we stayed there eight
or nine days then they blew up the levee with dynamite
so we had to leave." That was all. But he remembered
it, but quietly now, with the cigar now, the good one
the Warden had given him (though not lighted yet) in
his peaceful and steadfast hand, remembering that first
morning when he waked on the thin pallet beside his
host (the woman and baby had the one bed) with the
fierce sun already latticed through the warped rough
planking of the wall, and stood on the rickety porch
looking out upon that flat fecund waste neither earth
nor water, where even the senses doubted which was
which, which rich and massy air and which mazy and
impalpable vegetation, and thought quietly, *He must
do something here to eat and live. But I dont know
what. And until I can go on again, until I can find*

where I am and how to pass that town without them seeing me I will have to help him do it so we can eat and live too, and I dont know what. And he had a change of clothing too, almost at once on that first morning, not telling any more than he had about the skiff and the levee how he had begged borrowed or bought from the man whom he had not laid eyes on twelve hours ago and with whom on the day he saw him for the last time he still could exchange no word, the pair of dungaree pants which even the Cajan had discarded as no longer wearable, filthy, buttonless, the legs slashed and frayed into fringe like that on an 1890 hammock, in which he stood naked from the waist up and holding out to her the mud-caked and soot-stained jumper and overall when the woman waked on that first morning in the crude bunk nailed into one corner and filled with dried grass, saying, "Wash them. Good. I want all them stains out. All of them."

"But the jumper," she said. "Aint he got ere old shirt too? That sun and them mosquitoes—" But he did not even answer, and she said no more either, though when he and the Cajan returned at dark the garments were clean, stained a little still with the old mud and soot, but clean, resembling again what they were supposed to resemble as (his arms and back already a fiery red which would be blisters by tomorrow) he spread the garments out and examined them and then rolled them up carefully in a six-months-old New Orleans paper and thrust the bundle behind a rafter, where it remained while day followed day and the blisters on

his back broke and suppurated and he would sit with
his face expressionless as a wooden mask beneath the
sweat while the Cajan doped his back with something on
a filthy rag from a filthy saucer, she still saying nothing since she too doubtless knew what his reason was,
not from that rapport of the wedded conferred upon her
by the two weeks during which they had jointly suffered
all the crises emotional social economic and even moral
which do not always occur even in the ordinary fifty
married years (the old married: you have seen them,
the electroplate reproductions, the thousand identical
coupled faces with only a collarless stud or a fichu
out of Louisa Alcott to denote the sex, looking in pairs
like the winning braces of dogs after a field trial, out
from among the packed columns of disaster and alarm
and baseless assurance and hope and incredible insensi-
tivity and insulation from tomorrow propped by a thousand morning sugar bowls or coffee urns; or singly,
rocking on porches or sitting in the sun beneath the
tobacco-stained porticoes of a thousand county court-
houses, as though with the death of the other having
inherited a sort of rejuvenescence, immortality; relict,
they take a new lease on breath and seem to live forever, as though that flesh which the old ceremony or
ritual had morally purified and made legally one had
actually become so with long tedious habit and he or
she who entered the ground first took all of it with him
or her, leaving only the old permanent enduring bone,
free and tramelless)—not because of this but because

she too had stemmed at some point from the same dim hill-bred Abraham.

So the bundle remained behind the rafter and day followed day while he and his partner (he was in partnership now with his host, hunting alligators on shares, on the halvers he called it—"Halvers?" the plump convict said. "How could you make a business agreement with a man you claim you couldn't even talk to?" "I never had to talk to him," the tall one said. "Money aint got but one language.") departed at dawn each day, at first together in the pirogue but later singly, the one in the pirogue and the other in the skiff, the one with the battered and pitted rifle, the other with the knife and a piece of knotted rope and a lightwood club the size and weight and shape of a Thuringian mace, stalking their pleistocene nightmares up and down the secret inky channels which writhed the flat brass-colored land. He remembered that too: that first morning when turning in the sunrise from the rickety platform he saw the hide nailed drying to the wall and stopped dead, looking at it quietly, thinking quietly and soberly, *So that's it. That's what he does in order to eat and live*, knowing it was a hide, a skin, but from what animal, by association, ratiocination or even memory of any picture out of his dead youth, he did not know but knowing that it was the reason, the explanation, for the little lost spider-legged house (which had already begun to die, to rot from the legs upward almost before the roof was nailed on) set in that teeming and myriad desolation, enclosed and lost within the furious embrace of flowing mare earth and stallion sun, divining through pure rapport of kind for kind, hill-billy and bayou-rat, the two one and identical because of the same grudged dispensation and niggard fate of hard and unceasing travail not to gain future security, a balance in the bank or even in a buried soda can for slothful and easy old age, but just permission to endure and endure to buy air to feel and sun to drink for each's little while, thinking (the convict), *Well, anyway I am going to find out what it is sooner than I expected to,* and did so, re-entered the house where the woman was just waking in the one sorry built-in straw-filled bunk which the Cajan had surrendered to her, and ate the breakfast (the rice, a semi-liquid mess violent with pepper and mostly fish considerably high, the chicory-thickened coffee) and, shirtless, followed the little scuttling bobbing bright-eyed rotten-toothed man down the crude ladder and into the pirogue. He had never seen a pirogue either and he believed that it would not remain upright—not that it was light and precariously balanced with its open side upward but that there was inherent in the wood, the very log, some dynamic and unsleeping natural law, almost will, which its present position outraged and violated—yet accepting this too as he had the fact that that hide had belonged to something larger than any calf or hog and that anything which looked like that on the outside would be more than likely to have teeth and claws too, accepting this, squatting in the pirogue, clutching both gunwales, rigidly immobile as though he had an egg filled with nitroglycerin in his mouth and scarcely breathing, thinking, *If that's it, then I can do it too and even if he cant tell me how I reckon I can watch him and find out*. And he did this too, he remembered it, quietly even yet, thinking, *I thought that was how to do it and I reckon I would still think that even if I had it to do again now for the first time*— the brazen day already fierce upon his naked back, the crooked channel like a voluted thread of ink, the pirogue moving steadily to the paddle which both entered and left the water without a sound; then the sudden cessation of the paddle behind him and the fierce hissing gobble of the Cajan at his back and he squatting bate-breathed and with that intense immobility of complete sobriety of a blind man listening while the frail wooden shell stole on at the dying apex of its own parted water. Afterward he remembered the rifle too—the rust-pitted single-shot weapon with a clumsily wired stock and a muzzle you could have driven a whiskey cork into, which the Cajan had brought into the boat—but not now; now he just squatted, crouched, immobile, breathing with infinitesimal care, his sober unceasing gaze going here and there constantly as he thought, *What? What? I not only dont know what I am looking for, I dont even know where to look for it*. Then he felt the motion of the pirogue as the Cajan moved and then the tense gobbling hissing actually, hot rapid and repressed, against his neck and ear, and glancing downward saw projecting between his own arm and body from behind the Cajan's hand holding the knife, and glaring up again saw the flat thick spit of mud which as he looked

at it divided and became a thick mud-colored log which
in turn seemed, still immobile, to leap suddenly against
his retinae in three—no, four—dimensions: volume,
solidity, shape, and another: not fear but pure and intense speculation and he looking at the scaled motionless shape, thinking not, *It looks dangerous* but *It looks
big*, thinking, *Well, maybe a mule standing in a lot looks
big to a man that never walked up to one with a halter
before*, thinking, *Only if he could just tell me what to
do it would save time*, the pirogue drawing nearer now,
creeping now, with no ripple now even and it seemed to
him that he could even hear his companion's held breath
and he taking the knife from the other's hand now and
not even thinking this since it was too fast, a flash; it
was not a surrender, not a resignation, it was too calm,
it was a part of him, he had drunk it with his mother's
milk and lived with it all his life: *After all a man cant
only do what he has to do, with what he has to do it with,
with what he has learned, to the best of his judgment.
And I reckon a hog is still a hog, no matter what it looks
like. So here goes*, sitting still for an instant longer until
the bow of the pirogue grounded lighter than the falling
of a leaf and stepped out of it and paused just for one
instant while the words *It does look big* stood for just a
second, unemphatic and trivial, somewhere where some
fragment of his attention could see them and vanished,
and stooped straddling, the knife driving even as he
grasped the near foreleg, this all in the same instant
when the lashing tail struck him a terrific blow upon
the back. But the knife was home, he knew that even on

his back in the mud, the weight of the thrashing beast longwise upon him, its ridged back clutched to his stomach, his arm about its throat, the hissing head clamped against his jaw, the furious tail lashing and flailing, the knife in his other hand probing for the life and finding it, the hot fierce gush: and now sitting beside the profound up-bellied carcass, his head again between his knees in the old attitude while his own blood freshened the other which drenched him, thinking, *It's my durn nose again.*

So he sat there, his head, his streaming face, bowed between his knees in an attitude not of dejection but profoundly bemused, contemplative, while the shrill voice of the Cajan seemed to buzz at him from an enormous distance; after a time he even looked up at the antic wiry figure bouncing hysterically about him, the face wild and grimacing, the voice gobbling and high; while the convict, holding his face carefully slanted so the blood would run free, looked at him with the cold intentness of a curator or custodian paused before one of his own glass cases, the Cajan threw up the rifle, cried "Boom-boom-boom!" flung it down and in pantomime re-enacted the recent scene then whirled his hands again, crying "Magnifique! Magnifique! Cent d'argent! mille d'argent! Tout l'argent sous le ciel de Dieu!" But the convict was already looking down again, cupping the coffee-colored water to his face, watching the constant bright carmine marble it, thinking, *It's a little late to be telling me that now,* and not even thinking this long because presently they were in the pirogue again, the

convict squatting again with that unbreathing rigidity as
though he were trying by holding his breath to decrease
his very weight, the bloody skin in the bows before him
and he looking at it, thinking, *And I cant even ask him
how much my half will be.*

But this not for long either, because as he was to tell
the plump convict later, money has but one language.
He remembered that too (they were at home now, the
skin spread on the platform, where for the woman's
benefit now the Cajan once more went through the pantomime—the gun which was not used, the hand-to-hand
battle; for the second time the invisible alligator was
slain amid cries, the victor rose and found this time
that not even the woman was watching him. She was
looking at the once more swollen and inflamed face of
the convict. "You mean it kicked you right in the face?"
she said.

"Nah," the convict said harshly, savagely. "It never
had to. I done seem to got to where if that boy was to
shoot me in the tail with a bean blower my nose would
bleed.")—remembered that too but he did not try to
tell it. Perhaps he could not have—how two people who
could not even talk to one another made an agreement
which both not only understood but which each knew
the other would hold true and protect (perhaps for this
reason) better than any written and witnessed contract.
They even discussed and agreed somehow that they
should hunt separately, each in his own vessel, to double
the chances of finding prey. But this was easy: the convict could almost understand the words in which the

Cajan said, "You do not need me and the rifle; we will
only hinder you, be in your way." And more than this,
they even agreed about the second rifle: that there was
someone, it did not matter who—friend, neighbor, perhaps one in business in that line—from whom they
could rent a second rifle; in their two patois, the one
bastard English, the other bastard French—the one
volatile, with his wild bright eyes and his voluble mouth
full of stumps of teeth, the other sober, almost grim,
swollen-faced and with his naked back blistered and
scoriated like so much beef—they discussed this, squatting on either side of the pegged-out hide like two members of a corporation facing each other across a
mahogany board table, and decided against it, the convict deciding: "I reckon not," he said. "I reckon if I
had knowed enough to wait to start out with a gun, I still
would. But since I done already started out without one,
I dont reckon I'll change." Because it was a question of
the money in terms of time, days. (Strange to say, that
was the one thing which the Cajan could not tell him:
how much the half would be. But the convict knew it was
half.) He had so little of them. He would have to move
on soon, thinking (the convict), *All this durn foolish-
ness will stop soon and I can get on back*, and then suddenly he found that he was thinking, *Will have to get on
back*, and he became quite still and looked about at the
rich strange desert which surrounded him, in which he
was temporarily lost in peace and hope and into which
the last seven years had sunk like so many trivial pebbles
into a pool, leaving no ripple, and he thought quietly,

with a kind of bemused amazement, *Yes. I reckon I had done forgot how good making money was. Being let to make it.*

So he used no gun, his the knotted rope and the Thuringian mace, and each morning he and the Cajan took their separate ways in the two boats to comb and creep the secret channels about the lost land from (or out of) which now and then still other pint-sized dark men appeared gobbling, abruptly and as though by magic from nowhere, in other hollowed logs, to follow quietly and watch him at his single combats—men named Tine and Toto and Theule, who were not much larger than and looked a good deal like the muskrats which the Cajan (the host did this too, supplied the kitchen too, he expressed this too like the rifle business, in his own tongue, the convict comprehending this too as though it had been English: "Do not concern yourself about food, O Hercules. Catch alligators; I will supply the pot.") took now and then from traps as you take a shoat pig at need from a pen, and varied the eternal rice and fish (the convict did tell this: how at night, in the cabin, the door and one sashless window battened against mosquitoes—a form, a ritual, as empty as crossing the fingers or knocking on wood—sitting beside the bug-swirled lantern on the plank table in a temperature close to blood heat he would look down at the swimming segment of meat on his sweating plate and think, *It must be Theule. He was the fat one.*)—day following day, unemphatic and identical, each like the one before and the one which would follow while his

theoretical half of a sum to be reckoned in pennies,
dollars, or tens of dollars he did not know, mounted—
the mornings when he set forth to find waiting for him
like the *matador* his *aficianados* the small clump of
constant and deferential pirogues, the hard noons when
ringed half about by little motionless shells he fought
his solitary combats, the evenings, the return, the pirogues departing one by one into inlets and passages
which during the first few days he could not even distinguish, then the platform in the twilight where before
the static woman and the usually nursing infant and
the one or two bloody hides of the day's take the Cajan
would perform his ritualistic victorious pantomime before the two growing rows of knifemarks in one of the
boards of the wall; then the nights when, the woman
and child in the single bunk and the Cajan already
snoring on the pallet and the reeking lantern set close,
he (the convict) would sit on his naked heels, sweating
steadily, his face worn and calm, immersed and indomitable, his bowed back raw and savage as beef
beneath the suppurant old blisters and the fierce welts
of tails, and scrape and chip at the charred sapling
which was almost a paddle now, pausing now and then
to raise his head while the cloud of mosquitoes about it
whined and whirled, to stare at the wall before him
until after a while the crude boards themselves must
have dissolved away and let his blank unseeing gaze go
on and on unhampered, through the rich oblivious darkness, beyond it even perhaps, even perhaps beyond the
seven wasted years during which, so he had just realised,

he had been permitted to toil but not to work. Then he
would retire himself, he would take a last look at the
rolled bundle behind the rafter and blow out the lantern
and lie down as he was beside his snoring partner, to
lie sweating (on his stomach, he could not bear the
touch of anything to his back) in the whining ovenlike
darkness filled with the forlorn bellowing of alligators,
thinking not, *They never gave me time to learn* but *I
had forgot how good it is to work*.

Then on the tenth day it happened. It happened for
the third time. At first he refused to believe it, not that
he felt that now he had served out and discharged his
apprenticeship to mischance, had with the birth of the
child reached and crossed the crest of his Golgotha and
would now be, possibly not permitted so much as ignored, to descend the opposite slope free-wheeling. That
was not his feeling at all. What he declined to accept
was the fact that a power, a force such as that which had
been consistent enough to concentrate upon him with
deadly undeviation for weeks, should with all the wealth
of cosmic violence and disaster to draw from, have been
so barren of invention and imagination, so lacking in
pride of artistry and craftmanship, as to repeat itself
twice. Once he had accepted, twice he even forgave, but
three times he simply declined to believe, particularly
when he was at last persuaded to realise that this third
time was to be instigated not by the blind potency of
volume and motion but by human direction and hands:
that now the cosmic joker, foiled twice, had stooped in

its vindictive concentration to the employing of dynamite.

He did not tell that. Doubtless he did not know himself how it happened, what was happening. But he doubtless remembered it (but quietly above the thick rich-
colored pristine cigar in his clean steady hand), what
he knew, divined of it. It would be evening, the ninth
evening, he and the woman on either side of their host's
empty place at the evening meal, he hearing the voices
from without but not ceasing to eat, still chewing
steadily, because it would be the same as though he were
seeing them anyway—the two or three or four pirogues
floating on the dark water beneath the platform on which
the host stood, the voices gobbling and jabbering, incomprehensible and filled not with alarm and not exactly
with rage or ever perhaps absolute surprise but rather
just cacophony like those of disturbed marsh fowl, he
(the convict) not ceasing to chew but just looking up
quietly and maybe without a great deal of interrogation
or surprise too as the Cajan burst in and stood before
them, wild-faced, glaring, his blackened teeth gaped
against the inky orifice of his distended mouth, watching (the convict) while the Cajan went through his
violent pantomime of violent evacuation, ejection, scoop-
ing something invisible into his arms and hurling it out
and downward and in the instant of completing the
gesture changing from instigator to victim of that which
he had set into pantomimic motion, clasping his head
and, bowed over and not otherwise moving, seeming to
be swept on and away before it, crying "Boom! Boom!

Boom!", the convict watching him, his jaw not chewing now, though for just that moment, thinking, *What? What is it he is trying to tell me?* thinking (this a flash too, since he could not have expressed this, and hence did not even know that he had ever thought it) that though his life had been cast here, circumscribed by this environment, accepted by this environment and accepting it in turn (and he had done well here—this quietly, soberly indeed, if he had been able to phrase it, think it instead of merely knowing it—better than he had ever done, who had not even known until now how good work, making money, could be) yet it was not his life, he still and would ever be no more than the water bug upon the surface of the pond, the plumbless and lurking depths of which he would never know, his only actual contact with it being the instants when on lonely and glaring mudspits under the pitiless sun and amphitheatred by his motionless and riveted semicircle of watching pirogues, he accepted the gambit which he had not elected, entered the lashing radius of the armed tail and beat at the thrashing and hissing head with his lightwood club, or this failing, embraced without hesitation the armored body itself with the frail web of flesh and bone in which he walked and lived and sought the raging life with an eight-inch knife-blade.

So he and the woman merely watched the Cajan as he acted out the whole charade of eviction—the little wiry man gesticulant and wild, his hysterical shadow leaping and falling upon the rough wall as he went through the pantomime of abandoning the cabin, gather-

ing in pantomime his meagre belongings from the walls
and corners—objects which no other man would want
and only some power or force like blind water or earth-
quake or fire would ever dispossess him of, the woman
watching too, her mouth slightly open upon a mass of
chewed food, on her face an expression of placid astonishment, saying, "What? What's he saying?"

"I dont know," the convict said. "But I reckon if it's
something we ought to know we will find it out when it's
ready for us to." Because he was not alarmed, though
by now he had read the other's meaning plainly enough.
He's fixing to leave, he thought. *He's telling me to leave
too*—this later, after they had quitted the table and the
Cajan and the woman had gone to bed and the Cajan
had risen from the pallet and approached the convict
and once more went through the pantomime of abandoning the cabin, this time as one repeats a speech which
may have been misunderstood, tediously, carefully
repetitional as to a child, seeming to hold the convict
with one hand while he gestured, talked, with the other,
gesturing as though in single syllables, the convict
(squatting, the knife open and the almost-finished paddle
across his lap) watching, nodding his head, even speaking in English: "Yah; sure. You bet. I got you."—
trimming again at the paddle but no faster, with no
more haste than on any other night, serene in his belief
that when the time came for him to know whatever it
was, that would take care of itself, having already and
without even knowing it, even before the possibility, the
question, ever arose, declined, refused to accept even

the thought of moving also, thinking about the hides, thinking, *If there was just some way he could tell me where to carry my share to get the money* but thinking this only for an instant between two delicate strokes of the blade because almost at once he thought, *I reckon as long as I can catch them I wont have no big trouble finding whoever it is that will buy them.*

So the next morning he helped the Cajan load his few belongings—the pitted rifle, a small bundle of clothing (again they traded, who could not even converse with one another, this time the few cooking vessels, a few rusty traps by definite allocation, and something embracing and abstractional which included the stove, the crude bunk, the house or its occupancy—something— in exchange for one alligator hide)—into the pirogue, then, squatting and as two children divide sticks they divided the hides, separating them into two piles, one-for- me-and-one-for-you, two-for-me-and-two-for-you, and the Cajan loaded his share and shoved away from the platform and paused again, though this time he only put the paddle down, gathered something invisibly into his two hands and flung it violently upward, crying "Boom? Boom?" on a rising inflection, nodding violently to the half-naked and savagely scoriated man on the platform who stared with a sort of grim equability back at him and said, "Sure. Boom. Boom." Then the Cajan went on. He did not look back. They watched him, already pad- dling rapidly, or the woman did; the convict had already turned.

"Maybe he was trying to tell us to leave too," she said.

"Yah," the convict said. "I thought of that last night. Hand me the paddle." She fetched it to him—the sapling, the one he had been trimming at nightly, not quite finished yet though one more evening would do it (he had been using a spare one of the Cajan's. The other had offered to let him keep it, to include it perhaps with the stove and the bunk and the cabin's freehold, but the convict had declined. Perhaps he had computed it by volume against so much alligator hide, this weighed against one more evening with the tedious and careful blade.) and he departed too with his knotted rope and mace, in the opposite direction, as though not only not content with refusing to quit the place he had been warned against, he must establish and affirm the irrevocable finality of his refusal by penetrating even further and deeper into it. And then and without warning the high fierce drowsing of his solitude gathered itself and struck at him.

He could not have told this if he had tried—this not yet midmorning and he going on, alone for the first time, no pirogue emerging anywhere to fall in behind him, but he had not expected this anyway, he knew that the others would have departed too; it was not this, it was his very solitude, his desolation which was now his alone and in full since he had elected to remain; the sudden cessation of the paddle, the skiff shooting on for a moment yet while he thought, *What? What?* Then, *No. No. No,* as the silence and solitude and emptiness roared down upon him in a jeering bellow: and now

reversed, the skiff spun violently on its heel, he the betrayed driving furiously back toward the platform where
he knew it was already too late, that citadel where the
very crux and dear breath of his life—the being allowed
to work and earn money, that right and privilege which
he believed he had earned to himself unaided, asking
no favor of anyone or anything save the right to be let
alone to pit his will and strength against the sauric
protagonist of a land, a region, which he had not asked
to be projected into—was being threatened, driving the
home-made paddle in grim fury, coming in sight of the
platform at last and seeing the motor launch lying
alongside it with no surprise at all but actually with a
kind of pleasure as though at a visible justification of
his outrage and fear, the privilege of saying *I told you
so* to his own affronting, driving on toward it in a dreamlike state in which there seemed to be no progress at all,
in which, unimpeded and suffocating, he strove dreamily
with a weightless oar, with muscles without strength or
resiliency, at a medium without resistance, seeming to
watch the skiff creep infinitesimally across the sunny
water and up to the platform while a man in the launch
(there were five of them in all) gobbled at him in that
same tongue he had been hearing constantly now for
ten days and still knew no word of, just as a second man,
followed by the woman carrying the baby and dressed
again for departure in the faded tunic and the sunbonnet, emerged from the house, carrying (the man carried
several other things but the convict saw nothing else)
the paper-wrapped bundle which the convict had put

behind the rafter ten days ago and no other hand had
touched since, he (the convict) on the platform too now,
holding the skiff's painter in one hand and the bludgeon-
like paddle in the other, contriving to speak to the
woman at last in a voice dreamy and suffocating and
incredibly calm: "Take it away from him and carry it
back into the house."

"So you can talk English, can you?" the man in the
launch said. "Why didn't you come out like they told
you to last night?"

"Out?" the convict said. Again he even looked,
glared, at the man in the launch, contriving even again to
control his voice: "I aint got time to take trips. I'm
busy," already turning to the woman again, his mouth
already open to repeat as the dreamy buzzing voice of
the man came to him and he turning once more, in a
terrific and absolutely unbearable exasperation, crying,
"Flood? What flood? Hell a mile, it's done passed me
twice months ago! It's gone! What flood?" and then
(he did not think this in actual words either but he
knew it, suffered that flashing insight into his own character or destiny: how there was a peculiar quality of
repetitiveness about his present fate, how not only the
almost seminal crises recurred with a certain monotony,
but the very physical circumstances followed a stupidly
unimaginative pattern) the man in the launch said,
"Take him" and he was on his feet for a few minutes
yet, lashing and striking in panting fury, then once
more on his back on hard unyielding planks while the
four men swarmed over him in a fierce wave of hard

bones and panting curses and at last the thin dry vicious
snapping of handcuffs.

"Damn it, are you mad?" the man in the launch said.
"Cant you understand they are going to dynamite that
levee at noon today?—Come on," he said to the others.
"Get him aboard. Let's get out of here."

"I want my hides and boat," the convict said.

"Damn your hides," the man in the launch said. "If
they dont get that levee blowed pretty soon you can hunt
plenty more of them on the capitol steps at Baton
Rouge. And this is all the boat you will need and you
can say your prayers about it."

"I aint going without my boat," the convict said. He
said it calmly and with complete finality, so calm, so
final that for almost a minute nobody answered him,
they just stood looking quietly down at him as he lay,
half-naked, blistered and scarred, helpless and manacled
hand and foot, on his back, delivering his ultimatum in
a voice peaceful and quiet as that in which you talk to
your bedfellow before going to sleep. Then the man in
the launch moved; he spat quietly over the side and said
in a voice as calm and quiet as the convict's:

"All right. Bring his boat." They helped the woman,
carrying the baby and the paper-wrapped parcel, into
the launch. Then they helped the convict to his feet and
into the launch too, the shackles on his wrists and ankles
clashing. "I'd unlock you if you'd promise to behave
yourself," the man said. The convict did not answer this
at all.

"I want to hold the rope," he said.

"The rope?"

"Yes," the convict said. "The rope." So they lowered him into the stern and gave him the end of the painter after it had passed the towing cleat, and they went on. The convict did not look back. But then, he did not look forward either, he lay half sprawled, his shackled legs before him, the end of the skiff's painter in one shackled hand. The launch made two other stops; when the hazy wafer of the intolerable sun began to stand once more directly overhead there were fifteen people in the launch; and then the convict, sprawled and motionless, saw the flat brazen land begin to rise and become a greenish-black mass of swamp, bearded and convoluted, this in turn stopping short off and there spread before him an expanse of water embraced by a blue dissolution of shore line and glittering thinly under the noon, larger than he had ever seen before, the sound of the launch's engine ceasing, the hull sliding on behind its fading bow-wave. "What are you doing?" the leader said.

"It's noon," the helmsman said. "I thought we might hear the dynamite." So they all listened, the launch lost of all forward motion, rocking slightly, the glitter-broken small waves slapping and whispering at the hull, but no sound, no tremble even, came anywhere under the fierce hazy sky; the long moment gathered itself and turned on and noon was past. "All right," the leader said. "Let's go." The engine started again, the hull began to gather speed. The leader came aft and stooped over the convict, key in hand. "I guess you'll have to behave now, whether you want to or not," he said, unlocking the manacles. "Wont you?"

"Yes," the convict said. They went on; after a time the shore vanished completely and a little sea got up. The convict was free now but he lay as before, the end of the skiff's painter in his hand, bent now with three or four turns about his wrist; he turned his head now and then to look back at the towing skiff as it slewed and bounced in the launch's wake; now and then he even looked out over the lake, the eyes alone moving, the face grave and expressionless, thinking, *This is a greater immensity of water, of waste and desolation, than I have ever seen before;* perhaps not; thinking three or four hours later, the shoreline raised again and broken into a clutter of sailing sloops and power cruisers, *These are more boats than I believed existed, a maritime race of which I also had no cognizance* or perhaps not thinking it but just watching as the launch opened the shored gut of the ship canal, the low smoke of the city beyond it, then a wharf, the launch slowing in; a quiet crowd of people watching with that same forlorn passivity he had seen before and whose race he did recognise even though he had not seen Vicksburg when he passed it— the brand, the unmistakable hallmark of the violently homeless, he more so than any, who would have permitted no man to call him one of them.

"All right," the leader said to him. "Here you are."

"The boat," the convict said.

"You've got it. What do you want me to do—give you a receipt for it?"

"No," the convict said. "I just want the boat."

"Take it. Only you ought to have a bookstrap or something to carry it in." ("Carry it in?" the plump convict said. "Carry it where? Where would you have to carry it?")

He (the tall one) told that: how he and the woman disembarked and how one of the men helped him haul the skiff up out of the water and how he stood there with the end of the painter wrapped around his wrist and the man bustled up, saying, "All right. Next load! Next load!" and how he told this man too about the boat and the man cried, "Boat? Boat?" and how he (the convict) went with them when they carried the skiff over and racked, berthed, it with the others and how he lined himself up by a coca-cola sign and the arch of a draw bridge so he could find the skiff again quick when he returned, and how he and the woman (he carrying the paper-wrapped parcel) were herded into a truck and after a while the truck began to run in traffic, between close houses, then there was a big building, an armory—

"Armory?" the plump one said. "You mean a jail."

"No. It was a kind of warehouse, with people with bundles laying on the floor." And how he thought maybe his partner might be there and how he even looked about for the Cajan while waiting for a chance to get back to the door again, where the soldier was and how he got back to the door at last, the woman behind him and his chest actually against the dropped rifle.

"Gwan, gwan," the soldier said. "Get back. They'll give you some clothes in a minute. You cant walk around

the streets that way. And something to eat too. Maybe
your kinfolks will come for you by that time." And he
told that too: how the woman said,

"Maybe if you told him you had some kinfolks here
he would let us out." And how he did not; he could not
have expressed this either, it too deep, too ingrained;
he had never yet had to think it into words through all
the long generations of himself—his hill-man's sober
and jealous respect not for truth but for the power, the
strength, of lying—not to be niggard with lying but
rather to use it with respect and even care, delicate quick
and strong, like a fine and fatal blade. And how they
fetched him clothes—a blue jumper and overalls, and
then food too (a brisk starched young woman saying,
"But the baby must be bathed, cleaned. It will die if you
dont" and the woman saying, "Yessum. He might holler
some, he aint never been bathed before. But he's a good
baby.") and now it was night, the unshaded bulbs harsh
and savage and forlorn above the snorers and he rising,
gripping the woman awake, and then the window. He
told that: how there were doors in plenty, leading he
did not know where, but he had a hard time finding a
window they could use but he found one at last, he
carrying the parcel and the baby too while he climbed
through first—"You ought to tore up a sheet and slid
down it," the plump convict said. But he needed no
sheet, there were cobbles under his feet now, in the rich
darkness. The city was there too but he had not seen it
yet and would not—the low constant glare; Bienville
had stood there too, it had been the figment of an emas-

culate also calling himself Napoleon but no more,
Andrew Jackson had found it one step from Pennsyl-
vania Avenue. But the convict found it considerably
further than one step back to the ship canal and the skiff,
the coca-cola sign dim now, the draw bridge arching
spidery against the jonquil sky at dawn: nor did he tell,
any more than about the sixty-foot levee, how he got the
skiff back into the water. The lake was behind him now;
there was but one direction he could go. When he saw
the River again he knew it at once. He should have; it
was now ineradicably a part of his past, his life; it
would be a part of what he would bequeath, if that were
in store for him. But four weeks later it would look different from what it did now, and did: he (the old man)
had recovered from his debauch, back in banks again,
the Old Man, rippling placidly toward the sea, brown
and rich as chocolate between levees whose inner faces
were wrinkled as though in a frozen and aghast amazement, crowned with the rich green of summer in the
willows; beyond them, sixty feet below, slick mules
squatted against the broad pull of middle-busters in the
richened soil which would not need to be planted, which
would need only to be shown a cotton seed to sprout and
make; there would be the symmetric miles of strong
stalks by July, purple bloom in August, in September
the black fields snowed over, spilled, the middles
dragged smooth by the long sacks, the long black limber
hands plucking, the hot air filled with the whine of gins,
the September air then but now June air heavy with
locust and (the towns) the smell of new paint and the

sour smell of the paste which holds wall paper—the towns, the villages, the little lost wood landings on stilts on the inner face of the levee, the lower storeys bright and rank under the new paint and paper and even the marks on spile and post and tree of May's raging water-height fading beneath each bright silver gust of summer's loud and inconstant rain; there was a store at the levee's lip, a few saddled and rope-bridled mules in the sleepy dust, a few dogs, a handful of negroes sitting on the steps beneath the chewing tobacco and malaria medicine signs, and three white men, one of them a deputy sheriff canvassing for votes to beat his superior (who had given him his job) in the August primary, all pausing to watch the skiff emerge from the glitter-glare of the afternoon water and approach and land, a woman carrying a child stepping out, then a man, a tall man who, approaching, proved to be dressed in a faded but recently washed and quite clean suit of penitentiary clothing, stopping in the dust where the mules dozed and watching with pale cold humorless eyes while the deputy sheriff was still making toward his armpit that gesture which everyone present realised was to have produced a pistol in one flashing motion for a considerable time while still nothing came of it. It was apparently enough for the newcomer, however.

"You a officer?" he said.

"You damn right I am," the deputy said. "Just let me get this damn gun—"

"All right," the other said. "Yonder's your boat, and here's the woman. But I never did find that bastard on the cottonhouse."

Wild Palms

THIS TIME THE DOCTOR AND THE MAN CALLED HARRY walked out of the door together, onto the dark porch, into the dark wind still filled with the clashing of invisible palms. The doctor carried the whiskey—the pint bottle half full; perhaps he did not even know it was in his hand, perhaps it was only the hand and not the bottle which he shook in the invisible face of the man standing above him. His voice was cold, precise, and convinced —the puritan who some would have said was about to do what he had to do because he was a puritan, who perhaps believed himself he was about to do it to protect the ethics and sanctity of his chosen profession, but who was actually about to do it because though not old yet he believed he was too old for this, too old to be wakened at midnight and dragged, haled, unwarned and still dull with sleep, into this, this bright wild passion which had somehow passed him up when he had been young enough, worthy enough, and to whose loss he believed he had not only become reconciled but had been both fortunate and right in having been elected to lose.

"You have murdered her," he said.

"Yes," the other said, almost impatiently; this the doctor noticed now, this alone. "The hospital. Will you telephone, or—"

"Yes, murdered her! Who did this?"

"I did. Dont stand here talking. Will you tel—"

"Who did this, I say? Who performed it? I demand to know."

"I did, I tell you. Myself. In God's name, man!" He took the doctor's arm, he gripped it, the doctor felt it, felt the hand, he (the doctor) heard his own voice too:

"What?" he said. "You? *You* did it? Yourself? But I thought you were the—" *I thought you were the lover* was what he meant. *I thought you were the one who* because what he was thinking was *This is too much! There are rules! Limits! To fornication, adultery, to abortion, crime* and what he meant was *To that of love and passion and tragedy which is allowed to anyone lest he become as God Who has suffered likewise all that Satan can have known.* He even said some of it at last, flinging the other's hand violently off, not exactly as if it has been a spider or a reptile or even a piece of filth, but rather as if he had found clinging to his sleeve a piece of atheistic or Communist propaganda—something not violating so much as affronting that profound and now deathless desiccated spirit which had contrived to retire into pure morality. "This is too much!" he cried. "Stay here! Dont try to escape! You cannot hide where you will not be found!"

"Escape?" the other said. "Escape? Will you telephone for the ambulance, in God's dear name?"

"I'll telephone, never you fear!" the doctor cried. He was on the earth below the porch now, in the hard black wind, already moving away, beginning to run suddenly and heavily on his thick sedentary legs. "Dont you dare to try!" he cried back. "Dont you dare to try!" He still had the flashlight; Wilbourne watched the beam of it jouncing on toward the oleander hedge as though it too, the little futile moth-light beam, struggled too against the constant weight of the black pitiless wind. *He didn't forget that,* Wilbourne thought, watching it. *But then he probably never forgot anything in his life except that he was alive once, must have been born alive at least.* Then at that word he became aware of his heart, as though all profound terror had merely waited until he should prompt himself. He could feel the hard black wind too as he blinked after the floundering light until it passed through the hedge and vanished; he blinked steadily in the black wind, he could not stop it. *My lachrymae are not functioning,* he thought, hearing his roaring and laboring heart. *As though it were pumping sand not blood, not liquid,* he thought. *Trying to pump it. It's just this wind I think I cant breathe in, it's not that I really cant breathe, find something somewhere to breathe because apparently the heart can stand anything anything anything.*

He turned and crossed the porch. This time as before he and the black steady wind were like two creatures trying to use the same single entrance. *Only it dont really want to come in,* he thought. *Dont need to. Dont have to. It's just interfering for the fun, the hell of it.* He could feel it on the door when he touched the knob, then, close, he could hear it too, a sibilance, a whisper. It was risible, it was almost a chuckling, leaning its weight on the door along with his weight, making the door easy, too

easy, surreptitious, making its weight really felt only
when he came to close the door and this time just too
easy because so steady, just risible and chuckling; it did
not really want to come in. He closed the door, watching
the faint light which fell into the hall from the lamp
inside the bedroom suck, shift and recover steadily as
what of the wind might have remained in the house if it
had wanted to, might have been trapped inside the house
by the closing door, licked quietly out through the ultimate closing crack, risible and constant, not at all departing, and turned listening, his head slanted a little
toward the bedroom door with listening. But no sound
came from beyond it, no sound in the hall but the wind
murmuring against the door of the barren rented hall
where he stood, quiet with listening, thinking quietly, *I
guessed wrong. It's incredible, not that I should have
had to guess but that I should have guessed so wrong*
not meaning the doctor, not thinking about the doctor
now (With a part of his mind he was not using now he
could see it: the other neat, tight, brown-stained wind-
proof tongue-and-groove hall, the flashlight still burning on the table beside the hurried bag, the thick bulging varicose planted calves as he had first seen them
beneath the nightshirt, planted outraged and convinced
and unassuageable by anything else but this; he could
even hear the voice not raised but risen, a little shrill,
unappeasable too, into the telephone: "And a policeman. A *policeman*. Two if necessary. Do you hear?"
He'll wake her too, he thought, seeing this too: the
upper room, the gorgon-headed woman in the gray high-

necked gown risen onto her elbow in the stale gray bed, her head cocked to listen and without surprise, who would be hearing only what she had been expecting for four days to hear. *She will come back with him—if he himself comes back*, he thought. *If he dont just sit outside with the pistol to guard the exits. And maybe she will even be there too.*) Because this didn't matter, it was just like putting a letter into the mail; it didn't matter what box, only that he should have waited so late to mail the letter, he, after the four years and then the twenty months, the almost two years more and then done, complete. *I have made a bust even of that part of my life which I threw away*, he thought, motionless in the risible murmur of the waiting and unhurried wind, his head turned slightly toward the bedroom door with listening, thinking with that trivial layer of his mind which he did not need to use, *So it's not just the wind I cant breathe in so maybe forever after I have gained, earned, some little of suffocation*, beginning to breathe not faster but deeper, he could not stop it, each breath shallower and shallower and harder and harder and nearer and nearer the top of his lungs until in a moment it would escape the lungs altogether and there would indeed be no breath left anywhere forever, blinking steadily and painfully at the sudden granulation of his lids as though the black sand dammed forever of any moisture at which his strong heart scooped and surged were about to burst out of him through all his ducts and pores as they say the sweat of agony does, thinking. *Steady now.*

*Careful now. When she comes back this time she will
have to begin to hold on.*

He crossed the hall to the bedroom door. There was
still no sound save the wind (there was a window, the
sash did not fit; the black wind whispered and murmured at it but did not enter, it did not want to, did not
need to). She lay on her back, her eyes closed, the
nightgown (that garment which she had never owned,
never worn before) twisted about her just under the
arms, the body not sprawled, not abandoned, but on the
contrary even a little tense. The whisper of the black
wind filled the room but coming from nothing, so that
presently it began to seem to him that the sound was
rather the murmur of the lamp itself sitting on an up-
ended packing case beside the bed, the rustle and murmur of faint dingy light itself on her flesh—the waist
ever narrower than he had believed, anticipated, the
thighs merely broad since they were flat too, the swell
and neat nip of belly between the navel's flattened crease
and the neat close cupping of female hair, and nothing
else, no croaching shadow of ineradicable blackness, no
shape of death cuckolding him; nothing to see, yet it was
there, he not permitted to watch his own cuckolding but
only to look down upon the invisible pregnancy of his
horning. And then he could not breathe and he began
to back away from the door but it was too late because
she was lying on the bed looking at him.

He didn't move. He couldn't help his breathing but
he didn't move, one hand on the door frame and his foot
already lifted for the first step back, the eyes open full

upon him though still profoundly empty of sentience.
Then he saw it begin: the *I*. It was like watching a fish
rise in water—a dot, a minnow, and still increasing; in
a second there would be no more pool but all sentience.
He crossed to the bed in three strides, fast but quiet; he
put his hand flat on her chest, his voice quiet, steady,
insistent: "No, Charlotte. Not yet. You can hear me. Go
back. Go back, now. It's all right now," quiet and urgent
and contained out of his need, as though departure only
followed farewell, and good-bye was not something to
precede the going away—provided there was time for
it. "That's right," he said. "Go back. It's not time yet.
I will tell you when the time comes." And she heard him
from somewhere because at once the fish became the
minnow again and then the dot; in another second the
eyes would be empty again and blank. Only he lost her.
He watched it: the dot growing too fast this time, no
serene minnow but a vortex of cognizant pupil in the
yellow stare spinning to blackness while he watched,
the black shadow not on the belly but in the eyes. Her
teeth caught her lower lip, she rolled her head and tried
to rise, struggling against the flat of his hand on her
breast.

"I'm hurting. Jesus, where is he? Where's he gone?
Tell him to give me something. Quick."

"No," he said. "He cant. You've got to hurt. That's
what you've got to hold on to." Now it must have been
laughing; it couldn't have been anything else. She lay
back and began to thresh from hip to hip, still threshing

as he untwisted the gown and drew it down and covered her.

"I thought you said you would do the holding."

"I am. But you've got to hold on too. You've got to do most of it for a while. Just a little while. The ambulance will be here soon, but you must stay here and hurt now. Do you hear? You cant go back now."

"Then take the knife and cut it out of me. All of it. Deep. So there wont be anything left but just a shell to hold the cold air, the cold—" Her teeth, glinting in the lamplight, caught her lower lip again; a thread of blood appeared at the corner of her mouth. He took a soiled handkerchief from his hip and leaned to her but she rolled her head away from his hand. "All right," she said. "I'm holding on. You say the ambulance is coming?"

"Yes. In a minute we will hear it. Let me—" She rolled her head again away from the handkerchief.

"All right. Now get to hell out. You promised."

"No. If I leave, you wont hold on. And you've got to hold on."

"I am holding on. I'm holding on so you can go, get out of here before they come. You promised me you would. I want to see you go. I want to watch you."

"All right. But dont you want to say good-bye first?"

"All right. But Jesus God, dont touch me. It's like fire, Harry. It doesn't hurt. It's just like fire. Just dont touch me." So he knelt beside the bed; she stopped her head now; her lips lay still under his for a moment, hot and dry to the taste, with the thin sweetish taste of the blood. Then she pushed his face away with her hand, it hot and dry too, he hearing her heart still, even now, a little too fast, a little too strong. "Jesus, we had fun, didn't we, bitching, and making things? In the cold, the snow. That's what I'm thinking about. That's what I'm holding on to now: the snow, the cold, the cold. But it doesn't hurt; it's just like fire; it's just—Now go. Get to hell out. Quick." She began to roll her head again. He rose from his knees.

"All right. I'm going. But you must hold on. You will have to hold on a long time. Can you do it?"

"Yes. But go. Go quick. We've got enough money for you to get to Mobile. You can lose yourself quick there; they cant find you there. But go. Get to hell away from here quick for God's sake." This time when the teeth caught the bright thin blood spurted all the way to her chin. He didn't move at once. He was trying to remember something out of a book, years ago, of Owen Wister's, the whore in the pink ball dress who drank the laudanum and the cowboys taking turns walking her up and down the floor, keeping her on her feet, keeping her alive, remembering and forgetting it in the same instant since it would not help him. He began to move toward the door.

"All right," he said. "I'm going now. But remember, you will have to hold on by yourself then. Do you hear? Charlotte?" The yellow eyes were full on him, she released the bitten lip and as he sprang back toward the bed he heard over the chuckling murmur of the wind the two voices at the front door, the porch—the plump-calved doctor's high, almost shrill, almost breaking, that of the gray gorgon wife cold and level, at a baritone pitch a good deal more masculine than the man's voice, the two of them unorientable because of the wind like the voices of two ghosts quarrelling about nothing, he (Wilbourne) hearing them and losing them too in the same instant as he bent over the wide yellow stare in the head which had ceased to roll, above the relaxed bleeding lip. "Charlotte!" he said. "You cant go back now. You're hurting. You're hurting. It wont let you go back. You can hear me." He slapped her, fast, with two motions of the same hand. "You're hurting, Charlotte."

"Yes," she said. "You and your best doctors in New Orleans. When anybody with one mail-order stethoscope could give me something. Come on, Rat. Where are they?"

"They're coming. But you've got to hurt now. You're hurting now."

"All right. I'm holding on. But you mustn't hold him. That was all I asked. It wasn't him. Listen, Francis— See, I called you Francis. If I were lying to you do you think I would call you Francis instead of Rat?—Listen, Francis. It was the other one. Not that Wilbourne bastard. Do you think I would let that bloody bungling bastard that never even finished hospital poke around in me with a knife—" The voice stopped; there was nothing in the eyes at all now though they were still open—no minnow, no dot even—nothing. *But the heart,* he thought. *The heart.* He laid his ear to her chest, hunting the wrist pulse with one hand; he could hear it be-

fore his ear touched her, slow, strong enough still but
each beat making a curious hollow reverberation as
though the heart itself had retreated, seeing at the same
moment (his face was toward the door) the doctor enter,
still carrying the scuffed bag in one hand and in the
other a cheap-looking nickel-plated revolver such as
you could find in almost any pawnshop and which, as
far as serviceability was concerned, should still have
been there, and followed by the gray-faced Medusa-
headed woman in a shawl. Wilbourne rose, already
moving toward the doctor, his hand already extended
for the bag. "It will last this time," he said, "but the
heart's—Here. Give me the bag. What do you carry?
Strychnine?" He watched the bag as it fled, snatched,
behind the thick leg, the other hand he did not even look
at as it came up but only in the next instant, at the cheap
pistol pointed at nothing and being shaken in his face
as the whiskey bottle had been.

"Dont move!" the doctor cried.

"Put that thing down," the wife said, in that same
cold baritone. "I told you not to bring it. Give him the
bag if he wants it and can do anything with it."

"No!" the doctor cried. "I'm a doctor. He is not.
He's not even a successful criminal!" Now the gray wife
spoke to Wilbourne so abruptly that for a moment he
did not even know he was being addressed:

"Is there anything in that bag that would cure her?"

"Cure her?"

"Yes. Get her on her feet and get both of you out of

this house." The doctor turned on her now, speaking in that shrill voice on the point of breaking:

"Can't you understand that this woman is dying?"

"Let her die. Let them both die. But not in this house. Not in this town. Get them out of here and let them cut on one another and die as much as they please." Now Wilbourne watched the doctor shaking the pistol in the wife's face as the other had shaken it in his.

"I will not be interfered with!" he cried. "This woman is dying and this man must suffer for it."

"Suffer fiddlesticks," the wife said. "You're mad because he used a scalpel without having a diploma. Or did something with it the Medical Association said he mustn't. Put that thing down and give her whatever it is so she can get out of that bed. Then give them some money and call a taxi-cab, not an ambulance. Give him some of my money if you wont your own."

"Are you mad?" the doctor cried. "Are you insane?" The wife looked at him coldly with her gray face beneath the screws of gray hair.

"So you will aid and abet him to the last, wont you? I'm not surprised. I never yet saw one man fail to back up another, provided what they wanted to do was just foolish enough." Again she turned on (not to) Wilbourne with that cold abruptness which for an instant left him unaware that he was being addressed: "You haven't eaten anything, I imagine. I'm going to heat some coffee. You'll probably need it by the time he and those others get through with you."

"Thank you," Wilbourne said. "I couldn't—" But

she was already gone. He caught himself about to say, "Wait I'll show you" then forgot this without even having to think that she would know the kitchen better than he since she owned it, moving aside as the doctor passed him and went to the bed, following the doctor, watching him set the bag down then seem to discover the pistol in his hand and look about for something to lay it upon before remembering, then remembering and turning over his shoulder his dishevelled face.

"Dont you move!" he cried. "Dont you dare to move!"

"Get your stethoscope," Wilbourne said. "I had thought about something now, but maybe we had better wait. Because she will come out of it once more, wont she? She'll rally another time. Of course she will. Go on. Get it out."

"You should have thought of that before!" The doctor still watched Wilbourne, glaring, still holding the pistol while he fumbled the bag open and extracted the stethoscope; then, still holding the pistol he ducked into the pronged tubes and leaned, seeming to forget the pistol again because he actually laid it on the bed, his hand still resting upon it but unconscious of the pistol, merely supporting his leaning weight, because there was peace in the room now, the fury gone; Wilbourne could now hear the gray wife at the stove in the kitchen and he could hear the black wind again, risible, jeering, constant, inattentive, and it even seemed to him that he could hear the wild dry clashing of the palms in it. Then he heard the ambulance, the first faint mounting wail,

far away yet, on the highway from the village, and almost immediately the wife came in, carrying a cup.

"Here comes your joyride," she said. "It never had
time to get hot. But it will be something in your
stomach."

"I thank you," Wilbourne said. "I do thank you. It
wouldn't stay down, you see."

"Nonsense. Drink it."

"I do thank you." The ambulance was wailing louder,
it was coming fast, it was close now, the wail sinking into a grumble as it slowed, then rising into the wail
again. It seemed to be just outside the house, loud and
peremptory and with an illusion of speed and haste even
though Wilbourne knew it was now merely crawling up
the rutted weed-choked lane which led from the highway
to the house; this time when it sank to the groan it was
just outside the house, the sound now possessing a baffled
grunting tone almost like the voice of an animal, a large
one, bewildered, maybe even injured. "I do thank you.
I realise there is always a certain amount of inevitable
cleaning up in vacating a house. It would be foolish to
add to it this late." Now he heard the feet on the porch,
hearing them above his heart, the profound strong cease-
less shallow dredging at air, breath on the point of escaping his lungs altogether; now (there was no knock)
they were in the hall, the trampling; three men entered,
in civilian clothes—a youth with a close cap of curly
hair, in a polo shirt and no socks, a neat wiry man of no
age and fully dressed even to a pair of horn glasses,
pushing a wheeled stretcher, and behind them a third

man with the indelible mark of ten thousand Southern
deputy sheriffs, urban and suburban—the snapped hat-
brim, the sadist's eyes, the slightly and unmistakably
bulged coat, the air not swaggering exactly but of a
formally pre-absolved brutality. The two men with the
stretcher wheeled it up to the bed in a business-like manner; it was the officer whom the doctor addressed, indi-
cating Wilbourne with his hand, and now Wilbourne
knew the other had really forgot that the hand still held
the pistol.

"This is your prisoner," the doctor said. "I will pre-
fer formal charges against him as soon as we get to
town. As soon as I can."

"Look out, Doc— Evening, Miss Martha," the officer
said. "Put that thing down. It might go off at any time.
That fellow you got it from might of pulled the trigger
before he turned it over to you." The doctor looked at
the pistol, then Wilbourne seemed to remember him
stowing it methodically into the scuffed bag along with
the stethoscope; he just seemed to remember this because he had followed the stretcher to the bed.

"Easy now," he said. "Dont rouse her up. She
wont—"

"I'll take charge of this," the doctor said, in that
weary voice which had become peaceful at last after a
fashion, as if it had worn itself out yet which would
have, could have risen again at need quick and easy, as
if it had renewed itself, renewed the outragement. "This
case has been turned over to me, remember that. I didn't
ask for it." He approached the bed (it was now that

Wilbourne seemed to remember him putting the pistol
into the bag) and lifted Charlotte's wrist. "Go as easy
with her as you can. But hurry. Doctor Richardson will
be there and I will follow in my car." The two men lifted
Charlotte onto the stretcher. It was on rubber-tired
wheels; with the hatless youth pushing it seemed to cross
the room and vanish into the hall with incredible rapidity, as though sucked there and not pushed (the very
wheels making a sucking sound on the floor), by no
human agency but by time perhaps, by some vent-pipe
through which the irrevocable seconds were fleeing,
crowding; even the night itself.

"All right," the officer said. "What's your name?
Wilson?"

"Yes," Wilbourne said. It went through the hall too
that way, sucked through, where the wiry man now had
a flashlight; the risible dark wind chuckled and murmured into the open door, leaning its weight against him
like a black palpy hand, he leaning into it, onto it. There
would be the porch, the steps beyond. "She's light,"
Wilbourne said in a thin anxious voice. "She's lost a lot
of weight lately. I could carry her if they would—"

"They can too," the officer said. "Besides, they are
being paid for it. Take it easy."

"I know. But that short one, that small one with the
light—"

"He saves his strength for this. He likes it. You dont
want to hurt his feelings. Take it easy."

"Look," Wilbourne said thinly, murmuring, "why
dont you put the handcuffs on me? Why dont you?"

"Do you want them?" the officer said. And now the stretcher without stopping sucked off the porch too, into space, still on the same parallel plane as though it possessed displacement perhaps but no weight; it didn't even pause, the white shirt and trousers of the youth seemed merely to walk behind it as it moved on behind the flashlight, toward the corner of the house, toward what the man from whom he had rented the house called the drive. Now he could hear the threshing of the invisible palms, the wild dry sound of them.

The hospital was a low building, vaguely Spanish (or Los Angeles), of stucco, almost hidden by a massy lushness of oleander. There were more of the shabby palms too, the ambulance turning in at speed, the siren's wail dying into the grunting animal-like fall, the tires dry and sibilant in oyster shells; when he emerged from the ambulance he could hear the palms rustling and hissing again as if they were being played upon by a sand-blower and he could smell the sea still, the same black wind, but not so strong since the sea was four miles away, the stretcher coming out fast and smooth again as though sucked out, the feet of the four of them crisp in the dry fragile shells; and now in the corridor he began to blink again at his sanded lids, painfully in the electric light, the stretcher sucking on, the wheels whispering on the linoleum, so that it was between two blinks that he saw that the stretcher was now propelled by two nurses in uniform, a big one and a little one, he thinking how apparently there was no such thing as a matched stretcher team, how apparently all the stretchers in the

world must be propelled not by two physical bodies in
accord but rather by two matched desires to be present
and see what was going on. Then he saw an open door
fierce with light, a surgeon already in operating tunic
beside it, the stretcher turning in, sucked through the
door, the surgeon looking at him once, not with curiosity
but as you memorise a face, then turning and following
the stretcher as Wilbourne was about to speak to him,
the door (it sounded rubber-tired too) clapping to
soundlessly in his face, almost slapping his face, the
officer at his elbow saying, "Take it easy." Then there
was another nurse; he had not heard her, she did not
look at him at all, speaking briefly to the officer.
"Okay," the officer said. He touched Wilbourne's elbow.
"Straight ahead. Just take it easy."

"But let me—"

"Sure. Just take it easy." It was another door, the
nurse turning and stepping aside, her skirts crisp and
sibilant too like the oyster shells; she did not look at
him at all. They entered, an office, a desk, another man
in sterilised cap and tunic seated at the desk with a blank
form and a fountain pen. He was older than the first
one. He did not look at Wilbourne either.

"Name?" he said.

"Charlotte Rittenmeyer."

"Miss?"

"Mistress." The man at the desk wrote on the pad.

"Husband?"

"Yes."

"Name?"

"Francis Rittenmeyer." Then he told the address too.
The pen flowed, smooth and crisp. *Now it's the fountain
pen I cant breathe in,* Wilbourne thought. "Can I—"

"He will be notified." Now the man at the desk looked
up at him. He wore glasses, the pupils behind them
distorted slightly and perfectly impersonal. "How do
you account for it? Instruments not clean?"

"They were clean."

"You think so."

"I know it."

"Your first attempt?"

"No. Second."

"Other one come off? But you wouldn't know."

"Yes. I know. It did."

"Then how do you account for this failure?" He
could have answered that: *I loved her.* He could have
said it: *A miser would probably bungle the blowing of
his own safe too. Should have called in a professional,
a cracksman who didn't care, didn't love the very iron
flanks that held the money.* So he said nothing at all,
and after a moment the man at the desk looked down
and wrote again, the pen travelling smoothly across the
card. He said, still writing, without looking up: "Wait
outside."

"I aint to take him in now?" the officer said.

"No." The man at the desk still did not look up.

"Couldn't I—" Wilbourne said. "Will you let—" The
pen stopped, but for a time longer the man at the desk
looked at the card, perhaps reading what he had written. Then he looked up.

"Why? She wouldn't know you."

"But she might come back. Rouse one more time. So I could—we could—" The other looked at him. The eyes were cold. They were not impatient, not quite palpably patient. They merely waited until Wilbourne's voice ceased. Then the man at the desk spoke:

"Do you think she will—Doctor?" For a moment Wilbourne blinked painfully at the neat scrawled card beneath the day-colored desk lamp, the clean surgeon's hand holding the uncapped pen beside it.

"No," he said quietly. The man at the desk looked down again, at the card too since the hand holding the pen moved to it and wrote again.

"You will be notified." Now he spoke to the officer, not looking up, writing steadily: "That's all."

"I better get him out of here before that husband blows in with a gun or something, hadn't I, Doc?" the officer said.

"You will be notified," the man at the desk repeated without looking up.

"All right, Jack," the officer said. There was a bench, slotted and hard, like in old-time open trolley cars. From it he could see the rubber-tired door. It was blank, it looked final and impregnable as an iron portcullis; he saw with a kind of amazement that even from this angle it hung in its frame by only one side, lightly, so that for three-quarters of its circumference there was an unbroken line of Klieg light. *But she might*, he thought. *She might*. "Jesus," the officer said. He held an unlighted cigarette in his hand now (Wilbourne had felt the movement against his elbow). "—Jesus, you played—What did you say your name was? Webster?"

"Yes," Wilbourne said. *I could get there. I could trip him if necessary and get there. Because I would know. I would. Surely they would not.*

"You played hell, didn't you. Using a knife. I'm old-fashioned; the old way still suits me. I dont want variety."

"Yes," Wilbourne said. There was no wind in here, no sound of it, though it seemed to him that he could smell, if not the sea, at least the dry and stubborn lingering of it in the oyster shells in the drive: and then suddenly the corridor became full of sound, the myriad minor voices of human fear and travail which he knew, remembered—the carbolised vacuums of linoleum and rubber soles like wombs into which human beings fled before something of suffering but mostly of terror, to surrender in little monastic cells all the burden of lust and desire and pride, even that of functional independence, to become as embryos for a time yet retaining still a little of the old incorrigible earthy corruption—the light sleeping at all hours, the boredom, the wakeful and fretful ringing of little bells between the hours of midnight and the dead slowing of dawn (finding perhaps at least this good use for the cheap money with which the world was now glutted and cluttered); this for a while, then to be born again, to emerge renewed, to bear the world's weight for another while as long as courage lasted. He could hear them up and down the corridor—the tinkle of the bells, the immediate sibilance

of rubber heels and starched skirts, the querulous murmur of voices about nothing. He knew it well: and now
still another nurse came down the hall, already looking
full at him, slowing as she passed, looking at him, her
head turning as she went on like an owl's head, her eyes
quite wide and filled with something beyond just curiosity and not at all shrinking or horror, going on. The
officer was running his tongue around inside his teeth as
though seeking the remnants of food; possibly he had
been eating somewhere when the call came. He still held
the unlighted cigarette.

"These doctors and nurses," he said. "What a fellow
hears about hospitals. I wonder if there's as much laying
goes on in them as you hear about."

"No," Wilbourne said. "There never is any place."

"That's so. But you think of a place like a hospital.
All full of beds every which way you turn. And all the
other folks flat on their backs where they cant bother
you. And after all doctors and nurses are men and
women. And smart enough to take care of themselves or
they wouldn't be doctors and nurses. You know how it is.
How you think."

"Yes," Wilbourne said. "You've just told me." *Because after all*, he thought, *they are gentlemen. They
must be. They are stronger than we are. Above all this.
Above clowning. They dont need to be anything else but
gentlemen.* And now the second doctor or surgeon—the
one of the fountain pen—came out of the office and
down the corridor, the skirts of his tunic sucking and
snicking behind him too. He did not look at Wilbourne

at all, even when Wilbourne, watching his face, rose as
he passed and stepped toward him, about to speak, the
officer rising hurriedly too, surging up. Then the doctor
merely paused long enough to look back at the officer
with one cold brief irascible glance through the glasses.

"Aren't you in charge of this man?" he said.

"Sure, Doc," the officer said.

"Then what's the trouble?"

"Come on now, Watson," the officer said. "Take it
easy, I tell you." The doctor turned; he had scarcely
paused even. "How about smoking, Doc?" The doctor
didn't answer at all. He went on, his smock flicking.
"Come on here," the officer said. "Sit down before you
get yourself in a jam or something." Again the door went
inward on its rubber tires and returned, clapped silently
to with that iron finality and that illusion of iron im-
pregnability which was so false since even from here
he could see how it swung in its frame by one side only,
so that a child, a breath, could move it. "Listen," the
officer said. "Just take it easy. They'll fix her up. That
was Doc Richardson himself. They brought a sawmill
nigger in here couple three years ago where somebody
hit him across the guts with a razor in a crap game.
Well, what does Doc Richardson do, opens him up, cuts
out the bad guts, sticks the two ends together like you'd
vulcanise an inner tube, and the nigger's back at work
right now. Of course he aint got but one gut and it aint
but two feet long so he has to run for the bushes almost
before he quits chewing. But he's all right. Doc'll fix her
up the same way. Aint that better than nothing? Huh?"

"Yes," Wilbourne said. "Yes. Do you suppose we could go outside a while?" The officer rose with alacrity, the cigarette still unlighted in his hand.

"That's an idea. We could smoke then." But then he could not.

"You go on. I'll stay right here. I'm not going to leave. You know that."

"Well, I dont know. Maybe I could stand at the door yonder and smoke."

"Yes. You can watch me from there." He looked up and down the corridor, at the doors. "Do you know where I could go if I get sick?"

"Sick?"

"Should have to vomit."

"I'll call a nurse and ask her."

"No. Never mind. I wont need it. I dont suppose I've got anything more to lose. Worth the trouble. I'll stay right here until they call me." So the officer went on down the corridor, on past the door hung in its three fierce slashes of light, and on toward the entrance through which they had come. Wilbourne watched the match snap under his thumb-nail and flare against his face, beneath the hat-brim, face and hat slanted to the match (not a bad face either exactly, just that of a fourteen-year-old boy who had to use a razor, who had begun too young to carry the authorised pistol too long), the entrance door apparently still open because the smoke, the first puff of it, streamed back up the corridor, fading: so that Wilbourne discovered that he really could smell the sea, the black shallow slumbering

Sound without surf which the black wind blew over. Up
the corridor, beyond an elbow, he could hear the voices
of two nurses, two nurses not two patients, two females
but not necessarily two women even, then beyond the
same elbow one of the little bells tinkled, fretful,
peremptory, the two voices murmuring on, then they
both laughed, two nurses laughing not two women, the
little querulous bell becoming irascible and frenzied,
the laughter continuing for half a minute longer above
the bell, then the rubber soles on the linoleum, hissing
faint and fast; the bell ceased. It was the sea he smelled;
there was the taste of the black beach the wind blew
over in it, in his lungs, up near the top of his lungs,
going through that again but then he had expected to
have to, each fast strong breath growing shallower and
shallower as if his heart had at last found a receptacle,
a dumping-place, for the black sand it dredged and
pumped at: and now he got up too, not going anywhere;
he just got up without intending to, the officer at the entrance turning at once, snapping the cigarette backward.
But Wilbourne made no further move and the officer
slowed; he even paused at the light-slashed door and
flattened his hat-brim against it, against the crack for
a moment. Then he came on. He came on, because Wilbourne saw him; he saw the officer as you see a lamp
post which happens to be between you and the street
because the rubber-tired door had opened again, outward this time (*The Kliegs are off*, he thought. *They are
off. They are off now.*) and the two doctors emerged, the
door clashing soundlessly to behind them and oscillat-

ing sharply once but opening again before it could have
resumed, re-entered immobility, to produce two nurses
though he saw them only with that part of vision which
still saw the officer because he was watching the faces
of the two doctors coming up the corridor and talking to
one another in clipped voices through their mouth-pads,
their smocks flicking neatly like the skirts of two women,
passing him without a glance and he was sitting down
again because the officer at his elbow said, "That's right.
Take it easy," and he found that he was sitting, the two
doctors going on, pinch-waisted like two ladies, the
skirts of the smocks snicking behind them, and then one
of the nurses passed too, in a face-pad also, not looking at him either, her starched skirts rustling on, he
(Wilbourne) sitting on the hard bench, listening: so that
for a moment his heart evacuated him, beating strong
and slow and steady but remote, leaving him globed in
silence, in a round vacuum where only the remembered
wind murmured, to listen in, for the rubber soles to
sibilate in, the nurse stopping at last beside the bench
and now he looked up after a space.

"You can go in now," she said.

"All right," he said. But he didn't move at once. *It's
the same one who didn't look at me*, he thought. *She's
not looking at me now. Only she is looking at me now.*
Then he got up; it was all right, the officer rising too,
the nurse looking at him now.

"Do you want me to go in with you?"

"All right." It was all right. Probably a breath would
do it yet when he put his hand on the door he found that

his whole weight would not do it, that is, he could not seem to get any of his weight into it, the door actually like a fixed iron plate in the wall except at that moment it fled suddenly before him on its rubber tires and he saw the nurse's hand and arm and the operating table, the shape of Charlotte's body just indicated and curiously flattened beneath the sheet. The Kliegs were off, the standards shoved away into a corner and only a single dome light burned, and there was another nurse—he had not remembered four of them—drying her hands at a sink. But she dropped the towel into a bin at that moment and passed him, that is, walked into then out of his vision, and was gone. There was a blower, a ventilator, going somewhere near the ceiling too, invisible or at least concealed, camouflaged, then he reached the table, the nurse's hand came and folded back the sheet and after a moment he looked back past her, blinking his dry painful eyelids, to where the officer stood in the door. "It's all right now," he said. "He can smoke now, cant he?"

"No," the nurse said.

"Never mind," he said. "You'll be through soon. Then you—"

"Come," the nurse said. "You only have a minute." Only this was not a cool wind blowing into the room but a hot one being forced out, so there was no smell in it of black sand it had blown over. But it was a wind, steady, he could feel it and see it, a lock of the dark savagely short hair stirring in it, heavily because the hair was still wet, still damp, between the closed eyes

and the neat surgeon's knot in the tape which supported
her lower jaw. Only it was more than this. It was more
than just a slackening of joints and muscles, it was a
collapsing of the entire body as undammed water col
lapses, arrested for the moment for him to look at
but still seeking that profound and primal level much
lower than that of the walking and upright, lower than
the prone one of the little death called sleep, lower even
than the paper-thin spurning sole; the flat earth itself
and even this not low enough, spreading, disappearing,
slow at first then increasing and at last with incredible
speed: gone, vanished, no trace left above the insatiable
dust. The nurse touched his arm. "Come," she said.

"Wait," he said; "wait." But he had to step back;
it came fast as before, the same stretcher on its rubber
tires, the wiry man hatless now too, his hair parted
neatly with water, brushed forward then curved back
at the brow like an old time barkeeper's, the flashlight
in his hip pocket, the rim of his coat caught up behind
it, the stretcher wheeling rapidly up broadside to the
table as the nurse drew the sheet up again. "I wont
need to help those two," he said. "Will I?"

"No," the nurse said. There was no especial shape
beneath the sheet now at all and it came onto the stretcher
as if it had no weight either. The stretcher whispered
into motion again, wheeling sibilantly, sucking through
the door again when the officer now stood with his hat
in his hand. Then it was gone. He could hear it for a
moment longer. Then he could not. The nurse reached
her hand to the wall, a button clicked and the hum of

the blower stopped. It cut short off as if it had run full-
tilt into a wall, blotted out by a tremendous silence which
roared down upon him like a wave, a sea, and there was
nothing for him to hold to, picking him up, tossing and
spinning him and roaring on, leaving him blinking
steadily and painfully at his dry granulated lids.
"Come," the nurse said. "Doctor Richardson says you
can have a drink."

"Sure, Morrison." The officer put his hat back on.
"Just take it easy."

The jail was somewhat like the hospital save that
it was of two storeys, square, and there were no oleanders. But the palm was there. It was just outside his
window, bigger, more shabby; when he and the officer
passed beneath it to enter, with no wind to cause it it
had set up a sudden frenzied clashing as though they
had startled it, and twice more during the night while
he stood, shifting his hands from time to time as that
portion of the bars which they clasped grew warm and
began to sweat on his palms, it clashed again in that
brief sudden inexplicable flurry. Then the tide began
to fall in the river and he could smell that too—the
sour smell of salt flats where oyster shells and the heads
of shrimp rotted, and hemp and old piling. Then dawn
began (he had been hearing the shrimp boats putting
out for some time) and he could see the draw bridge on
which the railroad to New Orleans crossed standing
suddenly against the paling sky and he heard the train
from New Orleans and watched the approaching smoke
then the train itself crawling across the bridge, high and

toylike and pink like something bizarre to decorate a cake with, in the flat sun that was already hot. Then the train was gone, the pink smoke. The palm beyond the window began to murmur, dry and steady, and he felt the cool morning breeze from the sea, steady and filled with salt, clean and iodinic in the cell above the smell of creosote and tobacco-spit and old vomit; the sour smell of the flats went away and now there would be a glitter on the tide-chopped water, the gars roiling sluggishly up and then down again among the floating garbage. Then he heard feet on the stairs and the jailer entered with a tin mug of coffee and a piece of factory-made coffee cake. "You want anything else?" he said. "Any meat?"

"Thanks," Wilbourne said. "Just the coffee. Or if you could get me some cigarettes. I haven't had any since yesterday."

"I'll leave you this until I go out." The jailer produced a cloth tobacco-sack and papers from his shirt. "Can you roll them?"

"I dont know," Wilbourne said. "Yes. Thanks. This will be fine." But he didn't make much of a job of it. The coffee was weak, oversweet and hot, too hot to drink or even hold in the hand, possessing seemingly a dynamic inherent inexhaustible quality of renewable heat impervious even to its own fierce radiation. So he set the cup on his stool and sat on the cot's edge above it; without realising it he had assumed the immemorial attitude of all misery, crouching, hovering not in grief but in complete guttish concentration above a scrap, a bone which would require protection not from anything which walked upright but from creatures which moved on the same parallel plane with the protector and the protected, pariah too, which would snap and snarl with the protector for it in the dust. He poured from the cloth sack into the creased paper as he knew, without being able to remember at all when and where he had seen the process, it should be done, watching in mild alarm as the tobacco sprayed off the paper in the light wind which blew in the window, turning his body to shelter the paper, realising that his hand was beginning to tremble though not concerned about it yet, laying the sack carefully and blindly aside, watching the tobacco as if he were holding the grains in the paper by the weight of his eyes, putting the other hand to the paper and finding they were both trembling now, the paper parting suddenly between his hands with an almost audible report. His hands were shaking badly now; he filled the second paper with a terrific concentration of will, not of desire for tobacco but just to make the cigarette; he deliberately raised his elbows from his knees and held the filled paper before his calm unshaven faintly haggard face until the trembling stopped. But as soon as he relaxed them to roll the tobacco into the paper they began to tremble again but this time he did not even pause, turning the tobacco carefully into the paper, the tobacco raining faintly and steadily from either end of the paper but the paper turning on. He had to hold it in both hands to lick it and then as soon as his tongue touched the paper his head seemed to catch from the contact the same faint uncontrollable

jerking and he sat for an instant, looking at what he had
accomplished—the splayed raddled tube already half
empty of tobacco and almost too damp to take fire. It
took both hands to hold the match to it too, it not smoke
but a single thin lance of heat, of actual fire, which shot
into his throat. Nevertheless, the cigarette in his right
hand and his left hand gripping his right wrist, he took
two more draws before the coal ran too far up the dry
side of the paper to draw again and dropped it, about
to set his foot on it before he remembered, noticed,
that he was still barefoot, and so letting it burn while
he sat looking at the coffee mug with a kind of despair,
who had shown none before this and perhaps had not
even begun to feel it yet, then taking up the mug, holding it as he had held the cigarette, wrist in hand, and
brought it to his mouth, concentrated not on the coffee
but on the drinking of it so that he perhaps forgot to
remember that the coffee was too hot to drink, making
contact between the cup-rim and his steadily and faintly
jerking head, gulping at the still wellnigh scalding
liquid, driven back each time by the heat, blinking, gulping again, blinking, a spoonful of the coffee sloshing out
of the cup and onto the floor, spashing over his feet and
ankles like a handful of dropped needles or maybe ice
particles, realising that he had begun to blink again too
and setting the mug carefully—it took both hands to
make contact with the stool too—on the stool again and
sitting over it again, hunched a little and blinking steadily
at that granulation behind his lids, hearing the two pair
of feet on the stairs this time though he did not even

look toward the door until he heard it open then clash again then looking around and up, at the double-breasted coat (it was of gray palm beach now), the face above it freshy shaved but which had not slept either, thinking (Wilbourne), *He had so much more to do. I just had to wait. He had to get out at a minute's notice and find someone to stay with the children.* Rittenmeyer carried the suitcase—that one which had come out from under the cot in the intern's quarters a year ago and had traveled to Chicago and Wisconsin and Chicago and Utah and San Antonio and New Orleans again and now to jail—and he came and set it beside the cot. But even then the hand at the end of the smooth gray sleeve was not done, the hand going now inside the coat.

"There are your clothes," he said. "I have made your bond. They will let you out this morning." The hand emerged and dropped onto the cot a sheaf of banknotes folded neatly twice. "It's the same three hundred dollars. You carried it long enough to have gained adverse possession. It should get you a long way. Far enough, anyhow. I'd say Mexico, but then you can probably stay hidden anywhere if you're careful. But there wont be any more. Understand that. This is all."

"Jump it?" Wilbourne said. "Jump the bail?"

"Yes!" Rittenmeyer said violently. "Get to hell away from here. I'll buy you a railroad ticket and send it to you—"

"I'm sorry," Wilbourne said.

"—New Orleans; you could even ship out on a boat—"

"I'm sorry," Wilbourne said. Rittenmeyer ceased. He was not looking at Wilbourne; he was not looking at anything. After a moment he said quietly:

"Think of her."

"I wish I could stop. I wish I could. No I dont. Maybe that's it. Maybe that's the reason—" Maybe that was; that was the first time when he almost touched it. But not yet: and that was all right too; it would return; he would find it, hold it, when the time was ready.

"Then think about me," Rittenmeyer said.

"I wish I could stop that too. I feel—"

"Not me!" the other said, with that sudden violence again; "dont you feel sorry for me. See? See?" And there was something else but he didn't say it, couldn't or wouldn't. He began to shake too, in the neat dark sober beautiful suit, murmuring, "Jesus. Jesus. Jesus."

"Maybe I'm sorry because you cant do anything. And I know why you cant. Anybody else would know why you cant. But that doesn't help any. And I could do it and that would help some, not much maybe but some. Only I cant either. And I know why I cant too. I think I do. Only I just havent—." He ceased too. He said quietly: "I'm sorry." The other ceased to tremble; he spoke as quietly as Wilbourne:

"So you wont go."

"Maybe if you could tell me why," Wilbourne said. But the other didn't answer. He took an immaculate handkerchief from his breast pocket and wiped his face carefully with it and Wilbourne noticed too that the morning breeze from the sea had dropped, gone on, as if the bright still cumulus-stippled bowl of sky and earth were an empty globe, a vacuum, and what wind there was was not enough to fill it but merely ran back and forth inside it with no schedule, obeying no laws, unpredictable and coming from and going nowhere, like a drove of bridleless horses in an empty plain. Rittenmeyer went to the door and rattled it, not looking back. The jailer appeared and unlocked the door. He was not going to look back. "You've forgotten the money," Wilbourne said. The other turned and came back and took up the neat fold of notes. After a moment he looked at Wilbourne.

"So you wont do it," he said. "You wont."

"I'm sorry," Wilbourne said. *Only if he had just told me why*, Wilbourne thought. *Maybe I would have*. Only he knew he would not have. Yet he continued to think it from time to time while the last days of that June accomplished and became July—the dawns while he listened to the heavy beat of the shrimper engines standing down the river toward the Sound, the brief cool hour of morning while the sun was still at his back, the long glare of brazen afternoons while the salt-impinged sun slanted full and fierce into his window, printing his face and upper body with the bars to which he held—and he had even learned to sleep again, finding sometimes that he had slept between two shiftings of his hands upon the sweating bars. Then he stopped thinking it. He didn't know when; he did not even remember that Rittenmeyer's visit had gone completely out of his mind.

One day—it was toward sunset, how he had failed to

see it before he did not know, it had been there twenty
years—he saw, beyond the flat one-storey border of the
river, across the river and toward the sea, the concrete
hull of one of the emergency ships built in 1918 and
never finished, the hull, the hulk; it had never moved,
the ways rotted out from under it years ago, leaving it
sitting on a mudflat beside the bright glitter of the river's
mouth with a thin line of drying garments across the
after well deck. The sun was setting behind it now and
he could not distinguish much, but the next morning he
discovered the projecting slant of stove pipe with smoke
coming out of it and he could distinguish the color of
the garments flapping in the morning sea-wind and
watched later a tiny figure which he knew to be a woman
taking the garments from the line, believing he could
distinguish the gesture with which she put the clothes
pins one by one into her mouth, and he thought, *If we
had known it we could probably have lived there for
the four days and saved ten dollars*, thinking, *Four days.
It could not possibly have been just four days. It could
not;* and watching, one evening saw the dory come alongside and the man mount the ladder with a long skein of
net cascading downward from his climbing shoulder,
fragile and fairy-like, and watched the man mend the net
under a morning's sun, sitting on the poop, the net across
his knees, the sun on the mazy blond webbing tawnily
silver. And a moon began and waxed nightly while he
stood there, and he stood there in the dying light while
night by night it waned; and one afternoon he saw the
flags, set one above another, rigid and streaming from

the slender mast above the Government station at the river mouth, against a flat steel-colored scudding sky and all that night a buoy outside the river moaned and bellowed and the palm beyond the window threshed and clashed and just before dawn, in a driving squall, the tail of the hurricane struck. Not the hurricane; it was galloping off somewhere in the Gulf, just the tail of it, a flick of the mane in passing, driving up the shore ten feet of roiled and yellow tide which did not fall for twenty hours and driving fiercely through the wild frenzied palm which still sounded dry and across the roof of the cell, so that all that second night he could hear the boom of seas against the breakwater in the crashing darkness and the buoy too, gurgling now between bellows; he could even seem to hear the roar of water streaming from it as it surged up again with each choking cry, the rain driving on, into the next dawn but with less fury now, on across the flat land before the east wind. It would be even quieter inland, it would become only a bright silver summer murmur among the heavy decorous trees, upon the clipped sward; it would be clipped; he could imagine it, it would be a good deal like the park where he had waited, maybe even with children and nurses at times, the best, the very best; there would even be a headstone soon, at just exactly the right time, when restored earth and decorum stipulated, telling nothing; it would be clipped and green and quiet, the body, the shape of it under the drawn sheet, flat and small and moving in the hands of two men as if without weight though it did, nevertheless bearing and quiet be-

neath the iron weight of earth. *Only that cant be all of it,*
he thought. *It cant be. The waste. Not of meat, there is al-*
ways plenty of meat. They found that out twenty years
ago preserving nations and justifying mottoes—granted
the nations the meat preserved are worth the preserving
with the meat it took gone. But memory. Surely memory
exists independent of the flesh. But this was wrong too.
Because it wouldn't know it was memory, he thought. *It*
wouldn't know what it was it remembered. So there's
got to be the old meat, the old frail eradicable meat for
memory to titillate.

That was the second time he almost got it. But it
escaped him again. But he was not trying yet; it was
still all right, he was not worried; it would return when
the time was ready and even stand still to his hand. Then
one night he was allowed a bath, and a barber (they
had taken his razor blades away from him) came early
the next morning and shaved him, and in a new shirt and
manacled to an officer on one side and his court-desig-
nated lawyer on the other he walked through the still
early sun, up the street where people—malaria-ridden
men from the sawmill swamps and the wind- and sun-
bitten professional shrimpers—turned to look after
him, toward the courthouse from the balcony of which
a bailiff was already crying. It was like the jail in its
turn, of two storeys, of the same stucco, the same smell
of creosote and tobacco spittle but not the vomit, set
in a grassless plot with a half dozen palms and oleanders
again too, blooming pink and white above a low thick
mass of lantana. Then an entry filled yet, for a while yet,

with shadow and a cellar-like coolness, the tobacco stronger, the air filled with a steady human sound, not exactly speech but that droning murmur which might have been the very authentic constant unsleeping murmur of functioning pores. They mounted stairs, a door; he walked up an aisle between filled benches while heads turned and the bailiff's voice still chanted from the balcony, and sat at a table between his lawyer and the officer then a moment later rose and stood again while the gownless judge in a linen suit and the high black shoes of an old man came with a short quick purposeful stride and took the Bench. It did not take long, it was businesslike, brief, twenty-two minutes to get a jury, his appointed lawyer (a young man with a round moon face and myópic eyes behind glasses, in a crumpled linen suit) challenging monotonously but it just took twenty-two minutes, the judge sitting high behind a pine counter grained and stained to resemble mahogany with his face which was not a lawyer's face at all but that of a Methodist Sunday School superintendent who on week days was a banker and probably a good banker, a shrewd banker, thin, with neat hair and a neat moustache and old-fashioned gold-rimmed spectacles. "How does the indictment read?" he said. The clerk read it, his voice droning, almost drowsy among the redundant verbiage:
". . . against the peace and dignity of the State of Mississippi . . . manslaughter . . ." A man rose at the far end of the table. He wore a suit of crumpled, almost disreputable, seersucker. He was quite fat and his was the lawyer's face, a handsome face, almost noble,

cast for footlights, forensic shrewd and agile: the District Attorney.

"We believe we can prove murder, Your Honor."

"This man is not indicted for murder, Mr. Gower. You should know that. Arraign the accused." Now the plump young lawyer rose. He had neither the older one's stomach nor the lawyer's face, not yet anyway.

"Guilty, Your Honor," he said. And now Wilbourne heard it from behind him—the long expulsion, the sigh.

"Is the accused trying to throw himself upon the mercy of this Court?" the judge said.

"I just plead guilty, Your Honor," Wilbourne said. He heard it again behind him, louder, but already the judge was hammering sharply with his child's croquet mallet.

"Dont speak from there!" he said. "Does the accused wish to throw himself on the mercy of the Court?"

"Yes, Your Honor," the young lawyer said.

"Then you dont need to make a case, Mr. Gower. I will instruct the jury—" This time it was no sigh. Wilbourne heard the caught breath, then it was almost a roar, not that loud of course, not yet, the little hard wooden mallet furious against the wood and the bailiff shouting something too, and there was movement, a surging sound of feet in it too; a voice cried, "That's it! Go ahead! Kill him!" and Wilbourne saw it—the gray buttoned coat (the same one) moving steadily toward the Bench, the face, the outrageous face: the man who without any warning had had to stand the wrong sort of suffering, the one suffering for which he was not fitted, who even now must be saying to himself, *But why me? Why? What have I done? What in the world can I have done in my life?* coming steadily on then stopping and beginning to speak, the roar cutting short off as he opened his mouth:

"Your Honor—If the Court please—"

"Who is this?" the judge said.

"I am Francis Rittenmeyer," Rittenmeyer said. Now it was a roar again, the gavel going again, the judge himself shouting now, shouting the roar into silence:

"Order! Order! One more outbreak like this and I will clear the room! Disarm that man!"

"I'm not armed," Rittenmeyer said. "I just want—" But already the bailiff and two other men were upon him, the smooth gray sleeves pinioned while they slapped at his pockets and sides.

"He's not armed, Your Honor," the bailiff said. The judge turned upon the District Attorney, trembling too, a neat orderly man too old for this too.

"What is the meaning of this clowning, Mr. Gower?"

"I dont know, Your Honor. I didn't—"

"You didn't summons him?"

"I didn't consider it necessary. Out of consideration for his—"

"If the Court please," Rittenmeyer said. "I just want to make a—" The judge lifted his hand; Rittenmeyer ceased. He stood motionless, his face calm as a carving, with something about it of the carved faces on Gothic cathedrals, the pale eyes possessing something of the same unpupilled marble blankness. The judge stared at

the District Attorney. It (the District Attorney's) was
the lawyer's face now, completely, completely watchful,
completely alert, the thinking going fast and secret behind it. The judge looked at the young lawyer, the plump
one, hard. Then he looked at Rittenmeyer. "This case
is closed," he said. "But if you still wish to make a
statement, you may do so." Now there was no sound at
all, not even that of breathing that Wilbourne could hear
save his own and that of the young lawyer beside him,
as Rittenmeyer moved toward the witness box. "This
case is closed," the judge said. "The accused is waiting
sentence. Make your statement from there." Rittenmeyer
stopped. He was not looking at the judge, he was not
looking at anything, his face calm, impeccable, outrageous.

"I wish to make a plea," he said. For a moment the
judge did not move, staring at Rittenmeyer, the gavel
still clutched in his fist like a sabre, then he leaned slowly
forward, staring at Rittenmeyer: and Wilbourne heard
it begin, the long in-sucking, the gathering of amazement and incredulity.

"You what?" the judge said. "A what? A plea? For
this man? This man who wilfully and deliberately performed an operation on your wife which he knew might
cause her death and which did?" And now it did roar,
in waves, renewed; he could hear the feet in it and the
separate screaming voices, the officers of the Court
charging into the wave like a football team: a vortex
of fury and turmoil about the calm immobile outrageous
face above the smooth beautifully cut coat: "Hang them!

Hang them both!" "Lock them up together! Let the
son of a bitch work on him this time with the knife!"
roaring on above the trampling and screaming, dying
away at last but still not ceasing, just muffled beyond
the closed doors for a time, then rising again from outside the building, the judge standing now, his arms
propped on the bench, still clutching the gavel, his head
jerking and trembling, the head of an old man indeed
now. Then he sank slowly back, his head jerking as the
heads of old men do. But his voice was quite calm,
cold: "Give that man protection out of town. See that he
leaves at once."

"I dont think he better try to leave the building right
now, Judge," the bailiff said. "Listen at them." But
nobody had to listen to hear it, not hysterical now, just
outraged and angry. "They aint hanging mad, just tar-
and-feathering mad. But anyway—"

"All right," the judge said. "Take him to my cham-
bers. Keep him there until after dark. Then get him
out of town.—Gentlemen of the jury, you will find the
prisoner guilty as charged and so bring in your verdict,
which carries with it a sentence at hard labor in the
State Penitentiary at Parchman for a period of not less
than fifty years. You may retire."

"I reckon there's no need of that, Judge," the foreman
said. "I reckon we are all—" The judge turned upon
him, the old man's thin and trembling fury:

"You will retire! Do you wish to be held in contempt?"
They were gone less than two minutes, hardly long

enough for the bailiff to close and then open the door. From outside the sound beat on, rising and falling.

That afternoon it rained again, a bright silver curtain roaring out of nowhere before the sun could be hidden, galloping on vagrom and coltlike, going nowhere, then thirty minutes later roaring back, bright and harmless in its own steaming footsteps. But when, shortly after dark, he was returned to his cell the sky was ineffable and stainless above the last green of twilight, arching the evening star, the palm merely murmuring beyond the bars, the bars still cool to his hands though the water, the rain, had long evaporated. So he had learned what Rittenmeyer meant. And now he learned why. He heard the two pairs of feet again but he did not turn from the window until the door had opened then clanged and clashed to and Rittenmeyer entered and stood for a moment, looking at him. Then Rittenmeyer took something from his pocket and crossed the cell, the hand extended. "Here," he said. It was a small box for medicine, unlabelled. It contained one white tablet. For a moment Wilbourne looked down at it stupidly, though only for a moment. Then he said quietly:

"Cyanide."

"Yes," Rittenmeyer said. He turned, he was already going: the face calm outrageous and consistent, the man who had been right always and found no peace in it.

"But I dont—" Wilbourne said. "How will my just being dead help—" Then he believed he understood. He said, "Wait." Rittenmeyer reached the door and put his hand on it. Nevertheless he paused, looking back.

"It's because I have got stale. I dont think good. Quick."
The other looked at him, waiting. "I thank you. I do
thank you. I wish I knew I would do the same for you in
my turn." Then Rittenmeyer shook the door once and
looked again at Wilbourne—the face consistent and
right and damned forever. The jailer appeared and
opened the door.

"I'm not doing it for you," Rittenmeyer said. "Get
that out of your damned head." Then he was gone, the
door clashed; and it was no flash of comprehension, it
was too quiet for that, it was just a simple falling of a
jumbled pattern. *Of course,* Wilbourne thought. *That
last day in New Orleans. He promised her. She said,
Not that bungling bastard Wilbourne, and he promised
her.* And that was it. That was all. It fell into the quiet
pattern and remained just long enough for him to see it
then flowed, vanished, gone out of all remembering forever and so there was just memory, forever and inescapable, so long as there was flesh to titillate. And now he
was about to get it, think it into words, so it was all right
now and he turned to the window and, holding the open
box carefully beneath and pinching the tablet in a
folded cigarette paper between thumb and finger he
rubbed the tablet carefully into powder on one of the
lower bars, catching the last dust in the box and wiping
the bar with the cigarette paper, and emptied the box
onto the floor and with his shoe-sole ground it into the
dust and old spittle and caked creosote until it had
completely vanished and burned the cigarette paper and
returned to the window. It was there, waiting, it was all

right; it would stand to his hand when the moment came. Now he could see the light on the concrete hulk, in the poop porthole which he had called the kitchen for weeks now, as if he lived there, and now with a preliminary murmur in the palm the light offshore breeze began, bringing with it the smell of swamps and wild jasmine, blowing on under the dying west and the bright star; it was the night. So it wasn't just memory. Memory was just half of it, it wasn't enough. *But it must be somewhere,* he thought. *There's the waste. Not just me. At least I think I dont mean just me. Hope I dont mean just me. Let it be anyone,* thinking of, remembering, the body, the broad thighs and the hands that liked bitching and making things. It seemed so little, so little to want, to ask. *With all the old graveward-creeping, the old wrinkled withered defeated clinging not even to the defeat but just to an old habit; accepting the defeat even to be allowed to cling to the habit—the wheezing lungs, the troublesome guts incapable of pleasure.* But after all memory could live in the old wheezing entrails: and now it did stand to his hand, incontrovertible and plain, serene, the palm clashing and murmuring dry and wild and faint and in the night but he could face it, thinking, *Not could. Will. I want to. So it is the old meat after all, no matter how old. Because if memory exists outside of the flesh it wont be memory because it wont know what it remembers so when she became not then half of memory became not and if I become not then all of remembering will cease to be.—Yes,* he thought, *between grief and nothing I will take grief.*

Old Man

ONE OF THE GOVERNOR'S YOUNG MEN ARRIVED AT THE
Penitentiary the next morning. That is, he was fairly
young (he would not see thirty again though without
doubt he did not want to, there being that about him
which indicated a character which never had and never
would want anything it did not, or was not about to,
possess), a Phi Beta Kappa out of an Eastern university,
a colonel on the Governor's staff who did not buy it with
a campaign contribution, who had stood in his negligent
Eastern-cut clothes and his arched nose and lazy con-
temptuous eyes on the galleries of any number of little
lost backwoods stores and told his stories and received
the guffaws of his overalled and spitting hearers and
with the same look in his eyes fondled infants named
in memory of the last administration and in honor (or
hope) of the next, and (it was said of him and doubtless not true) by lazy accident the behinds of some who
were not infants any longer though still not old enough
to vote. He was in the Warden's office with a briefcase,
and presently the deputy warden of the levee was there
too. He would have been sent for presently though not
yet, but he came anyhow, without knocking, with his
hat on, calling the Governor's young man loudly by a
nickname and striking him with a flat hand on the back
and lifted one thigh to the Warden's desk, almost be-

tween the Warden and the caller, the emissary. Or the
vizier with the command, the knotted cord, as began to
appear immediately.

"Well," the Governor's young man said, "you've
played the devil, haven't you?" The Warden had a
cigar. He had offered the caller one. It had been refused,
though presently, while the Warden looked at the back
of his neck with hard immobility even a little grim,
the deputy leaned and reached back and opened the
desk drawer and took one.

"Seems straight enough to me," the Warden said.
"He got swept away against his will. He came back as
soon as he could and surrendered."

"He even brought that damn boat back," the deputy
said. "If he'd a throwed the boat away he could a walked
back in three days. But no sir. He's got to bring the boat
back. 'Here's your boat and here's the woman but I
never found no bastard on no cottonhouse.' " He slapped
his knee, guffawing. "Them convicts. A mule's got twice
as much sense."

"A mule's got twice as much sense as anything except
a rat," the emissary said in his pleasant voice. "But that's
not the trouble."

"What is the trouble?" the Warden said.

"This man is dead."

"Hell fire, he aint dead," the deputy said. "He's up
yonder in that bunkhouse right now, lying his head off
probly. I'll take you up there and you can see him."
The Warden was looking at the deputy.

"Look," he said. "Bledsoe was trying to tell me something about that Kate mule's leg. You better go up to the stable and—"

"I done tended to it," the deputy said. He didn't even look at the Warden. He was watching, talking to, the emissary. "No sir. He aint—"

"But he has received an official discharge as being dead. Not a pardon nor a parole either: a discharge. He's either dead, or free. In either case he doesn't belong here." Now both the Warden and the deputy looked at the emissary, the deputy's mouth open a little, the cigar poised in his hand to have its tip bitten off. The emissary spoke pleasantly, extremely distinctly: "On a report of death forwarded to the Governor by the Warden of the Penitentiary." The deputy closed his mouth, though otherwise he didn't move. "On the official evidence of the officer delegated at the time to the charge and returning of the body of the prisoner to the Penitentiary." Now the deputy put the cigar into his mouth and got slowly off the desk, the cigar rolling across his lip as he spoke:

"So that's it. I'm to be it, am I?" He laughed shortly, a stage laugh, two notes. "When I done been right three times running through three separate administrations? That's on a book somewhere too. Somebody in Jackson can find that too. And if they cant, I can show—"

"Three administrations?" the emissary said. "Well, well. That's pretty good."

"You damn right it's good," the deputy said. "The woods are full of folks that didn't." The Warden was again watching the back of the deputy's neck.

"Look," he said. "Why dont you step up to my house and get that bottle of whiskey out of the sideboard and bring it down here?"

"All right," the deputy said. "But I think we better settle this first. I'll tell you what we'll do—"

"We can settle it quicker with a drink or two," the Warden said. "You better step on up to your place and get a coat so the bottle—"

"That'll take too long," the deputy said. "I wont need no coat." He moved to the door, where he stopped and turned. "I'll tell you what to do. Just call twelve men in here and tell him it's a jury—he never seen but one before and he wont know no better—and try him over for robbing that train. Hamp can be the judge."

"You cant try a man twice for the same crime," the emissary said. "He might know that even if he doesn't know a jury when he sees one."

"Look," the Warden said.

"All right. Just call it a new train robbery. Tell him it happened yesterday, tell him he robbed another train while he was gone and just forgot it. He couldn't help himself. Besides, he wont care. He'd just as lief be here as out. He wouldn't have nowhere to go if he was out. None of them do. Turn one loose and be damned if he aint right back here by Christmas like it was a reunion or something, for doing the very same thing they caught him at before." He guffawed again. "Them convicts."

"Look," the Warden said. "While you're there, why dont you open the bottle and see if the liquor's any good. Take a drink or two. Give yourself time to feel it. If it's not good, no use in bringing it."

"O. K.," the deputy said. He went out this time.

"Couldn't you lock the door?" the emissary said. The Warden squirmed faintly. That is, he shifted his position in his chair.

"After all, he's right," he said. "He's guessed right three times now. And he's kin to all the folks in Pittman County except the niggers."

"Maybe we can work fast then." The emissary opened the briefcase and took out a sheaf of papers. "So there you are," he said.

"There what are?"

"He escaped."

"But he came back voluntarily and surrendered."

"But he escaped."

"All right," the Warden said. "He escaped. Then what?" Now the emissary said look. That is, he said,

"Listen. I'm on per diem. That's tax-payers, votes. And if there's any possible chance for it to occur to anyone to hold an investigation about this, there'll be ten senators and twenty-five representatives here on a special train maybe. On per diem. And it will be mighty hard to keep some of them from going back to Jackson by way of Memphis or New Orleans—on per diem."

"All right," the Warden said. "What does he say to do?"

"This. The man left here in charge of one specific officer. But he was delivered back here by a different one."

"But he surren—" This time the Warden stopped of
his own accord. He looked, stared almost, at the emissary.
"All right. Go on."

"In specific charge of an appointed and delegated
officer, who returned here and reported that the body
of the prisoner was no longer in his possession; that, in
fact, he did not know where the prisoner was. That's
correct, isn't it?" The Warden said nothing. "Isn't that
correct?" the emissary said, pleasantly, insistently.

"But you cant do that to him. I tell you he's kin to
half the—"

"That's taken care of. The Chief has made a place for
him on the highway patrol."

"Hell," the Warden said. "He cant ride a motorcycle.
I dont even let him try to drive a truck."

"He wont have to. Surely an amazed and grateful
State can supply the man who guessed right three times
in succession in Mississippi general elections with a car
to ride in and somebody to run it if necessary. He wont
even have to stay in it all the time. Just so he's near
enough so when an inspector sees the car and stops and
blows the horn of it he can hear it and come out."

"I still dont like it," the Warden said.

"Neither do I. Your man could have saved all of this
if he had just gone on and drowned himself, as he seems
to have led everybody to believe he had. But he didn't.
And the Chief says do. Can you think of anything better?" The Warden sighed.

"No," he said.

"All right." The emissary opened the papers and un-

capped a pen and began to write. "Attempted escape
from the Penitentiary, ten years' additional sentence,"
he said. "Deputy Warden Buckworth transferred to
Highway Patrol. Call it for meritorious service even if
you want to. It wont matter now. Done?"

"Done," the Warden said.

"Then suppose you send for him. Get it over with."
So the Warden sent for the tall convict and he arrived
presently, saturnine and grave, in his new bed-ticking,
his jowls blue and close under the sunburn, his hair recently cut and neatly parted and smelling faintly of the
prison barber's (the barber was in for life, for murder-
ing his wife, still a barber) pomade. The Warden called
him by name.

"You had bad luck, didn't you?" The convict said
nothing. "They are going to have to add ten years to
your time."

"All right," the convict said.

"It's hard luck. I'm sorry."

"All right," the convict said. "If that's the rule." So
they gave him the ten years more and the Warden gave
him the cigar and now he sat, jackknifed backward
into the space between the upper and lower bunks, the
unlighted cigar in his hand while the plump convict and
four others listened to him. Or questioned him, that is,
since it was all done, finished, now and he was safe again,
so maybe it wasn't even worth talking about any more.

"All right," the plump one said. "So you come back
into the River. Then what?"

"Nothing. I rowed."

"Wasn't it pretty hard rowing coming back?"

"The water was still high. It was running pretty hard still. I never made much speed for the first week or two. After that it got better." Then, suddenly and quietly, something—the inarticulateness, the innate and inherited reluctance for speech, dissolved and he found himself, listened to himself, telling it quietly, the words coming not fast but easily to the tongue as he required them: How he paddled on (he found out by trying it that he could make better speed, if you could call it speed, next the bank—this after he had been carried suddenly and violently out to midstream before he could prevent it and found himself, the skiff, travelling back toward the region from which he had just escaped and he spent the better part of the morning getting back inshore and up to the canal again from which he had emerged at dawn) until night came and they tied up to the bank and ate some of the food he had secreted in his jumper before leaving the armory in New Orleans and the woman and the infant slept in the boat as usual and when daylight came they went on and tied up again that night too and the next day the food gave out and he came to a landing, a town, he didn't notice the name of it, and he got a job. It was a cane farm—

"Cane?" one of the other convicts said. "What does anybody want to raise cane for? You cut cane. You have to fight it where I come from. You burn it just to get shut of it."

"It was sorghum," the tall convict said.

"Sorghum?" another said. "A whole farm just rais-

ing sorghum? *Sorghum?* What did they do with it?"
The tall one didn't know. He didn't ask, he just came
up the levee and there was a truck waiting full of niggers
and a white man said, "You there. Can you run a shovel
plow?" and the convict said, "Yes," and the man said,
"Jump in then," and the convict said, "Only I've got a—"

"Yes," the plump one said. "That's what I been aiming to ask. What did—" The tall convict's face was grave,
his voice was calm, just a little short:

"They had tents for the folks to live in. They were
behind." The plump one blinked at him.

"Did they think she was your wife?"

"I dont know. I reckon so." The plump one blinked
at him.

"Wasn't she your wife? Just from time to time kind
of, you might say?" The tall one didn't answer this at
all. After a moment he raised the cigar and appeared
to examine a loosening of the wrapper because after
another moment he licked the cigar carefully near the
end. "All right," the plump one said. "Then what?" So
he worked there four days. He didn't like it. Maybe that
was why: that he too could not quite put credence in
that much of what he believed to be sorghum. So when
they told him it was Saturday and paid him and the
white man told him about somebody who was going to
Baton Rouge the next day in a motor boat, he went to
see the man and took the six dollars he had earned and
bought food with it and tied the skiff behind the motor
boat and went to Baton Rouge. It didn't take long and
even after they left the motor boat at Baton Rouge and

he was paddling again it seemed to the convict that the
River was lower and the current not so fast, so hard,
so they made fair speed, tying up to the bank at night
among the willows, the woman and baby sleeping in the
skiff as of old. Then the food gave out again. This time it
was a wood landing, the wood stacked and waiting, a
wagon and team being unladen of another load. The
men with the wagon told him about the sawmill and
helped him drag the skiff up the levee; they wanted to
leave it there but he would not so they loaded it onto
the wagon too and he and the woman got on the wagon
too and they went to the sawmill. They gave them
one room in a house to live in here. They paid two dollars a day and furnish. The work was hard. He liked it.
He stayed there eight days.

"If you liked it so well, why did you quit?" the
plump one said. The tall convict examined the cigar
again, holding it up where the light fell upon the rich
chocolate-colored flank.

"I got in trouble," he said.

"What trouble?"

"Woman. It was a fellow's wife."

"You mean you had been toting one piece up and
down the country day and night for over a month, and
now the first time you have a chance to stop and catch
your breath almost you got to get in trouble over another one?" The tall convict had thought of that. He
remembered it: how there were times, seconds, at first
when if it had not been for the baby he might have,
might have tried. But they were just seconds because in

the next instant his whole being would seem to flee the
very idea in a kind of savage and horrified revulsion;
he would find himself looking from a distance at this
millstone which the force and power of blind and risible
Motion had fastened upon him, thinking, saying aloud
actually, with harsh and savage outrage even though it
had been two years since he had had a woman and that
a nameless and not young negress, a casual, a straggler
whom he had caught more or less by chance on one of
the fifth-Sunday visiting days, the man—husband or
sweetheart—whom she had come to see having been shot
by a trusty a week or so previous and she had not heard
about it: "She aint even no good to me for that."

"But you got this one, didn't you?" the plump convict said.

"Yah," the tall one said. The plump one blinked at
him.

"Was it good?"

"It's all good," one of the others said. "Well? Go on.
How many more did you have on the way back? Sometimes when a fellow starts getting it it looks like he
just cant miss even if—" That was all, the convict told
them. They left the sawmill fast, he had no time to buy
food until they reached the next landing. There he spent
the whole sixteen dollars he had earned and they went
on. The River was lower now, there was no doubt of it,
and sixteen dollars' worth looked like a lot of food and
he thought maybe it would do, would be enough. But
maybe there was more current in the River still than it
looked like. But this time it was Mississippi, it was cot-

ton; the plow handles felt right to his palms again, the strain and squat of the slick buttocks against the middle buster's blade was what he knew, even though they paid but a dollar a day here. But that did it. He told it: they told him it was Saturday again and paid him and he told about it—night, a smoked lantern in a disc of worn and barren earth as smooth as silver, a circle of crouching figures, the importunate murmurs and ejaculations, the meagre piles of worn bills beneath the crouching knees, the dotted cubes clicking and scuttering in the dust; that did it. "How much did you win?" the second convict said.

"Enough," the tall one said.

"But how much?"

"Enough," the tall one said. It was enough exactly; he gave it all to the man who owned the second motor boat (he would not need food now), he and the woman in the launch now and the skiff towing behind, the woman with the baby and the paper-wrapped parcel beneath his peaceful hand, on his lap; almost at once he recognised, not Vicksburg because he had never seen Vicksburg, but the trestle beneath which on his roaring wave of trees and houses and dead animals he had shot, accompanied by thunder and lightning, a month and three weeks ago; he looked at it once without heat, even without interest as the launch went on. But now he began to watch the bank, the levee. He didn't know how he would know but he knew he would, and then it was early afternoon and sure enough the moment came and he said to the launch owner: "I reckon this will do."

"Here?" the launch owner said. "This dont look like anywhere to me."

"I reckon this is it," the convict said. So the launch put inshore, the engine ceased, it drifted up and lay against the levee and the owner cast the skiff loose.

"You better let me take you on until we come to something," he said. "That was what I promised."

"I reckon this will do," the convict said. So they got out and he stood with the grapevine painter in his hand while the launch purred again and drew away, already curving; he did not watch it. He laid the bundle down and made the painter fast to a willow root and picked up the bundle and turned. He said no word, he mounted the levee, passing the mark, the tide-line of the old raging, dry now and lined, traversed by shallow and empty cracks like foolish and deprecatory senile grins, and entered a willow clump and removed the overalls and shirt they had given him in New Orleans and dropped them without even looking to see where they fell and opened the parcel and took out the other, the known, the desired, faded a little, stained and worn, but clean, recognisable, and put them on and returned to the skiff and took up the paddle. The woman was already in it.

The plump convict stood blinking at him. "So you come back," he said. "Well well." Now they all watched the tall convict as he bit the end from the cigar neatly and with complete deliberation and spat it out and licked the bite smooth and damp and took a match from his pocket and examined the match for a moment as

though to be sure it was a good one, worthy of the cigar
perhaps, and raked it up his thigh with the same deliberation—a motion almost too slow to set fire to it, it would
seem—and held it until the flame burned clear and free
of sulphur, then put it to the cigar. The plump one
watched him, blinking rapidly and steadily. "And they
give you ten years more for running. That's bad. A
fellow can get used to what they give him at first, to
start off with, I dont care how much it is, even a hundred and ninety-nine years. But ten more years. Ten
years more, on top of that. When you never expected it.
Ten more years to have to do without no society, no
female companionship—" He blinked steadily at the
tall convict. But he (the tall convict) had thought of that
too. He had had a sweetheart. That is, he had gone to
church singings and picnics with her—a girl a year or
so younger than he, short-legged, with ripe breasts and
a heavy mouth and dull eyes like ripe muscadines, who
owned a baking-powder can almost full of ear-rings
and brooches and rings bought (or presented at sugges-
tion) from ten-cent stores. Presently he had divulged
his plan to her, and there were times later when, musing,
the thought occurred to him that possibly if it had not
been for her he would not actually have attempted it—
this a mere feeling, unworded, since he could not have
phrased this either: that who to know what Capone's
uncandled bridehood she might not have dreamed to be
her destiny and fate, what fast car filled with authentic
colored glass and machine guns, running traffic lights.
But that was all past and done when the notion first oc-

curred to him, and in the third month of his incarceration she came to see him. She wore ear-rings and a bracelet or so which he had never seen before and it never became quite clear how she had got that far from home, and she cried violently for the first three minutes though presently (and without his ever knowing either exactly how they had got separated or how she had made the acquaintance) he saw her in animated conversation with one of the guards. But she kissed him before she left that evening and said she would return the first chance she got, clinging to him, sweating a little, smelling of scent and soft young female flesh, slightly pneumatic. But she didn't come back though he continued to write to her, and seven months later he got an answer. It was a postcard, a colored lithograph of a Birmingham hotel, a childish X inked heavily across one window, the heavy writing on the reverse slanted and primer-like too: *This is where were honnymonning at. Your friend (Mrs) Vernon Waldrip*

The plump convict stood blinking at the tall one, rapidly and steadily. "Yes, sir," he said. "It's them ten more years that hurt. Ten more years to do without a woman, no woman a tall a fellow wants—" He blinked steadily and rapidly, watching the tall one. The other did not move, jacknifed backward between the two bunks, grave and clean, the cigar burning smoothly and richly in his clean steady hand, the smoke wreathing upward across his face saturnine, humorless, and calm. "Ten more years—"

"Women ---t!" the tall convict said.